THE BRIGHT DAY

On the night Neil Moray is returned as an
Independent Member of Parliament for the sea-
side town of Scotney, William Lomax, editor of
the local paper, is visited by a woman with an
unsavoury tale to tell about Moray's campaign
manager, Rodney Cope. Lomax takes a hard
look at the set-up in Moray's camp. The development of the West Front is a major issue and a
suspicion persists that Cope may have a special
interest in it. Then the woman who started it all
is found dead. Moray realises that the real enemy
is within, while his secretary, Hannah, with the
prospect of personal happiness at hand, finds herself dangerously close to the dark things that wait
at the end of the bright day.

THE
BRIGHT DAY

by

MARY HOCKING

1975

CHATTO & WINDUS
LONDON

Published by
Chatto & Windus Ltd
40/42 William IV Street
London WC2N 4DF

ISBN 0 7011 2072 X

Printed in Great Britain by
Cox & Wyman Limited, London
Fakenham and Reading

To
Jack and Effie

. . . . . the bright day is done
And we are for the dark

Acknowledgement

The lines from the song, 'Lord of the Dance', are reproduced by kind permission of the publisher, © 1963 Stainer & Bell Ltd

The excerpts from 'The Ballad of East and West' by Rudyard Kipling are reproduced by kind permission of Mrs. George Bambridge, Messrs. A. P. Watt & Son and Eyre Methuen Ltd

The lines from the song, 'For All We Know', are reproduced by kind permission of Francis Day & Hunter Ltd. Copyright 1934 Leo Feist Inc., U.S.A.

I

THERE was one star in the sky, pale and dying. Soon it would be light. It was difficult to believe that during the day they were up there, stars in their millions; difficult to believe that the world doesn't just turn over with the coming of day and leave them behind along with all our dreams and nightmares.

There are those who don't leave their dreams behind with the coming of day, visionaries, poets, maniacs, spinsters in their late thirties—like Hannah Joyce Mason— not sure who they are or where they are going.

These thoughts were in Hannah's mind as she left her brother's house in Picton's Quay soon after dawn. It was the kind of thinking that was the despair of her relatives.

'It's time she got married and settled down,' the two women agreed as they discussed her over an hour later.

'If she's not careful, she'll come to a bad end like her Aunt Maud.'

The dining-room curtains had been pulled back revealing another grey day. It had been a bad spring and no one guessed what a hot summer was to follow.

'The trouble with Hannah is that she's an ordinary person trying to be extraordinary. She has to make gestures to keep up her courage.'

'I wish she'd make a gesture and come down to breakfast.'

The window was open and there was a faint breeze. The younger woman said, 'I can smell the river today. I wish it wasn't tidal. I'm sure we get Scotney's refuse carried inland.'

'I thought Scotney was really nasty the last time I went there. Loud and vulgar, and something else as well. It quite frightened me. What does Hannah want to live there for?'

'She says it has "life".'

9

'It had a high life once.' The older woman began to talk about Scotney in the days of its Edwardian elegance while her daughter went upstairs to wake Hannah, who by this time had reached the marshes.

It was usually misty over the marshes in the early morning, but today it was clear and the Downs on the far side of the valley looked near enough for rain. The river was the colour of sedge and it flowed very quickly towards the sea, silent save where it swirled round a few small rocks and made a noise as though a plug had been pulled out somewhere beneath. The banks rose steeply on either side; there were a lot of stones in the dun-coloured earth. Hannah, who had been walking for some time, paused and looked down at her reflection, but she had dislodged some of the stones and they plopped into the water so that her image broke up and bobbed about lamentably. She said, 'So much for Joyce!' But she didn't really believe she could jettison Joyce so easily: Joyce might be dull and unadventurous, but she was very resilient. Necessary, too. She worked hard for her living while Hannah dreamed her dreams.

The river twisted through a flat valley with the Downs rising on either side. The valley was treeless and rather drab with pylons striding across it. There were one or two herds of cattle. The only sign of human occupation was an old cottage standing beside what had once been a railway halt. It was a melancholy place, a half-way house between dream and nightmare; it had an attraction for Hannah which she could not define, except to say 'it speaks to my subconscious'. Whenever she came to Picton's Quay, she made a point of visiting the cottage; it was more than a habit, it was a ritual and if she didn't perform it she felt uneasy. Although she was normally fastidious, this place drew her by its very neglect. She had sometimes thought that she would like to sleep there, but contented herself with weaving fantasies about it. It was that kind of place.

She kicked another stone and a startled bird flew up from a clump of grass ahead of her. She turned on to the track that led away from the river towards the cottage. Her sister-in-law would be annoyed with her for going off like this before breakfast. Although Hannah was glad to have escaped from her relatives, she still behaved as though she was being watched by someone, a someone to whom she must demonstrate that she was 'different'. From early years, she had wanted to be different. It hadn't been easy. Being like other people was a condition of survival in her home. 'Hannah' had only been included to please her great-aunt; even though they agreed to call her Hannah, they expected her to behave like Joyce. Now, in spite of herself, she glanced at her watch. It would have to be a quick visit this morning; there was a difference between being late for breakfast and being unpardonably late. Her upbringing made her reject the unpardonable.

As it was, she did not have so much as a glance through one of the windows. When she was near the cottage, she heard voices and two people came into view. A man and a woman. They were quite near her, walking towards a car, the roof of which was now just visible over an untidy hedge. They did not see her, but she saw them. She recognised the man. It was a shock. This was *her* secret place, surely they could have found somewhere else. It would never be the same again. She turned away quickly and walked back to Picton's Quay. Her sister-in-law said she had given them all the most awful fright. Hannah spent the rest of the day trying to make up for it.

That was in March.

2

At one o'clock in the morning of the second of May there was a thin crowd outside the Town Hall to hear the result of the by-election declared. Few had made a special journey for this purpose, but it was a clear, warm night and there were still quite a number of people out in the town. Although the discrediting of Geoffrey Ormerod, the much-favoured Conservative candidate, had created a flurry, the campaign itself had roused little interest. Scotney was used to scandal. Apart from perennial vice and violence, its superintendent of police was suspended, the district auditor was after several of the councillors, and unsavoury rumours were circulating regarding the bribing of officials in connection with the development of the West Front. Scotney, whatever else it may have lacked, had vitality, and regardless of bad government it thrived. Nevertheless, there must have been a number of people who were sufficiently offended by the stench of corruption to have made their way to the polling booths that fine May day, because when the results were announced the reforming Independent candidate had won. To faint cheers from below, and frenzied acclaim from supporters on the balcony, Neil Moray stepped forward to let a few words float down to the dingy Victorian square. A breeze carried his words into the narrow alleyways of The Warren; farther away, to the east of the town, in the area known as 'Mario's half-mile', the breeze stirred a few pieces of dirty newspaper, discarded cigarette packets, sodden potato crisps, a half-eaten ham roll, but there was nothing to indicate that any of the citizens in this area, which Moray had promised to sweep clean, were unduly perturbed.

A party of young people who had stopped by the Town Hall on their way from smoking pot, and other activities of which he would not have approved, gave Neil Moray a good-humoured cheer. He was, as one of the girls said, 'quite a dish'. She deliberately phrased this in the style of what she took to be his period—he was thirty-three. The Conservative candidate did not appear on the balcony, and Neil Moray made no mention of its having been a fair-fought campaign, although he did shake hands with the Labour candidate.

In a quarter of an hour, he was drinking champagne in his headquarters with the handful of people most closely associated with his victory. There was not much space, as his headquarters consisted of a room ten by fifteen over a bakery, and Hannah Mason sat on the knees of Rodney Angevin Cope who had, in every sense of the words, master-minded the campaign. Most of those present were too tired to go back over the major events of the last few weeks, or to look to the future, and contented themselves with telling hilarious and largely apocryphal stories about their own canvassing exploits. The exception was Cope, one of those people who, at the very moment when others are flagging, seem to receive a fresh charge of energy. Hannah, usually able to generate nervous energy whenever she needed it, felt drained by his very proximity.

'You can afford to campaign about drug addiction,' she said. 'You don't need drugs!'

'I'm high on success,' he laughed.

Neil Moray, in contrast, seemed to be suffering a reaction.

'Wondering why the hell you did it?' Cope asked him. Cope was perceptive but not always tactful. Moray, who did not like to have his thoughts read, shrugged his shoulders and turned away, a rebuff which in no way troubled Cope. Someone refilled Moray's glass.

'You should go home to bed,' Hannah said to him.

The warmth of her concern seemed to irritate Moray; but he took her advice and began to make his farewells, going to each person in turn and greeting them according to his estimate of them. By the time he came to Hannah he had recovered his good-humour sufficiently to smile. He had a sensitive, diffident face and his expression tended to be a

13

little abstracted; the smile was charming and rare enough to come as a personal reward. There was, however, something enigmatic, if not a little cold, about the eyes as he looked at Hannah, assessing what was due to her. She had worked very hard during the campaign and no doubt many of those present considered that a hug and a kiss would be appropriate. Spontaneous gestures did not come easily to Moray, however, particularly if he suspected that they were eagerly awaited; so he pressed a forefinger to the tip of Hannah's nose and murmured, 'I'll have more to say to thee later.' Her heightened colour told him that she had expected him to be more demonstrative. He did not offer to drive her home, although he passed the end of her road.

Hannah moved away and began to talk gaily to Major and Mrs. Brophy, two of Moray's most loyal supporters. She waited until half an hour after Moray had gone before she said, 'Time for me to make tracks.'

'What!' Cope's eyes widened in exaggerated surprise. 'Not staying? I thought we were going to see the real Hannah Mason tonight.' He undid the zip of her dress a token three inches and peered down her back.

'Don't be silly.' She fumbled and said crossly, 'I can't do it up now.'

'You need a husband.'

'It's the one time I give it serious thought.'

'Dear Hannah! I don't think you've been thanked properly, have you?' He put his arms round her and hugged her. 'Bless you, my love. You've been an absolute darling in every way. Three cheers for our Hannah!'

They cheered her with a will; she was a cheerful worker and very popular.

'Do you want a lift home?' Cope asked her.

'No thanks, I'd sooner walk.'

'Sure?' His persistence was not altogether kind. 'You're not being brave?'

'I'm gasping for air, that's all.'

She waved a theatrically cheerful farewell to the others; Cope gave her a pat on the behind as she turned away and said. 'That's my girl!' He seemed determined to demonstrate that he was aware she had been hurt.

She was indeed hurt. She was an emotional person, although she tried to conceal the fact, and she had expected that in the moment of victory Moray would be more generous. She was also aware that he had made a greater effort to express gratitude to others than to herself. Self-pity was not one of her indulgences, however, and as she walked along the street she was saying to herself, 'You put yourself in the centre of the picture too much. You can't do a good job and keep quiet about it, you must have everyone standing around and applauding. No wonder you get hurt. People haven't time for that sort of thing.' In this fashion, she nagged herself home.

Home was in a narrow street off the seafront; there was a lock-up garage beneath her flat, an antique shop to the left, and a meeting place for an obscure religious sect to the right. Opposite was a municipal car park set rather picturesquely in the burnt-out ruins of an old church, the lower walls of which had been left standing as though they had all the value of Roman remains. Hannah had spent a long time trying to find the right environment for herself. She often stood on the doorstep when she came back at night, looking at the street curving to the crossroads where other streets fanned out, lined with shops and restaurants, antique markets, boutiques, pubs. Not a row of semi-detached houses in miles! But tonight, she was too tired and dispirited to congratulate herself on having escaped from the atmosphere of her childhood. As she walked up the stairs, it seemed to her that Hannah Mason hadn't become notably wiser since she left suburbia.

Out in the streets, the breeze died down. Even the few revellers had come to rest somewhere. The policeman walking down Pont Street where Moray had his headquarters found all the buildings in darkness, the last supporter gone. On the seafront, a few drop-outs huddled against the breakwaters. A sea-mist stole up and hid them from P.C. Turner's not very inquiring eyes. The clock of St. John's Church struck three.

As far as the staff of *The Scotney Gazette* were concerned, it had all happened now. Basil Todd, on his way out, was surprised to hear footsteps–not the slow, regular, flat-footed tread of P.C. Turner, or the shuffle of a late-night drunk, but the lighter tread of a woman's feet, well-shod. He waited, one hand on the office outer door, as she came towards him out of the mist.

He was young, ambitious, idealistic, embittered, endowed with a moderate talent and little idea how to make the most of it. War waged constantly within him. In the sick light of the street lamp, his face looked raw with the misery of it all. The editor had rejected a profile he had written, unrequested, on Rodney Cope. 'Clever' the editor had called it, as though there was something reprehensible about a journalist being clever! 'This sort of thing may be fashionable in the quality papers, so-called, but I find it highly self-conscious and rather irritating.' Pretentious ass! No, that wasn't quite right, Todd moodily corrected himself; he wasn't exactly pretentious, nor yet entirely an ass. Affected, precious, pedantic, pedagogic, mannered. . . . Todd couldn't hit on the right word, and while he was searching for it, the woman had come abreast of him and stopped, as he had somehow feared she might.

'I want to see the editor. Is he in there?' Her breath smelt of whisky. She turned her head aside, to conceal her identity or her drinking.

Todd regarded what he could see of her with curiosity: trousers, a boxy camel-hair jacket with the collar turned up, a scarf concealing her hair and part of her face. He had the feeling he should have recognised her, but didn't.

'You'll find him in his room–door at the end of this room here.' He made it sound as though it was a usual occurrence for people to make calls on the *Gazette* office at this time of night. The woman certainly behaved as though it was, she went past Todd and walked towards the door he had indicated.

'If it can wait until tomorrow. . . .' Todd said belatedly.

'Oh, bugger off! This is tomorrow.' She sounded like someone who has come a long way and lost a lot of enthusiasm.

Todd shrugged his shoulders. He didn't think the editor had earned any protection tonight; he went out and left him to the woman.

'Are you the editor?' the woman said, standing in the doorway. She knew that William Lomax was the editor of the *Gazette,* but had always thought he didn't look right for the job, more like the owner of an antique shop that wasn't doing well. She was vaguely troubled now by the sight of him sitting there, his features all awry with surprise; there was something ludicrous about him, one of the sadder Shakespearian jesters. He was thin, too. Not a robust man.

'Mrs. Ormerod!' In spite of a rather disorientated expression—he looked always as though he had taken a wrong turning in a strange town—William Lomax never forgot a face or a name. A disconcerting gift, even, at times, to its owner. He could smell the whisky, and could make a guess what had brought her here, though why she should come to him to bewail her husband's ignominious defeat, he could not imagine. He supposed there were not many of her friends who would be pleased to offer comfort at this hour of the night. He screwed his face up into a grimace which might equally have expressed pleasure or pain, and said, 'Won't you sit down?'

'Were you outside the Town Hall?' she asked.

'I was.'

'I thought I saw you.' She moved a sheaf of paper and sat down on the chair opposite Lomax's desk. The room was little more than a cubicle; it smelt of newsprint and the kitchen odours of the Indian restaurant next door. She undid her scarf slowly and then folded it with obsessive concern; her fingers were heavily stained with nicotine.

Lomax fidgeted with anything that came to hand, putting papers that did not belong in piles into piles, opening and closing drawers with a brisk sound. She said, the drink making her quick to take offence : 'It's all right. I haven't come for a chat.'

'No?' He settled back in his chair, regarding her furtively. A good many cranks came to the office, usually he tried to

17

get Todd or one of the others to deal with them. Mrs. Ormerod wasn't exactly a crank, but she wasn't well-adjusted, either. Lomax found unbalanced people rather disturbing, they always made one so aware of the problem of balance. Mrs. Ormerod looked decidedly ill. Her dark, straight hair had the lifelessness of ill-health, her sallow face was finely scored with the sharp lines of neurosis. He was rather shocked. She could be no more than thirty, if that, and he could remember her when she had a bright, gamin charm and he had thought her wasted on Ormerod who seemed to him a cold, inadequate sort of man. That was before his own marriage broke up: he wasn't so inclined to judge other men now.

She said, 'My husband lost the election by over eight thousand votes.' She put one hand between her eyes and held the palm pressed there, as though trying to keep some particularly unwelcome thoughts at bay.

Lomax said, 'Eight thousand, three hundred and two.'

'I've buggered up his life.' The scarf, which she had reduced to the size of a handkerchief, slid off her lap; she made a flapping motion at it, and then decided to let it have its freedom.

'Isn't that rather an exaggeration?' Lomax didn't want too much drama at this, or any, hour of the night.

She jerked her handbag open and he watched querulously while she scrabbled for cigarettes; she was the kind of woman who makes a total assault on the contents of a bag, instead of picking out the items which she requires. She had been biting her nails. Lomax's mouth screwed up fastidiously. He moved his thin body uneasily in his chair. He could, in spite of his frail appearance, be very tough with people who tried to intimidate him, but he was vulnerable to the assaults of the weak. She got the cigarette going, held her head back and breathed smoke through her nose; Lomax regarded the taut muscles in her thin neck with apprehension. Sympathy could be fatal, she'd be here all night. He looked at her sternly.

It turned out it wasn't sympathy she was after. Through the haze of cigarette smoke, her eyes studied his face with surprising shrewdness. Something about that glance made the hairs on the back of his neck prickle. It was a sensation he had had before, and it usually meant news.

'I've got to tell someone,' she said. 'I can't go on with all this on my mind.' In spite of this statement, she showed no inclination to unburden herself; it was obvious her mind had clouded after that one flash of shrewd calculation.

Lomax said cautiously, 'Mrs. Ormerod, your husband's troubles have been widely reported. They aren't news any more.'

She gave him a long stare; he thought she had taken offence again. Then she said, 'They say Mario Vicente bought my husband because he wanted favours from him. Geoffrey was on the council when they first met; he was chairman of the Planning Committee before he decided to stand for parliament.'

Lomax tapped his front teeth with his forefinger.

She said, 'Do you know how that information about my husband got into the hands of the blessed virgin Moray?'

'Yes.' As she waited for him to go on, he said rather primly, 'Someone sent details of certain financial transactions between your husband and Mario Vicente to Neil Moray's office.'

'A bloody charade!'

'The documents were real enough, Mrs. Ormerod. I saw them. Mario made lavish gifts to your husband; he also invested money in your husband's business and set him up in offices in Marshall Street.

'Oh, I don't doubt your word. You're incorruptible.' She delivered herself of this judgement with some contempt; it was plain that no one pleased her much tonight. Then her mind got snagged up on the harsh stuff of his incorruptibility. 'All that fuss over the appointment of Councillor Mark's wife as head of that school. . . . My husband tried to get Lord Cannock to sack you for what you wrote about that. Do you know what Lord Cannock told him? He'd raise your salary! Did he? You'd better be after him if he didn't.'

19

It was nearly half-past three. Lomax said with some asperity 'What about those documents, Mrs. Ormerod?'

'They were stolen.'

'Well, obviously someone took them,' he said impatiently. 'A member of your husband's staff who had a grudge against him, perhaps.'

She looked at him, that long look again, as though she had travelled a great distance from the little world he inhabited and could scarcely remember how it worked. 'They were stolen from our house,' she said in an off-hand way. 'He didn't keep them at the office.'

'You mean someone broke in? If so, the police will . . .'

'Geoffrey didn't report it to the police. They would have asked questions about what was missing.' She leant forward and crushed the cigarette stub in the ashtray, holding it down, and then twisting it as though it was something human she was extinguishing. Dear me, Lomax thought, how fanciful one becomes at half-past three in the morning! 'It was Rodney Cope,' she said.

'Rodney Cope.' He did not get her meaning at once.

Now that she had said it, she seemed momentarily to lose interest. She flicked the packet open and took another cigarette; before she lit it, she looked round the room as though surprised to find herself in it. Lomax, who had recovered himself, thought that the sooner he got her out of here, the better; she was obviously more unbalanced than he had realised.

'Cope certainly made brilliant use of that material,' he said, trying to sound persuasive and firm at the same time. 'But that is hardly sufficient reason. . . .'

'I had an affair with him.' She stared at Lomax with a listless resentment in her eyes which did more to convince him of the truth of this statement than any circumstantial evidence could have done. 'I knew he was using me . . . at least, I suppose I must have known. . . .' There was no doubt, looking at her harrowed face, that this had been dragging on for a long time; she was at the nerves' edge.

'Mrs. Ormerod,' he spoke gently because he was genuinely

20

sorry for her. 'You are overwrought. Don't you think you have allowed yourself to imagine things?'

She shook her head, the movement was barely perceptible, as though he had held out a hope that was so futile it was scarcely worth acknowledging.

'Your affair with him is finished, I take it?'

'I haven't seen him since March. I think I could take it as finished, don't you?'

'Does the fact that you haven't seen him lately really mean he was using you? Might he not have lost interest? It's the usual reason, although I know that doesn't make it any less painful.'

'Yes.' After a moment during which she inspected the idea as though it was standing somewhere in a corner of the room, she said, 'But then, it's difficult to see what attracted him in the first place, isn't it? Tell me, Mr. Lomax, do you think I'm the sort of woman whom Rodney Cope would find irresistible?'

'I'm not Rodney Cope, Mrs. Ormerod.'

She got up and wound the scarf round her neck. 'You don't believe my story.' She sounded unsurprised and not particularly disappointed. 'Oh well, I don't know what I expected, really.' It seemed to him she was almost relieved. 'It would be tough to take on Cope, wouldn't it? Not like quibbling over the appointment of a head teacher. I can see that.'

Lomax let her go. He began to sort through the papers he had mis-arranged on his desk and came across Todd's profile on Rodney Cope. He read it through again. Todd had not liked Cope. Cope had been to Eton and had had a short but colourful career in the Scots Guards: a deadly combination, guaranteed to light the fuse of Todd's hatred. Lomax did not run a newspaper for the purpose of allowing his staff to give vent to either their prejudices or their obsessions. Nevertheless, most of the information given about Cope was factual, and his manner and style of speaking had been accurately, if a trifle bitchily, recorded. Of course, it was written in the slick, laconic style young Todd so admired, and it was less original than many of the more quietly written appraisals which had appeared from time to time in the *Gazette*; but it made an impact—one wanted to kick either Cope or the writer. The *Gazette* had standards. Its material was, in a modest way, well-written and well-presented and this was appreciated by the more erudite of its readers; but what kept up its sales was the fact that in a town not noted for candour in public affairs, it had never refused to print unpalatable facts or been afraid to criticise the more powerful elements in Scotney society, be they local councillors, the tycoons who invested in property, the gangsters who ran protection rackets, or the accommodating policemen. Reluctantly, Lomax decided that this was no time for his own personal obsession with style to take precedence. He was not superstitious, but the fact of Cope being brought to his attention twice in one night was not something that should be overlooked.

Lomax picked up his pen and ran through the profile. And what, Todd wondered in conclusion, would Cope make of success? He was the kind who needed a challenge. Would he find it here in Scotney, helping to consolidate Moray's victory, a victory which owed not a little to the discrediting of Ormerod? Political opponents could not always be expected to be so helpful. From now on, people were going to look to Moray for results. A long, hot summer awaited Cope. 'Oh, no, it does not!' Lomax ejaculated. 'Not in this newspaper!'

'The words "long hot summer" should be banned for the next hundred years, at least,' he told Todd the next day. 'The rest of it is all right.'

He handed the copy to Todd who stared at it in dismay. It wasn't the long, hot summer that was bothering him, it was the whole damn thing. He had not for one moment imagined that Lomax would use it.

'Now, there are one or two things I should like to make clear,' he muttered, trying to summon to mind all the objections which ought to have occurred to Lomax but had so singularly escaped him. 'This presents Cope as something more than a whizz kid on the local political scene; there's a reference here to . . . where is it? Ah, yes. This bit about "a versatile man in a cosmopolitan town . . ." and it goes on to mention other versatile characters such as Mario Vicente. Now, you could read it that I'm saying Cope isn't so far removed from Mario. . . .'

'That, in fact, was how I did read it,' Lomax admitted mildly.

'But the whole emphasis of Moray's campaign was that he was as far removed from Mario as is heaven from hell!'

'Oh well, the purer the politician, the more devious must his campaign manager be.'

This piece of quiet cynicism so shocked Todd, who in spite of his constant denunciations was rather easily shocked, that he went out of the room.

As he walked back to his own desk his mind was going over some of the other things he had said about Cope–'that air of rather dangerously aimless enterprise which Eton gives to those of its pupils not destined for high office'. What had he meant by that? It was something he had felt genuinely at the time of writing; he had seen Cope's face before him, the brilliance of the eyes which never seemed to be focused on anything in particular, like the eyes of a very intelligent child that is not fully occupied and may, therefore, look for trouble just for the hell of it. But that was incredibly fanciful! One could not possibly put it forward to substantiate that comment about Eton. Todd sat down at his desk, gnawing his lip. He had come to the office that morning prepared to work up a grievance about the rejection of the profile, he had even thought of handing in his notice; but now he was worried. He had always been afraid to hit hard in case someone hit him harder. Cope laughed a lot. But how good was his sense of humour?

Todd got up and went back to Lomax's room.

'I don't want this to run us into any trouble,' he said.

'Why should it? It's not actionable.'

'Well, the *Gazette* has attacked corruption in this town often enough, and now we get a member of parliament who promises to do something about it and we turn sour on him before he's had a chance to get going.' Todd was good at working up resentment, already he felt the familiar swell and surge of bitterness within him.

'But you always maintain that the people concerned are flattered by these profiles. And, in any case, it's not about Moray. I'll see him and get him to give details of some of the reforms he means to carry out. He's done enough attacking, goodness only knows, he should be glad to offer some of his more constructive thoughts. Don't you think?'

Todd went out. There were times when he thought Lomax was not fit to run a newspaper.

3

HANNAH walked along the seafront. It was Sunday and a grey one, mist was coming in from the sea, overcoats and long-sleeved pullovers were the rig of the day. Few people had been caught out. The English know their weather; even their faces had been adapted to it today.

There were a few people down on the beach, walking dogs, or watching children throw pebbles at the incoming waves. Up on the promenade, the windows of the shelters were blurred with sea-mist.

Hannah looked from side to side as she walked. She never tired of Scotney. Each building facing the sea had been conceived and decorated according to its owner's predilection, with no care for its neighbour. A planner's nightmare. It should be allowed to happen occasionally, otherwise one would be left with the dreary monotony of nearby Hinton, mile upon mile of annihilating good taste. The commercial buildings along the front were interspersed with terraces of Victorian houses, and squares, some small and homely, others vastly pretentious. The squares that had tried and failed were inexplicably sandwiched between those that were coolly triumphant. 'It just happens,' people said. But William Lomax, who also strolled along the front every Sunday and occasionally chatted with Hannah, had a more interesting explanation. He said that Mario Vicente bought property here and there, and that a whole square could suddenly become fashionable because Mario owned one house or had a restaurant on the corner. Where Mario bought, money followed.

Hannah came to the pier. Children were gazing through the palings which fenced it off from the promenade, wistful as though locked out of paradise; those on the pier, already disillusioned, whined and snivelled in the drizzle. The flags above the pier hung limp. The clock said a quarter past twelve.

To the east of the pier there were no more graceful squares and terraces. The boarding houses were small and sullen, and the amusement arcades looked dingy as though the owners could not afford to buy new equipment or repair the old. Then, as one came to the harbour, the atmosphere changed abruptly. Immediately opposite the harbour the ground rose steeply and narrow streets were lofted crazily one above the other. This was the oldest part of the town, and some of the buildings were sixteenth-century; they clung together in crooked tiers and one or two seemed to lurch precariously over the tier below. This was the area known as 'Mario's half mile'. The properties were well-maintained, whitewashed, with doors and window frames picked out in bright colours. There were narrow restaurants which contrived to cater for more customers than one would have thought physically possible; they had names like *The Cod and Lobster, Smugglers' Rest, The Crossed Keys.* Most of the restaurants were good; they were also relatively inexpensive. Hannah came to this area every Sunday for lunch.

Guiseppe's was opposite the jetty. There were a few tables outside, sheltered by two large sunshades advertising *Cinzano.* The drizzle was persistent now, so Hannah went into the dining-room. This was a small room which had not been tricked out with any fancy décor; the walls were whitewashed and the wooden tables were covered with check cloths. The waiter, who knew Hannah, came over to her at once and asked, 'And what is it to be today?' He had once presumed to bring her a *Dubonnet* because she had asked for it three weeks running, but had learnt his lesson. Today she opted for a dry sherry.

It was half-past twelve and the restaurant was empty apart from a party of six sitting at the table near the serving hatch. From the way they sat at the table, chairs anyhow, tilted back, or pulled in close if the sitter was hunched over the table, it was apparent that they were frequent visitors. The three women and the girl were at one end of the table, dressed in black; the women smiled and talked, not in the bright social way in which English women behave in a restaurant, but in an intimate, relaxed way as though in their own home. The girl looked as though she would rather be doing something else, but she was dispirited rather than sullen; rebellion was obviously out of the question. The two men did not talk much; they leant back against the wall, smoking cigars, and staring with sad, dark eyes towards the harbour. Every now and again, one of them would make a comment without removing the cigar from his mouth or turning to his companion; the other would nod wisely or sigh expansively. The women were not drinking, but the men each had a dark green aperitif. The waiter, now leaning with arms folded against the serving hatch, watched them. One sensed that he was ready to accommodate them in any way. At the moment, they did not want him. They came here each week and sat and talked and sipped their drinks. When they ate, Hannah had no idea; sometimes the men went away and when she left she would see them drinking in another bar, at other times they were joined by other men and then there was a lot of hand-clasping and exchange of greetings with the women. It was all very foreign, but the fascinating thing about it was that they made you feel you were in their country. At this moment, Hannah caught the eye of the bulkier of the two men and he gave her a little bow; she came often enough for Mario Vicente to recognise her as a regular customer.

Hannah turned her attention to the menu, annoyed with herself for having betrayed an interest in the party. But perhaps today she could be forgiven her curiosity. Mario had, after all, suffered a serious setback recently. The development of the West Front was something in which he was reputed to be interested, so interested that he had lent a considerable sum of money to Geoffrey Ormerod, who was the director of an expanding property development company. Whatever favours Mario might have expected in return would not now be forthcoming since Ormerod was no longer a local councillor and had lost to Moray in the parliamentary election. Hannah knew that Moray was interested in a scheme for the West Front which had the backing of no less a person than Arthur Heffernan. Mario Vicente, Rodney Cope had assured Hannah, was small-time in comparison with Heffernan, who was making a national reputation for himself on the way to an international one. In fact, it was really something of a charitable enterprise for Heffernan to bother with Scotney at all.

Hannah thought about this as she ate her veal marsala. It was not easy, however, to gloat over Mario Vicente's misfortunes. He seemed so unassuming sitting there at ease, his body, almost as wide as it was long, over-spreading the small chair. His features were harsh; the thick, broad nose was blunted at the tip as though in the making of it the sculptor's chisel had slipped; the lips had received the same rough treatment, they were used to abuse and knew how to handle it. But, as snow will soften the rugged contour, so the heavy powdering of grey in the thick, curly hair had a mellowing effect. Although she could be very perceptive, there was a romantic vein in Hannah which insisted that a man who looks harsh is really gentle as a lamb. In her favour, in this case, were Mario's eyes. As he stared out towards the harbour with an expression of deep melancholy, he seemed to be contemplating the whole of his past life: the eyes said he had had no option but to be what he was, they asked your forgiveness. A difficult man to dislike.

One or two of the tables by the window had filled up. The restaurant was still empty down Hannah's end of the room when the woman came in. The waiter prised his shoulders from the wall. The woman looked at him and shook her head. She walked across to the table occupied by the Italians, no one of whom, man or woman, happened to have noticed either her entry or her approach.

'Is Geoffrey coming here?' She gave an irritable twitch of her head as she spoke; it was not clear whom she might be addressing, the waiter, Hannah, or one of the party at the table. 'I've locked myself out of the house.' She caught Hannah's eye and made a clownish grimace of despair.

She wore an ice-blue trouser suit which had probably looked good before she took to sleeping in it. She had no handbag, perhaps that was locked in the house; but in her right hand she carried car keys which she jingled all the while, like a leper ringing a bell. The people at the table certainly behaved as if she had some kind of disease, they weren't anxious to breathe the same air. The women had stopped talking; the older ones seemed to have become suddenly rather massive, looming at the head of the table like affronted deities. The girl sat with her knees together, toes pointed out, and examined her shoes as if they pinched. Mario's companion contemplated the table, thumb and forefinger pressed to the tip of his nose the better to aid meditation. Only Mario acknowledged the woman's remark. He moved his wide shoulders very leisurely and turned his head; slowly his eyes scanned the room, resting indifferently on the people in the window, Hannah in her corner, the waiter who had suddenly become engrossed in his order pad. When the circuit was complete, he made a slight, throwaway gesture with one hand; it was the kind of gesture he might have made if he had been asked whether he had found a piece of trashy jewellery left behind by a customer.

'But don't you know where he is?' The woman's voice was strident; she meant to have his attention.

He rewarded her with the faintest shrug of the shoulders. His indifference was humiliating; the woman had to scratch away at it, trying to draw a response. Hannah sympathised with her. The woman had got herself into a situation from which it was difficult to withdraw. Nevertheless, Hannah wished she would withdraw. There was something menacing about the scene, a feeling that violence was not far beneath the surface and might break out at any moment. Hannah wished she had sat by the window.

The woman began to shout. 'Sweet Jesus! Can't you say something? You're not a zombie, are you?'

The remark gave grave offence to the women, even the girl raised her head, fascinated in a cringing way.

'For God's sake! Geoffrey hasn't been home for two days. I don't claim many rights, but if I've been deserted I've a right to know. He is my husband.'

'But he is nothing to me.' Mario placed his hand on the table in front of him and studied it as though to assure himself it had the usual complement of fingers. There was a dark ruby ring on the third finger and a plain gold ring on the little finger. For some reason, the rings made Hannah realise more than anything else that she was in a situation quite alien to her. Mario said, 'I do not even remember your husband very well.'

'You remembered him well enough when he was useful to you.' She turned to the Italian women. Hannah, knowing instinctively that this was a mistake, held her breath. 'Can't you say something to him, can't you make him understand?'

Very slowly, with an air of one rousing himself with the utmost reluctance from a delicious lassitude, Mario got to his feet. The woman took a step back. Her manner changed. She put one hand to her hair, drawing it back from her forehead in a nervous, tentative gesture that was not unpleasing and had perhaps served her well in days when she was more sure of her attraction. She wheedled, 'I must see him. Really, I must. Do please help me, Mario.' His face was quite expressionless. He made a light flick of his hand in the direction of the door and said, 'Go.'

The woman turned away. 'I'll have a coffee,' she said defiantly. She moved jerkily towards Hannah's table. Perhaps the ridiculousness of her position flashed across her mind, for she made another wry grimace; her wrinkled face had momentarily a monkeyish charm, as she said, 'Do you mind if I join you?'

'Not at all.' Hannah moved her handbag from the vacant chair.

'No.' Mario came and stood by the table. 'Madame does not wish to be disturbed.'

'What the hell! She's drinking coffee, isn't she? I can have coffee, too. It's a restaurant. You can bloody well serve me. And since I can't pay for it, you can take it out of the allowance you pay Geoffrey!'

Mario's face was impassive, the eyes were black and still as though something, patience perhaps, had died within him. Then he raised his hand and at the same moment Hannah upset her coffee in her lap. She jumped to her feet, wailing loudly, and overturned her chair. She laughed about the incident afterwards, but at the time she was convinced that if she didn't spill her coffee, blood would be spilt. This was no doubt an exaggeration; Mario would probably have done no more than take the woman by the arm and turn her in the direction of the door. As it was, Hannah's action rendered even this gesture unnecessary. While Mario offered his handkerchief to Hannah, the woman turned and marched down the room, swinging the hand in which she carried the car keys in an exaggerated circular motion.

'How will she manage about getting into her house?' Hannah asked weakly.

'Oh, the police will let her in. They do it before, I believe. Now! Enrico! Another coffee for Madame. And you will have a brandy. Yes, yes, I insist!' As he walked away with Enrico, he said, just loud enough for Hannah to hear him, 'And no bill, you understand? This has been embarrassing for Madame.'

Hannah needed the coffee, but she did not enjoy the brandy and she would have preferred to pay for the meal. She looked across at Mario Vicente and wondered whether she should argue about it. He was stabbing a finger towards the harbour, perhaps he was drawing his companion's attention to one of the boats; the women were talking among themselves again, not busily going over the recent incident, but talking about something quite unconnected with it as though the woman had never been. Hannah decided it might be wiser for her to follow their example. Nevertheless, when the waiter passed her table, she said to him quietly, 'Was that Mrs. Ormerod?'

He nodded and went away quickly, plainly not wishing to be drawn into conversation on the subject.

Hannah had felt that the woman's face was familiar, but she had not realised that it was Mrs. Ormerod until she made the reference to the payment of an allowance to Geoffrey. Mrs. Ormerod had not supported her husband during the campaign and Hannah had never seen them together. So where had she seen Mrs. Ormerod? This bothered her for a while. But later, at evening service, as she sat half-listening to the sermon, she suddenly had a clear picture of Mrs. Ormerod in a happier mood, laughing in the early morning at the cottage near Picton's Quay, with Rodney Cope. Hannah was relieved. She had liked the woman, and was no less inclined to like her now; but she no longer felt quite so troubled at the thought of Mrs. Ormerod, deserted by her husband, and locked out of her house.

The minister said heavily, 'And there are those whose ears are tuned to the world's distractions, who never really listen. . . .' Hannah gave her attention to the minister for a few minutes, and then began to wonder if she had any change for the collection.

4

'I've had Lomax on the telephone,' Major Brophy told Moray. He and Moray were in the bar at *The Cod and Lobster*. 'Wife turfs me out on a Sunday evening,' Major Brophy said. 'Says I fidget during that serial they've got on BBC 2. Henry James. I liked the Forsyte Saga, and I didn't mind the Pallisers, either. They were real people; I knew what they were about. . . .' His voice trailed away and he looked unhappily into his beer. Life made less and less sense to him. 'I am an Edwardian' was one of his favourite statements, always uttered as though this was something peculiar to himself and had nothing to do with date of birth.

Moray had just returned to Scotney after a week-end away. Victory seemed to have caught him unprepared; he was tired and rather apprehensive about the future. He did not consider that a telephone call from Lomax was sufficient reason for the Major to intrude on his time. He suspected the man simply wanted a drinking companion. Moray hated intrusion and he was beginning to realise the extent to which he would now be subject to it. 'What did Lomax want?' he asked.

'An article introducing the new MP to his people, I suppose. That sort of thing.' The Major hadn't much idea of the way journalists thought, least of all Lomax who seemed to him as inscrutable as the grey sea beyond the window. He knew, however, that journalists as a breed were unreliable and therefore to be handled with care. 'Probably important to see him,' he said. 'But I told him, no sensational stuff. We want to ease up on all that now. Get back to normal.'

An extraordinary attitude! Moray thought. They had campaigned against vice and corruption, energetic action had been promised; and that, as far as the Major was concerned, was an end to it. The declaration of intent was in itself sufficient. Only a troublemaker would want to take the matter further. Troublemakers were more sinister than the property speculator, the dope pedlar, the men who ran the protection rackets, all of whom operated within the system; whereas the troublemaker aimed at destroying the system. Moray had become aware, in the few days that had elapsed since the election, that there were others who shared this view. He began to see that this deep suspicion of the persistent troublemaker was probably the one thing which could unite the warring elements; the disgruntled policemen, Ormerod's followers, the councillors—good and bad, even Moray's own followers, they had all had enough of trouble. It made him feel very depressed.

'We need to be constructive,' the Major said. 'This is a good town to live in. Got to make the people believe that. The trouble with newspapers is they only print the bad stuff.' It was Lomax whom he saw as the troublemaker. 'A nice enough fellow, but you've got to watch him. Not as mild as he looks. He's upset a lot of people in this town, influential people. I told him that once, and he said "I'll settle for that as a testimonial"—or some such piece of bravado. Of course, it was a shock for him, his wife going off like that. Made him bitter, I daresay; inclined to believe the worst of people.'

Moray made no comment. He had a rather better understanding of Lomax, but he did not like him. Lomax regarded most men, Moray included, as a bundle of endless possibilities, some good, some bad. Moray did not regard himself as being as other men; he did not think of himself as better, or worse, but as different—Neil Moray, someone set a little apart. He was piqued by Lomax's attitude. Nevertheless, he supposed he would have to see the man.

'I'd better telephone him.' It was an excuse to get away from the Major. He wanted what was left of the evening to himself; he had things to think about which were not connected with politics.

His flat was on the outskirts of the town. He drove slowly. To his right, across the flat fields, the Downs rose dramatically; a view that was dear to the hearts of the natives of Sussex. Neil Moray was not a native and the view seemed to him unduly challenging.

The week-end had not been a success. He had hoped that by the end of it he would have reached a decision about his relationship with his mistress, Lucy Jameson, but in fact he was more undecided than ever. Had she not been West Indian things would have been simpler. Suppose he decided not to marry her because they did not have enough in common? Could he be sure that it was not the different colour of their skins, rather than emotional and intellectual differences, that really bothered him? This was a difficult question to answer since the thing which had first drawn his attention to her had been the colour of her skin. He had been faithful to her for a long time, he had considered her feelings with great sensitivity; at every stage of their relationship he had been very aware of her as a West Indian. But this week-end, overwhelmed by victory, he had seen her simply as a woman and it had to be admitted that she had lost as a result. It wasn't that she was any worse than other women, only that she wasn't any better. A woman who was no better than the next was not the woman for Neil Moray to take to wife.

When he got back to his flat thoughts of Lucy were driven from his mind. He could scarcely open the door for the clutter of mail; as bad as Christmas, except that his Christmases had never been like that, his family's attitude to Christmas having been restrained in the extreme. He gathered up the letters and took them into the sitting-room. He would ask Hannah to deal with the bulk of them, but there was always a chance that one or two personal letters were hidden away in the heap. He kept his personal life very much to himself. It was not that he had anything of which to be ashamed, but rather that he regarded it as a possession; material possessions were not important to him, but his personality and everything which pertained to it was very important and closely guarded. An inspection of the mail revealed nothing more interesting than a letter from a Quaker aunt noting his election and exhorting the virtues of integrity and self-denial.

Self was reluctant to be denied. Moray telephoned Rodney Cope and told him about his conversation with Brophy. 'I can't have him making appointments for me like this,' he said fretfully.

'Of course you can't. Just the same, I think you should see Lomax.'

Cope dismissed the subject and went on to talk about something else. Obviously he assumed that Moray would accept his advice without question. It occurred to Moray that Cope had made a great success of organising the campaign and might now imagine he could organise the member of parliament.

Cope was giving more advice. '. . . must keep the dear girl happy. Good secretaries are hard to come by.' He went on to make suggestions as to how Hannah might be kept happy.

Hannah had worked hard during the campaign, and once or twice Moray had dined at her flat after a particularly gruelling evening's work. On these occasions she had been warmly sympathetic to him. Cope had wanted to know whether Moray had slept with her. Moray, who had not slept with Hannah (although he was sure that this was what she had wanted) had refused to be drawn. He was usually reserved about his affairs, but was capable of surprising his friends by suddenly recounting Rabelaisian anecdotes which gained in their effect by being so out of character. He was not unaware of the delight this occasioned. The moment, however, must be of his own choosing. Now, he interrupted Cope impatiently, 'First things first. I must telephone Lomax.'

He had meant to make amends to Hannah and had intended suggesting a celebration dinner; but Cope's intervention had made him feel that he had lost the initiative. It was because he was irritated with Cope, that on his way to the office the next day he decided to buy flowers for Hannah.

Hannah was opening the post when Moray came into the room. There was a large box of chocolates on her table and a bottle of wine.

'Is it your birthday?' he asked, rather taken aback.

'No. The chocolates are from Mrs. Brophy and the wine is from the Major.' She ripped open an envelope. 'Isn't it sweet of them?'

Moray wished he had thought of wine. 'As soon as I can see my way ahead we must have a real celebration.' He made room for the flowers on the table. 'In the meantime. . . .'

She gave the flowers a brief glance and said, 'Oh, thank you, Neil. You shouldn't have bothered. Don't forget you have a meeting with the Town Clerk at a quarter to ten, will you?'

It was apparent that as far as she was concerned the time for making amends had passed; the fact that she was pleasant about it only made the situation more uncomfortable for Moray. He went through the post quickly and left the office.

Cope arrived a few minutes later. 'Looks like a funeral parlour,' he said cheerfully.

'Yes,' Hannah agreed. 'Carnations always make me think of funerals. Something about the smell.'

'From Neil?' Cope plucked a flower. 'Not the chocolates and the wine as well, surely?'

'Just the flowers.'

'Insensitive brute!'

He sat down on a packing case and arranged the flower in his buttonhole while Hannah cleared the table. 'Would now be the time for me to ask you out to lunch?' he said when she had finished.

'Would you mind if I said no? I really have so much to do this week.'

He sighed. 'Ah, Hannah the breaker of hearts! How cruel you are to us poor men!'

She inserted paper in the typewriter and regarded him in much the same way as she might scan a draft, looking for spelling mistakes and split infinitives. He had a high fore-head from which the thick fair hair was receding in crisp

37

waves; the areas of skin left bare were unmarked, remarkably so for a man in his mid-thirties. He had a straight nose, a wide but not particularly sensual mouth, a long chin; it could have been the face of a comic, a visionary, or an antique Greek. The vivid blue eyes seemed unrelated to the rest of the face, as though they might break free of the sockets at any minute.

'Sure you're not the one who is cruel?' she asked.

'What a wounding thing to say.'

'Come now, Rodney! I wouldn't pierce your heart, would I?' She leant her elbows on the table, her chin nudging the top of the typewriter. Her eyes were bright with mischief. 'That's not something that's ever happened to you, is it?'

Normally, she tended to be sensitive where other people's feelings were concerned, even to the point of failing to protect her own interests. But Moray had upset her, and she was not disposed to be kind at this moment. The surprising thing about her, Cope thought, was that at such times she revealed a much shrewder mind than one would have imagined her to possess. The female of the species is always dangerous when roused; but this is often demonstrated by a spontaneous lashing out with the first weapon to hand. Hannah was selective. She chose her tools as a surgeon might, and she knew where to make the incision.

'You are something of a student of human nature, Hannah,' he said. 'I suspect you know more about Neil and myself than we would care to imagine.'

'*You* wouldn't care twopence!' she retorted.

'You must tell me why you think I am so unfeeling, so that I may mend my wicked ways.'

'You like to stir things up and see what happens.'

'Does that frighten you? Are you afraid of what might happen to you if I stirred things up?' Idly, on the whim of the moment, he decided to see to what extent he could disturb her. He had always felt that her emotional balance was rather precarious. 'I think people should be grateful to those who "stir things up". It's all experience. Perhaps you, too, have unplumbed depths of cruelty, dear Hannah. One should never retreat from experience. Do you retreat from experience?'

She made no reply.

'Hmm,' he said. 'I see you do.'

He leant back, studying her with arms folded. Her chestnut hair was its natural colour, or near enough—perhaps she used a rinse occasionally, but there were grey hairs here and there to indicate that she had decided in favour of growing old gracefully. She would make a joke of it and repeat it too often, but despite a few backward glances, she would do it. She had a trim figure and good clothes sense. She knew what suited her, although an occasional reluctance to leave youth behind betrayed itself in a too-short skirt or a frivolous blouse. Her make-up was sometimes a little too heavy—this was so today, but that was a defence not an indulgence. All fairly predictable. But there was a restlessness in the eyes, something unsatisfied about the mouth, that was slightly at variance with the rest of the picture.

'You know, Hannah,' he said, 'your trouble is that you are two people: an ardent, impulsive little woman that any sensible man would want to take to wife. . . .'

'Sensible? What a reward for ardour!' She managed to sound amused, but her colour was high. 'Tell me about the other half, Sigmund.'

'But there she speaks! Needle-sharp. Men don't like it, dear.'

'I should worry?' she asked, smiling but not with her eyes.

'Don't you, though? Not even a little in the long watches of the night.'

Intermittently, she had been typing. Now she took a buff form out of the typewriter and handed it to him.

'Could you sign your name in full, please. How did the Angevin creep in, by the way? I've always wanted to ask.'

'I come from a long and ancient line,' he said lightly.

'Ah well,' she said as he handed the form back. 'We all fantasise a little, don't we?'

Cope laughed. 'A nice touch, Hannah.' His interest in this

39

skirmish was beginning to wane; for it to become really exciting there must be a risk to himself as well as to Hannah and he could not see that developing. He might as well get down to the morning's work.

He took a pile of letters from the 'in' tray. 'You're not doing your stuff this morning, woman. You've not sorted the wheat from the chaff.' He read through one or two notes and said, 'I see Neil is lunching with Lomax tomorrow. We'd better get something out for him, I don't suppose he's had much time to work on anything himself. His first words to the citizenry will be important and Lomax is sharp as a tack.'

'I always think he's such a gentle man,' she protested.

'Gentleman! His father kept a tobacconist's shop.'

She looked genuinely startled for a moment, and then laughed. 'You really meant that, didn't you? I don't care if his father was a road-sweeper. It was disposition I was referring to, not breeding.'

'And quite apart from his parentage,' Cope was a little nettled, 'he isn't a particularly outstanding journalist. No enterprise, otherwise he wouldn't still be editing a local paper.'

'But it's a good one, and it sells.'

'Oh, he manages well enough. Not top rank, but well enough. For one thing, he gives bright boys their head. And then, he's never allowed himself to be owned by any particular faction.'

'Have we finished his obituary?' She was still making fun of him.

He looked at her angrily, and then laughed. 'We're back where all this started, aren't we? Talking about funerals. I must say I feel rather as though someone had died. Must be the election hangover. Let's get through this stuff quickly.'

The correspondence was varied and almost each letter called for a different approach. Cope made the necessary adjustments smoothly, striking exactly the right note in each case, selecting the information to be given, the points to be stressed, as though once he read a letter something clicked in his brain and everything was there at his disposal, words, tone, content. Hannah had never come across anyone whose brain worked so quickly or who could sustain mental effort for so long. Towards the end of this long session, however, she frowned over a letter to the local branch of the Transport and General Workers' Union.

'You don't think that sounds too accomplished?'

'Can one be too accomplished?'

'It's not quite the appeal Neil has had for people, I would think.'

'Read it back to me.'

He sat looking at the table, beating a tattoo with the fingers of his right hand while he listened. 'You're right,' he said eventually. He looked at her curiously. 'How much of all this do you believe, Hannah?' He waved a hand over the pile of letters.

She was confused, not having expected the question, indeed, not having asked it of herself. 'I've been a secretary for years,' she extemporised. 'One can't put one's heart and soul into each letter.'

'Somewhere, wriggling away at the back of your mind, Hannah, is a little worm of scepticism.'

'I shouldn't have worked the hours I have, *and* for so little pay, if that was true!' she protested. 'I think Neil is absolutely genuine in everything he says and does.'

'And me?'

'Someone has to attend to the business side of things.'

'Integrity is not enough, in other words.'

'If you want this before the end of the afternoon,' she dismissed the question of integrity, 'you had better leave me to get on with it. What about this last letter?'

'Just tone it down, or rough it up, or whatever you think it needs.' He looked at his watch. Ten past one. 'I shan't be back until about half-past four.'

After Cope had gone, Hannah decided to type one or two letters before eating her sandwiches; she had started on the second letter when the door opened and William Lomax came in.

'I'm supposed to be lunching with Moray,' he said, in answer to her surprised glance.

'Not today. Tomorrow.'

'Oh dear.' He sat on one of the packing cases. 'How silly of me. Yes, now I come to think of it, I do recall. . . .' His eyes swerved away from her and he gazed round the room. 'You haven't got much space, have you? I think we've got a little more space.' Space seemed to interest him; he got up and began to pace the room.

Hannah watched him. She was aware that he was never entirely at ease in her company. When she met him on the seafront he would greet her with lively enthusiasm, but this could quite suddenly, for no apparent reason, be replaced by nervous abruptness. At times, he was almost rude. Yet he continued to seek her company. This erratic behaviour had surprised Hannah, but at first she had not been disturbed by it. Lately, however, it seemed to have infected her, and as she walked through the town, or attended functions, she found herself looking out for him, eager, yet apprehensive in case he came upon her unawares. At the moment, perhaps because her encounter with Cope had put her on her guard, she was the calmer of the two.

Lomax said, 'Ten by fifteen.'

'You've just missed Rodney,' Hannah told him. 'He won't be back until half-past four and Neil won't be in again today.'

'Cope still with you, is he?' Lomax gazed up at the ceiling and down again, as though fascinated by the height–or lack of it–of the room. 'Man of enormous energy, he always seems to me. Not at all the type an independent candidate can usually hope to recruit for his campaign manager.'

'I think he enjoys the challenge.'

'Ah, maybe.' He nodded his head absently. 'But I suppose there won't be much for him to do now.'

'You have to be joking!' She grimaced wryly at the pile of letters on her desk.

'Lucky Mr. Moray! To be able to afford Rodney Cope and Hannah Mason.'

Hannah looked at him with a shade more reserve in her manner. He had a thin, rather bony face and a habit of holding his head a little to one side; the eyes were deeply sunk in the sockets and she had the impression that one was a little higher than the other. She realised, what she had lately overlooked, that in spite of the vague, unfinished way he left his sentences and his general air of not having quite got the gist of any conversation, he was very perceptive.

'Perhaps money doesn't matter to Rodney Cope,' she suggested.

'It can't do,' he agreed.

It would have been better to have left the conversation here, but she had to develop the theme. 'Perhaps it's power that fascinates him. He may like to feel he can influence events.'

Lomax pursed his lips and tilted his head even farther to one side as he appeared to consider this not very original suggestion. 'By persuading Moray to back Heffernan's scheme for the development of the West Front?'

'Neil *didn't* back Heffernan's scheme!' Hannah looked at Lomax angrily. 'If the editor of the *Gazette* can't get the picture straight, no wonder there has been so much misunderstanding.'

'Refresh my memory,' Lomax said meekly.

'Ormerod wanted Heffernan's scheme thrown out before it had ever been considered. Neil felt it should be considered objectively in relation to the needs of the town as a whole, not the needs of a few interested parties who stand to lose if it is adopted.'

Lomax gave her a sudden, unexpectedly sweet smile, as though, for some reason she could not understand, she had gladdened his heart. 'It's a wicked world, isn't it?' he said.

She responded to the smile, although she was not entirely mollified.

He looked round the room again, this time appearing fascinated by the low, sliding window. 'Do you find it difficult to get a window cleaner?' he asked. 'We have an awful job.'

He peered down from the window. 'You get a good view of The Warren, don't you?'

'By the time Neil has finished with it, it will be called The Honeycomb.'

'That's rather good.' He looked at her as though she had surprised him. Had she betrayed that scepticism of which Cope had accused her? While she was thinking about this, he said, 'By the way, do you know if Cope is friendly with Mrs. Ormerod?'

Hannah concentrated for a moment on the typewriter, realigning the paper, her tongue between her lips, her eyes intent. When she had done this to her satisfaction, she said, 'You would have to ask Rodney that. I've enough to do typing his correspondence, I don't concern myself with his friends.'

Lomax said, 'Ah, yes. . . .' He looked at his watch. 'Good gracious! Nearly two o'clock. Have you lunched?'

'I'm having a working lunch.'

'Ah well, another time. One day next week, perhaps?'

Hannah smiled.

Lomax stood staring gloomily at the window as though brooding on the cleaning problem; then he turned on his heel and went out of the room.

Hannah went on typing, her fingers moving very fast, her eyes flicking automatically from the pad to the typewriter. She kept this up for some twelve minutes, whisking paper rapidly in and out of the typewriter. Then she went to the window to eat her sandwiches. She slid the window back as far as it would go. It was ten past two. The narrow footways of The Warren ran off to the left and to the right. In the distance, between gaps in the low roofs opposite, she could see the plane trees in Scotney Square, where people would be eating sandwiches on the grass and admiring the elegant façade of the Victorian houses. It was surprisingly quiet, the pubs were still open, business in the shops was slack. The walls of the pub opposite, *The North Star*, had recently been painted a brilliant carnation; it made the Chinese restaurant next door, its windows covered by a net curtain which had not been washed since the day it was put up, look more dingy than ever. There was a jewellers' next to the Chinese restaurant, its windows protected by iron bars which must have been provided by a previous owner, since the array of second-hand junk in the window scarcely warranted such elaborate precautions. Farther on, Hannah could see The Lantern Shop, its window crammed with light shades of every kind, the lights themselves looking wan as electric light does in daytime. Hannah liked the way the sordid and the elegant rubbed shoulders in Scotney. Scotney was an exciting place to be.

5

WATER was sluicing down, the gutter must be blocked. It had been raining for several hours, if not all day; Pauline Ormerod had heard it when she woke in the morning, and again at midday. Now she could not hear the raindrops because of this cascade which had recently started. She sat up, resting her weight on one elbow. The light was bad, the room was full of shadow, and beyond the window the sky was a darker grey; she could just see the tops of trees moving, nothing else. If she sat upright, she would probably see the roofs of the houses on the far side of the London Road. That would be exciting! Instead, she turned over on her stomach and lay with her head hanging down the side of the bed. She had put her travelling clock on the floor, because she kept knocking it off the bedside table; now it stared up at her, eyeball to eyeball. Half-past five! A day gone. But not so far gone that she could just turn over and sleep through to the next day. She stared at the carpet; she was gradually sliding off the bed and she had a good view of the carpet, but it didn't present her with any answer to her problems. She put out a hand to stop herself falling, and lay for a moment or two meditating, her body supported by the one hand pressed on the floor. 'I can't stay like this for ever,' she thought drearily. She hauled herself back onto the bed, and sat huddled up, staring at the blurred windows. Her head was heavy and the room smelt stale. In the long mirror she could see her reflection, she raised a hand and made a rude gesture. It didn't solve anything. She looked around; there were her clothes strewn across the floor, a half-empty bottle of gin and an overturned glass under the dressing-table, the telephone directory for the Scotney area on Geoffrey's bureau (why did no one ever ask to have the telephone directory with them on their desert island? All those interesting people. . . .)

Geoffrey hadn't answered the telephone. He never answered the telephone now, in case it was her ringing. Perhaps he never went out in case he met her. Perhaps they were both living cooped up in bedrooms, sleeping the time away.

She got up and went very slowly into the bathroom. Any quick movement was painful. She did not wash or brush her teeth, that film of dirt was all she had left, her last protection. She went back to the bedroom and looked out of the window. She hadn't missed much of a day. Beyond the green –beg its pardon, The Green, God knew they had paid enough for a house fronting The Green. . . . Beyond The Green, the London Road was jammed with cars and buses in between which sleek black motor-cyclists wormed their way. There was a long queue at the bus stop, people huddled in raincoats, poking one another's eyes with umbrellas. What did they do it for? she wondered. Why didn't they all stay in bed on a day like this? Farther away, in the direction of Scotney Square, lights had come on in shops and office blocks. But by the time she had dressed it would be too late for visiting either shops or offices. She had meant to visit Geoffrey's solicitor. The first small grain of resolution stirred within her. When she had woken this morning, and thought how she must bathe to remove all odour, dress to make herself acceptable, take a taxi so that she didn't spoil the effect on the way, arrive at Slater and Wilberforce after ten in the hope that Mr. Slater would by that time have arrived, but would not yet be engaged with another client . . . she had turned over and gone to sleep again. Even at her best, she had never been good at observing the customary patterns of behaviour; other people did that kind of thing so much better than she did. But she would go to endless trouble, risk ridicule and humiliation, and even, on occasions, jeopardise her personal safety, simply in order to do something the wrong way. In the days when he had found her an irresistible madcap, Geoffrey had said she was one of those people who thought that 'No Entry' stood for 'Short-Cut'. Resolution hardened

47

into action. She had to see Mr. Slater. It was ludicrous to imagine that any convention about hours of business, any nonsense about professional etiquette, any social niceties about not calling on people unannounced, should stand in the way of her seeing Mr. Slater on a matter which affected her husband's future. She was now unwaveringly set upon her purpose. She dressed with little care for Mr. Slater's predilection for a well-turned out woman, but taking just as long as if sartorial elegance had been her object. By the time she emerged in long-sleeved, torn black sweater, out-of-date tartan mini-skirt and Cossack boots, a lot of thought had been expended, but the matter under consideration had been the clothes to suit her own mood and Mr. Slater was almost forgotten. She had to return to the house to look up his private address in the telephone directory. She and Geoffrey had dined at his house once, but it was an occasion which she had erased from her memory.

Her car was being serviced, so she set out on foot. She had forgotten to take her handbag with her. This was becoming a habit; she had run up bills all over the town. In her present mood, however, it suited her to walk in the rain and she set off across The Green towards the even more expensive area on the fringe of Gloucester Park where Mr. Slater lived. She arrived at his house at seven as he was relaxing with a drink before dinner.

'It's Pauline Ormerod, Mr. Slater,' she reminded him, and smiled graciously, just as though she was giving her name at a ball.

A gust of wind blew rain into Mr. Slater's face which was round and pink as a sugar plum. He had pale protruding eyes and an invariable smile. Even now, when he was far from pleased, the lips still smiled.

'You had better come in,' he said.

'I want to talk to you about Geoffrey.' She showed willingness to start a discussion there in the hall, which was as well from her point of view as he had no intention of allowing her a further foothold. The wind dislodged petals from the tulips in the window recess. Mr. Slater closed the front door.

'I cannot possibly talk to you about your husband, Mrs. Ormerod.' It was hard to tell whether the impropriety of her visit, or her slovenly attire, displeased him the most. Her boots made muddy welts on the highly polished parquet floor.

'But I can't contact him. He doesn't answer the telephone and he doesn't reply to my letters. So I *must* talk to you.'

'If your husband does not wish to communicate with you, that is nothing to do with me, Mrs. Ormerod.'

At this point, Mrs. Slater closed the drawing-room door and another tulip petal fell.

'But you are his solicitor. You must know what has happened to him.'

'Nothing has happened to him.' Mr. Slater smiled reprovingly. 'He is staying in London for the time being, that is all.'

'He hasn't been arrested?'

'There is no reason why he should be arrested, Mrs. Ormerod. He has committed no crime.'

'But he lost the election.'

'He lost the election because he did not get as many votes as Neil Moray,' Mr. Slater said tartly. 'He is unlikely to be arrested for that.'

'But people didn't vote for him because of the disclosures about his dealings with Mario Vicente. I'm not a fool, Mr. Slater.'

'If that is your reading of the situation. . . .' Mr. Slater shrugged his shoulders.

'What is *your* reading of it, then?'

'I have no idea why people vote for one candidate as opposed to another,' Mr. Slater smiled disdainfully. 'Nor am I concerned with it. Now, Mrs. Ormerod, if you don't mind. . . .'

'But I haven't nearly finished. It's no use trying to edge me out like that. I have information which is important. As my husband's legal representative. . . .'

'Really, this is quite intolerable!' Mr. Slater's face became a more hectic pink. 'I must ask you to leave.'

'But I am trying to tell you something that concerns my

49

husband. You are paid to represent him, after all!' She spoke as though he were a tradesman.

Mr. Slater left the tulips to their fate and opened the front door again.

'It's about the burglary,' she said.

'Burglary!' He was very angry. His smile agitated his features terribly. 'Was there really a burglary, Mrs. Ormerod?'

She stared at him. 'Of course there was.' The wind which surged into the hall seemed to have taken all her vehemence away. 'Those documents. . . .'

'The envelope in which those documents were posted was typed on the typewriter in your husband's study, Mrs. Ormerod, the one which *you* used to type his correspondence.'

She rested her hand on the little table where the telephone stood and drops of water from her sweater smeared the delicate cherry wood. 'You're not suggesting . . . you can't possibly mean. . . .'

'I am making no suggestions, Mrs. Ormerod.' He knew that he had already said too much and was anxious to get rid of her.

'Does Geoffrey believe that I . . .?'

'Mrs. Ormerod, I have merely given you one or two facts. . . .'

'But I must speak to Geoffrey, I must!'

Mr. Slater panicked as her voice shrilled into the garden and beyond. 'You must leave, Madam! Otherwise I shall call the police.'

She said, 'Oh God, what a bloody mess!'

Mr. Slater put out one hand to urge her forward and then bethought himself of what might happen if she resisted. The smell of damp earth drifted in and mingled with the odour of her wet pullover. For a moment which seemed to him interminable, they stood in silence in the doorway, then she walked past him, her head bowed in thought as though she had already forgotten he was there. He closed the door after her and then hurried to peer in undignified fashion through the dining-room curtains to make sure that she left his premises. He was relieved to see her open the garden gate; she left it swinging on its hinges and he did not venture out to close it until he was sure she would be some distance away. The rain was coming down harder than ever.

Pauline walked on the fringe of darkness beyond which lay Gloucester Park. She understood Geoffrey's behaviour now. When he became so bitter and spiteful, she thought he had guessed she was having an affair, while all the time he was thinking that it was she who had sent those documents to Neil Moray.

'You have never wanted me to go into politics, have you?' How often he had said that. 'You think it would make too many demands on you if I were to go into politics. You resented my business activities, but you couldn't do anything about that. . . .'

A bus swished by, splashing her with muddy water.

'Oh God!' she thought. 'What a bloody awful mess!'

It was still raining heavily when Hannah left her evening class at half-past nine. There were a few people sheltering in shop doorways near the bus stop, a girl and a boy running, laughing, coats drawn over their heads. Hannah looked down the road; it was a wide road in one of the busiest parts of the town, but there was little traffic about and no sign of a bus. She decided not to wait, it would only put her in a worse temper. She attended an astronomy class which for the first two years she had greatly enjoyed; she had bought a star map and, together with other members of the class, had gone onto the Downs at night, and had visited nearby observatories; she had saluted the seasons with such comments as 'Winter is upon us, Orion is coming up. . . .' Now, however, they were discussing galaxies that were so many million light years away that man would never see them from this planet, even with the aid of the largest telescope. Hannah liked her stars visible to man.

Tonight, toiling up the hill towards the church of St.

Stephen the Martyr, she felt very depressed. Everything came to an end. Even the stars, it seemed. It was no use young Mr. Ross lecturing about a limitless universe, as far as she was concerned she had come to the end of the stars on the night of 31st May, 1973.

She turned into Saddlers Row. She could hear water running in the gutters; the street lights were furred as though it was a November evening. In the car park opposite her flat, there were five cars, a lorry, and a caravan which had been abandoned for some six weeks. A dark, oily pool of water had collected at the entrance. She opened the door to one side of the garage and went up the narrow shaft that led to the flat. There was a smell of damp plaster and the handrail felt slippery. The light bulb flickered; she hoped it wasn't going out, it was difficult to reach the fitting. She felt she could not bear the extinguishing of another light.

It was a relief to get into the flat. Most of it was on view from where she stood just inside the front door; bedroom to her left, kitchen, which also contained the bath (an idiosyncrasy of design much deplored by her sister-in-law), the sitting-room, the long stroke of the L, to her right. There were no doors, but curtains could be drawn if she had visitors who fussed about such things. The lavatory was at the bottom of the stairs, which was a nuisance, indeed a hazard, when guests had had rather too much to drink; someone had once broken an ankle.

Hannah looked thankfully around her as she took off her wet cape and shoes. The stars might be lost to her, but she still had number 12a Saddlers Row. She went into the sitting-room and stretched out on the Victorian couch which she had bought in a country-house sale and had re-upholstered herself. The room was perhaps rather sparsely furnished for some tastes, Hannah hated to live in a clutter; but a lot of work and love had gone into it and each piece of furniture was a reward for determined forays into antique markets and auction rooms.

The open-plan living had its disadvantages, however; from where she was lying, the far corner of the bedroom was visible, showing a portion of unmade bed. Hannah did not live sluttishly, and it was rare for her to go out without making her bed. The bed had remained unmade because she had spent more time than usual reading *The Scotney Gazette*. Her reading had given her little pleasure.

The last three editions of the *Gazette* were on the top of the bookcase. She picked them up and began to read through the passages which had most offended her, in much the same way as one probes a bad tooth to make sure it can still be made to ache. She turned first to the profile on Rodney Cope. Cope had dismissed it with a shrug of the shoulders—'I told you Lomax encouraged his bright boys. This is Basil Todd flexing what he uses for muscle.' Perhaps there was some sense in this. The interview with Neil was on another page. His words had been faithfully and unambiguously recorded, but it was all a little dull, rather tired-sounding. Neil had been tired at the time, so perhaps one shouldn't complain about that. But things had not improved in subsequent weeks. The *Gazette* had become decidedly tetchy, looking back over the last few months and asking questions. Had the campaign against Ormerod been so strong that people had over-reacted? Did no one intend to examine Ormerod's objections to Heffernan's proposals objectively? Exactly what *was* proposed, and who would benefit? And so and so forth.

The previous Sunday, before she had begun to feel quite so uneasy, Hannah had met Lomax walking along the front. She had decided not to go to *Guiseppe's*, but to see whether there was a reasonably priced restaurant on the West Front.

'It's quite pleasant along here,' she acknowledged, albeit a little grudgingly because the harbour area was older and she preferred old buildings. The promenade here was wide, however, the property set well back, there were more trees, and farther away the great cliffs rose with dramatic suddenness.

'Make the most of it,' Lomax advised. 'There are changes on the way.'

'Perhaps we need change,' Hannah said. 'Neil thinks this

new enterprise will offer big opportunities, bring new blood to the town, a lot of business....

'It will bring the really big-time gamblers, the highly organised rackets.' He swung his rolled umbrella and held it, shouldering arms. 'Would you like that?' He looked at her intently, as though the whole scheme depended on her answer and if Hannah Mason were not pleased that would be an end to it.

'Surely that may not happen?' she protested, evading the necessity of making so momentous a decision.

'It will, it will!' he assured her with passion, and then stopped to poke some litter out of the way with the handle of the umbrella, following this up with a practice shot which left her undecided as to whether his game was golf or hockey. 'What Mario Vicente has done hasn't greatly altered the character of the town; in some ways, he has added a flavour to it, but...'

Hannah recalled that he was reputed to be friendly with Mario Vicente, some people said too friendly. Whatever the truth of the matter, it seemed likely that his judgement had been somewhat at fault in his association with Mario. It wasn't what one expected of him. Hannah, while regretting this flaw in the much-respected editor of the *Gazette,* found the man more interesting for being fallible. She took him up on his remarks about Mario. 'Neil says that Mario works undercover, that where he doesn't own, he controls. He thinks it is bad that Mario's influence isn't apparent, that it means people can't express a point of view about his dealings.'

'I would have thought that over the last few weeks people had heard much of Mario's dealings, and absolutely nothing of Heffernan's.' The editor of the *Gazette* dismissed Neil's views crisply; Will Lomax addressed himself to Hannah with some urgency. 'I think that under Heffernan's scheme you might be very aware of change. Scotney would seem less like your home, it would belong to the "international set"– ghastly phrase.' He looked at her keenly. 'Don't you think it's ghastly?' Before she could answer, he stopped abruptly, disconcerting a couple who were ambling close behind. 'Look!'

He took Hannah's arm and swung her round. They stood together, gazing back at the long line of the promenade, at the buildings, the pretentious and the restrained, the sober and the garish, which, in spite of their diversity, gave Scotney its identity. 'Do you want that to become "The California of the South Coast"?' His eyes told her that if she wanted it, she must have it, but he would be desperately disappointed in her.

Hannah made a joke of it and told him he had spoilt her Sunday morning stroll. But he had done rather more than that. He had disturbed her peace of mind. She found she was beginning to ask her own questions.

During the last few weeks, Neil had spent much of his time in London. He had made his maiden speech: on immigration. It was not a topic of much concern to his constituency which, apart from occasional cases of illegal entry into the country, was scarcely aware of the problem. 'I wish he didn't have these sudden rushes of idealism to the head,' Cope had said. Hannah wished she could see it as idealism. It seemed to her that Neil was putting off the time when he must come to terms with his election promises. She did not think that he was a coward, but she began to question whether he had sufficient grasp of the realities of the world in which he was now moving. The problems were considerable and had defeated many a good man before him. But it was scarcely conceivable that Neil Moray was but one of many good men.

Hannah had come under Neil's spell, and she was not alone in this. Politicians, in spite of their much-vaunted contempt for the media, tended more and more to court its favours, adapting their personalities to its demands, striving to create the right image. Unfortunately, what came across was as blandly unconvincing as the patter of the public relations officer. Neil Moray was different: thoughtful, tentative, apt to speak hesitantly, he gave the impression that he was bringing a fresh mind to bear on each problem put before him. He was a good listener, and his answers were never glib; yet he contrived to convince his audience that he *would*

55

find the answer. But there was more to his appeal than this. When he reflected silently on a question, he seemed to be holding in the balance one's own hope and despair. He was the kind of person who arouses that almost unbearable hope that here at last is someone who carries within him the secret power which turns this world's dross into gold. As soon as he stepped onto a platform, he projected to the audience that mysterious sense of secret power; even if he was only looking down at his notes while the speaker introduced him, he held the attention of the audience and aroused an exciting sense of expectancy. The fact that he never seemed quite to fulfil this promise at any one engagement did not detract from the success of his performance, but seemed only to whet the appetite. One day, his listeners felt, sometime, somewhere, he would do something really spectacular and they were resolved to be present on that occasion. Towards the end of his campaign his meetings were packed. 'He would have been a superb actor,' Cope had once said. 'Give him the part of the Officer and he'd steal the death scene from King Lear.'

But what would he have done with the part of Lear? Hannah was beginning to wonder.

She threw the copies of the *Gazette* on the floor. Was it possible that Neil was going to end up like all the other well-meaning but ineffectual people in parliament? That would be unutterably sad. So much bright hope, such high endeavour, all waning, the light and the dark running together to form a smudgy, all-pervading drabness. She couldn't bear to watch that happening slowly, week by week.

She went into the kitchen and made herself a cheese omelette. Before she went to bed, she opened all the windows, ventilation was a problem in the open-plan design. The noises of the town came to her ears, men shouting outside pubs at closing time, the screech of tyres on slippery roads, an occasional siren. The rain had stopped, and she saw a solitary star between the roof of the International Stores and the spire of St. Stephen the Martyr.

The time had come for a change, she thought. If she gave in her notice immediately, she could say that once the excitement of the election was over, the work no longer interested her. That would sound perfectly plausible; Neil had commented once or twice during the campaign on her lack of political conviction. She did not think he would mind if she left now; he would get a lot of his secretarial work done at Westminster. She felt better for having made the decision and slept well.

She got up early and set out for the office in the bright light of a fine June day. The possibility of change excited her. She might try commuting to London. She opened the post, sorted it and set to work clearing the backlog of letters which Cope had dictated to her yesterday. Cope telephoned to say he would not be in until the afternoon.

Neil came in at half-past nine.

'I came down with the newspapers,' he said. 'Have you ever done that?'

'Whatever for?'

'I was late at the House. I missed the last train.'

'Couldn't you have come down this morning?'

He shook his head. 'I had a lot to do. There's so much I have to catch up on, read about. . . .' He sat on the one upright chair. His voice was husky, but staccato, not his usual way of talking. 'The station is very odd at that hour. No drunks, even. And the cloakrooms and all-night coffee places were all closed because of the bomb scares. Some trains had been cancelled. Most of the people waiting had missed trains, too. I remember once when I was working with discharged prisoners, I had to meet a man at a railway booking office. I was sure I would recognise him, but when I got there all the people who were waiting looked so utterly destitute of hope I couldn't pick my fellow out. People always look like that when they're waiting and they've nothing to do, have you noticed? As though they are staring through a rent in life.' He closed his eyes. 'I'm so desperately tired. Would there be any coffee?' Hannah was shocked by his appearance. The colour had ebbed from his face and the slight tan merely made his skin look unhealthy, blotched with shadow.

Hannah filled the kettle. When she had made the coffee,

he said, 'Have you got the file on Heffernan? I forgot to take it with me.'

'Good Heavens! You were meeting him, weren't you?'

'It didn't matter.' His voice was dry, without humour. 'He did all the talking.'

'How did you get on?'

'I can't say I took to him.'

She put the file on the table, and he looked down at it, but did not touch it. Hannah sensed the desperate tiredness which comes from a reluctance to tackle something, and the thought crossed her mind that he would not be able to cope with public life. Afterwards, she told herself that this was fanciful, but no doubt it affected her reactions at the time.

He said, handing her the empty cup, 'That's better! What would I do without you, Hannah?'

Hannah said, 'Fortunately, you don't have to do without me; so the question doesn't arise.'

He did not do anything about the Heffernan file that morning.

6

'WELL now, I should like his help. You get me? I'd be very glad of his help. But if I don't get it, well, that's too bad. I'll be able to get along, though I can see it may take just that little bit longer. I wouldn't want anyone to think I was upset about this.' Arthur Heffernan broke off at this point to glare at Priscilla Fry. It was a hot day. The window (there was a lot of window) was open, something he rarely permitted, and already two flies had come in. He put his hand over the mouthpiece and hissed, 'Get them out of here.' While she made a brisk attack with a roll of paper, he returned to his telephone conversation with Rodney Cope.

'I don't take offence at this sort of thing, you know that. I've been in the business world too long to take offence at anything. But I like to know where I stand with someone, and I got the feeling I didn't rate very high with this Neil Moray. What was he before he stood for parliament, by the way? A Sunday school teacher or something? I know his kind, they preach humility but they don't practise it themselves, and I got the definite impression that in his quiet way, he thought rather a lot of himself.' He patted his pink, freckled head with a rolled handkerchief. 'Now, I just don't have time for that kind of thing, it doesn't impress me one bit. I like a man I can talk to fair and square; maybe we'll call each other a lot of names, but that doesn't matter, the tougher they come the more I like them. But it would take a month of Sundays to get to understand what goes on in that young man's mind, and I don't have that time to spare. . . .' He wriggled on his seat, pulling himself up by the shoulders; even on the telephone, he was very conscious of his lack of height. 'Yes, well, maybe, but I expected someone with more dynamism, and that wasn't the way he presented to me. I just can't see him in a fight. And we're going to need to fight this all the way. . . . All right, if you say so. You know him better than I do. But I don't often make mistakes. I understand about people; I've had a lot of dealings with people over the years and I don't back many losers. . . . All right, I'll leave it to you. But I don't want this to hang fire, it's important there shouldn't be any suggestion that we've run into difficulties. . . . Oh, I don't worry about that. Who reads a local paper, anyhow? Just the people who want to know if their football team won. But I wouldn't want Moray to back down, it wouldn't look good at this point in time. . . . Yes, do that, will you?'

He put the receiver down, brisk, to the point, that was always his way. His secretary said, 'I could buy some *aerosol.*'

Heffernan studied his hands; he had small, rather puffy hands with stubby fingers in which were surprisingly embedded finely rounded nails with a delicate sheen of pearl above the clear half-moons. His bulbous eyes looked angrily at the nails as though repelled by the sight of something so sensitive snared up in his flesh.

'What did you think of him? I always respect your judgement, you know that.' He looked at Priscilla Fry compellingly.

He was desperately thin-skinned, obsessed with projecting an image of himself quite at variance with the real person. This quiet, sad-faced middle-aged woman, who looked as though she had wandered into the wrong half of the century, had been the guardian of that image for many years and did not fail him now.

'Rather enigmatic?' she suggested. It would not do to lie; their relationship would have foundered long ago if it had been based on lies. Her attitude to him was that of a nanny, anxious for the well-being of her charge, but not wanting to spoil his little pleasures. She was careful to present him with little bits of truth, never too much at any one time, and always carefully mixed with less indigestible stuff. 'He doesn't give much of himself away to anyone, I would guess. Charming, and aware of it, but not making use of it as yet, perhaps

60

doesn't know how to. I would say a little immature. These people who live so within their shell often are, don't you think? And he hasn't had a failure.'

'Yes!' Heffernan snapped finger and thumb. 'That's it! He hasn't had a failure.' It was the thing which had got under his skin when he talked to Moray. Now that he was presented with a reason unconnected with class for that slight aura of superiority he no longer felt any resentment. The man who has not had a failure is only to be pitied; either he has risked too little, or is fast using up his reserves of luck.

'I hope he isn't going to be a nuisance.' He had Moray in perspective now.

'It would be difficult for him to turn round and march the other way, wouldn't it?' she mused. 'I don't think he's the kind who would find that very easy.'

'No. You're right there. He wouldn't find it easy.' Heffernan sounded satisfied.

He hadn't done his homework on Moray, Priscilla Fry reflected. It was unlike him. He usually went to so much trouble. He was not by nature a good judge of other people, his own personality got in the way, he was easily flattered and quick to take offence. He found social intercourse painful, he could never quite conquer the feeling that he was the one who must prove himself. It wasn't that his origins were bad, but rather that he wasn't conscious of originating anywhere. His parents had spent their life in an endeavour to move up the social scale so that he seemed to have rungs rather than roots. But what he lacked in intuition, he made up for by painstaking research. Even when he was dealing with relatively unimportant people, who would figure only briefly in one of his schemes, he would study all that he could find out about them, sometimes talking to people who had known them as children. The deepest clefts in personality are made in childhood. He had every reason to know that. His final decisions were never made over a good meal; those who suffered under the illusion that this was how business was done came in for a few shocks where he was concerned. He

61

knew his weakness: he didn't make decisions until the vibrations had died away—except in a few cases of which Priscilla Fry was one and Rodney Cope another.

'The local paper,' he said, putting Moray to one side. 'What's it called—*The Scotney News,* or *Gazette,* or *Weekly.* . . . or something.'

'*Gazette.*'

'Who owns it? We must have a record of that.'

'It's one of the Cannock papers.'

'Oh, *is* it!' Lord Cannock had a reputation for not interfering with his editors.

'I don't think you need worry. It's a very respectable paper. In the past they've run into a bit of trouble with some of the local big-wigs, but it's all been very low-keyed.'

'And the editor is William Lomax. Right?'

'Forty-three. Divorced. Wife wanted someone more enterprising, she's married to a Zurich broker now. No children. He lives alone. Mildly eccentric. Devoted to the *Gazette.*'

'No possibility that he might be on Vicente's pay roll?'

'He's been to Vicente's house once or twice, people talk, but there's no evidence of Vicente exerting any influence on the *Gazette.*'

'How would you sum up Lomax?'

'Staunch. But not a crusader.'

He nodded his head. 'Yes. I think that is probably right. I wouldn't be quite sure there is nothing between him and Vicente, though.' He found it hard to believe that anyone could come so close to money and not find some of it in his pocket. 'We might have a look at that angle, anyway. Just in case it should come in useful.'

7

THE long range weather forecast was good. There was no mention of storms. All seemed set for a long period of untroubled sunshine. Scotney was quick to get into the act; it had recorded temperatures in the top seventies yesterday. Not bad for the beginning of June.

Rodney Cope left his basement room in Cadogan Crescent, which in spite of its distinguished-sounding name, was on the 'wrong' side of the London Road, and walked towards Scotney Square. It was the morning rush hour and petrol fumes were already polluting the brisk morning air. In the centre of the busy concourse, a harassed traffic warden waved traffic on with a motion as though stirring a pudding. While he waited, Cope decided that he would take a stroll through The Warren. Neil would have to wait for him.

It didn't worry Cope that Neil showed signs of being difficult, or that the *Gazette* appeared to be mounting a campaign against the proposed development of the West Front. These things would have to be dealt with, but they didn't worry him. Neil was likely to be the most difficult problem. The *Gazette* would tire, newspapers seldom stayed with this kind of thing for long—even if the staff had the stamina, their readers didn't. Neil's resistance might be of a different order, and the fact that the part which he had to play was an active and not a passive one made his reactions crucial.

But none of this was in Rodney Cope's mind as he strolled through The Warren. He never planned moves in advance. If you plan, you start working out other people's moves and before you know where you are, you are adapting yourself to them. He didn't believe in adapting himself to other people. He preferred to be strong enough to enforce his will on them. Quite apart from these considerations, he hated planning.

It meant imposing a measure of discipline on yourself, telling yourself that you couldn't do this, or must do that, marking out a path for yourself which very soon had high brick walls on either side. You set limits for yourself and lived within them. He would rather be dead. And that wasn't one of those idle phrases. He had played around with death. When he had been on military service in the Near East he had been involved in a number of unofficial exploits any one of which might have ended his life. It had been a good time. Some of the men he had been with wouldn't admit that now. They suffered from a sense of shame, a need to explain away, now, in a civilised context, the savagery of warfare. When he listened to them he wondered what it was they were talking about, it had so changed in their minds that he was unable to recognise the incidents as the ones in which he had been involved. War and peace don't inhabit the same world, they require a different vocabulary, more than that, a different person. How can a peace-time man, moralising comfortably in his armchair, ever understand the man who is fighting outside the stockade? The immediacy of the moment, the quickened pulse, the sharpened senses, the heightened awareness of life that comes from an acquaintance with death, what does he know of this? But now, back here, where all the wheels were running down, it was a different kind of death; death had grown older, he too had tired and staled, he took you by inches.

It was the one thing which frightened Rodney Cope. Every so often he had to do something to demonstrate that he wasn't going to be shepherded into the pen. He had seen a painting once at a local exhibition; it had been called 'Pen Level'. He could remember now the stakes looming up, blocking the view of the long, bare hills beyond. Not for him.

All these thoughts were in his mind as he walked through The Warren. Sombre thoughts to be occasioned by an election victory. But Cope, looking back over the past few months, was uneasy. It had all started at a party. He had met Moray. A man called Ronald Singleton, who himself had unfulfilled political ambitions, had been trying to per-

suade Moray to stand as Independent candidate for Scotney. On an impulse, in the way that things happened to him,
Cope had told himself that *he* could persuade Moray to
stand. And when he succeeded, he had added, feeling that the
gesture needed rounding off, 'I'll be your campaign manager. You'll get in with a majority of over four thousand.'
He had been quite convinced of this and his assurance had
infected Moray. Moray did not want to handle the messy
part of the campaign. He saw in Cope a man capable of
taking this off his shoulders, whereas Ronald Singleton would
drag him down with him into the morass. One of the messiest
parts of the campaign was money-raising activities. 'I'll have
to leave all that to you,' Moray had said to Cope. One thing
led to another. The quest for money led Cope to Arthur
Heffernan, and from then on more was at stake than winning
an election. Cope had worked hard for both his masters. It
had been exhilarating, and the fact that Moray was not
aware of what was happening and would certainly not have
approved of it, had given added interest to the manoeuvre.
Yet, Cope was uneasy. When he was confronted with Heffernan's plans for the development of the West Front, he had
found himself thinking that this was a challenge of a different order to his other adventures, something he must see
through. He had never before caught himself thinking in
terms of seeing anything through. The corruption of civilisation was hard to withstand.

He stooped in the doorway of a print shop, a dark little
place which he seemed to fill like a giant in a fairy's cave. The
prints were good. He had no interest in them, he wasn't
going to put his head in culture's noose. But he liked the little
shops in The Warren which were mostly run by young people
who had stepped out of line. In the end, of course, the shops
would own them, but most of them were some way from that
yet. He bought articles here and there, half-aware of the in-
sidious nature of such philanthropic gestures. At the moment,
he was supposed to be collecting costume prints. He could
tell by the way the girl looked at him—not calculatingly, she
hadn't learnt to calculate a thing yet, but with a gentle

perplexity–that she couldn't fathom his motives. How long would it be before she was more interested in her sales than her customers' motives for buying? He caught himself in the act of making a value judgement. These were dangers one had to risk. He paid for the print and wandered on, past a café where they were putting out elegant white-painted chairs at coffee tables, threading his way between wickerware outside the next shop. The sun was bright, and although the rays were still too much on the slant to penetrate the narrow alleys, the forecast had promised a long, fine day and the shopkeepers were trustingly placing their wares on the gleaming cobblestones. He could smell the first whiff of *Ambre Solaire*.

Neil had been waiting for him for half an hour when he arrived at the office.

'I've been prospecting,' Cope told him. 'There's a new coffee place opened in The Warren. Shall we try it out?'

'We can't talk there.'

'Much safer than here,' Cope assured him. 'Hannah has probably bugged all the packing cases, haven't you, love?'

'If you want to be on your own, wouldn't it be better if I tried out the place in The Warren?' she suggested.

'Would you mind?' Moray asked awkwardly.

'I've got to go to the printers, anyway. That'll take some time.'

'What would we do without our Hannah?' Cope said lightly when she had gone.

'Perhaps we need to talk about that.'

'Doing without Hannah?'

'No. But about the future, for all of us.'

'Why yes. By all means, let's talk about the future.' Cope stretched his long legs out in front of him and waited.

Moray sat at Hannah's table; the weight of his slightly bowed shoulders rested on his left forearm, the right arm was extended across the desk, the fingers resting lightly on the wood. He studied the scratches on the surface of the table as though they were lines of music and he was waiting for the bar where he came in. Cope had no intention of giving him a cue. They had used each other, Cope and Moray; now they had to work out what use they still had for each other. After a moment, Moray raised his eyes and gave Cope a rueful, half-apologetic smile. It was charming, the kind of smile which can be a prelude to almost anything, including a kick in the teeth. Cope responded by raising his eyebrows.

Moray said, 'We've come quite a way together. I don't think I have said how grateful I am.' He looked rueful as a man who has recently gone through his accounts and found himself deeper in debt than he had imagined.

Cope did not intend to back out tactfully, like one of those figures in a Western, riding off into the sunset when all the bad men have been shot, leaving the good guy to make a nice, law-abiding town for all the honest little people to live in. He said, 'Let's not waste time on gratitude. There's quite a way to go yet.'

'I don't know how things are with you financially.' Moray sounded awkward; he hated talking money as much as a miser hates spending it.

'You don't need to worry about that,' Cope answered. 'It's a useful training for me in responsible citizenship. You must try to see me in the capacity of an apprentice.' As Moray still seemed uneasy, he said, 'Unless, of course, you feel you want to manage the whole show on your own from now on.'

'That's the last thing I want.' But Moray's tone suggested he had given it some thought. He began to list his reasons for rejecting the idea, more for his own satisfaction than Cope's. 'There's no organisation here to speak of as yet. I've made a few useful contacts in the town, but they need to be followed up, nursed, and God knows when I'll get the time for that. Then there are the issues I raised at the election, I've got to try to work out the best way of doing the things I promised. Some of them are so complicated, it needs a research unit working on them full-time! Planning. . . .'

The telephone rang. It was maddening for him, just as he had worked his way round to the thing which was really worrying him. Cope studied him as he dealt with the call, a reminder that he was to speak at a meeting sponsored by The Downland Association. He was tired, the slight twitch of his left eyelid was more pronounced than usual this morning, but he had too much respect for his caller—or himself—to betray weariness; although his manner was restrained, he managed to inject some interest into his words. He gives just enough, never an ounce more, Cope thought; I wonder whether he deliberately paces himself. How far could he go if he was really extended?

Moray put the receiver down, made a note on a pad in front of him, and said, 'I'm not very happy about this scheme of Heffernan's.'

Cope said idly, 'Or was it Heffernan you weren't keen on? Tycoons are seldom likable, that's why they get to be tycoons. But you don't need to worry too much about the impression Heffernan made on you. His scheme isn't a projection of his personality, he's not Mario. Other people will have worked the scheme out for him.'

Moray said stubbornly, 'He looked at me as though I was one of his possessions.'

'That's his way. In his eyes, people are either for him, or against him; there is no such thing as non-alignment.'

'No one,' Moray said, 'has ever behaved as though they possessed me.'

It must have been a devastating confrontation. For a moment, Cope could barely control the desire to laugh at the picture conjured up.

Moray went on, 'It made me wonder about his methods. I think we shall need to investigate his scheme very thoroughly.'

'You're a damn liar!' Cope thought. 'You're not thinking about the scheme even now. You are still suffering under this assault on your ego.'

'I've never committed myself to Heffernan's scheme.' Moray had been a member of parliament for just under a month, and already he was learning his lessons. 'I went through my speeches last night. I was very careful what I said on the subject.'

'You said,' Cope reminded him, 'that the proposals for the

development of the West Front should be considered coolly and objectively and not simply dismissed out of hand as some interested parties would like them to be.'

'That is just what I propose to do. Consider them coolly and objectively.'

'Not all of your meetings were cool and objective. I remember one at which someone accused you of defending the scheme in order to make capital out of Ormerod's difficulties. You replied, if you remember, by giving a number of reasons why you thought the scheme might be of advantage to the town. This was a matter which came up several times at question-and-answer sessions. You were asked to elaborate on your previous remarks. The next time you were asked to elaborate on your elaborations.'

'The reasons I gave were quite valid.'

'You don't think they suggested that you had already given very careful consideration to the scheme? I'm only mentioning this because if you withdraw now that is what people will say.'

'Are you saying I have committed myself to something from which I can't withdraw?' Moray asked stiffly.

'Don't let's put words into each other's mouths,' Cope laughed. 'You can always withdraw from anything.'

Moray bit his lip; the conversation had passed beyond the point where it would have been wise for him to object to the use of the word 'withdraw', it showed how easily one could be put in a false position.

'People have a tendency to think life is much simpler than it really is,' Cope said. 'Expose a man, and people will imagine that everything with which he is connected is contaminated; conversely, the things which he attacked must be good. It would be quite a tricky operation to convince people that Ormerod was right to attack the West Front development without making it seem that you were wrong.'

Moray looked ahead of him. The shutters were down, his face expressed very little. He said, 'You examined the scheme in some detail, didn't you? It was one of the matters I left to you.'

'It was, and I did. I thought it was good. I still think so. It's a little frightening, of course; nothing on this scale has ever been planned over here. But it's all perfectly feasible.'

'Feasible as an engineering project, you mean?'

'Yes. It's been done elsewhere. Tokyo.'

'Tokyo!'

'In miniature, of course.'

'It will dwarf the town!'

'We shall have a Scotney Upper and a Scotney Lower—Scotney Supra, if that sounds more picturesque.'

'It sounds dreadful either way.'

'I told you there would be lower and upper levels for the shops and . . .'

'I imagined it as something like Chester. . . .'

'Why borrow from the past? This is a twenty-first-century development.'

'You should have told me all this.' Up to this point, Moray had avoided recriminations. Now he looked very straight at Cope; there was a momentary glimpse of a man Cope hadn't yet encountered. 'Why didn't you tell me?'

'I thought I told you quite a lot about it,' Cope replied blandly. 'I didn't have any doubts. I put it to you the way I found it—exciting. I still find it exciting.'

Moray looked at him as though for him, also, this was an encounter with an unknown person. His momentary firmness foundered. 'I should have gone into it myself, of course. But it wasn't one of the main issues for me; I never meant to talk about it so much, but there was all that trouble about Ormerod, and at each meeting it seemed necessary to say just a little bit more. . . .' There were beads of sweat on his forehead, not from the heat, which hadn't yet penetrated the room, but panic.

Cope looked at him, fascinated. It is happening to you! he thought. To you of all people, Neil Moray! You, too, are looking back, cool and full of wisdom, to a time when you were fighting tooth and claw—well, not tooth and claw, perhaps, but as near as your kind will ever come to it. And now, in a totally different climate, you are being called to account. What can you say? That they wouldn't have voted for you if you had behaved as you are behaving now, cautious, non-committal, weighing every word. . . . You wouldn't have anything to answer for, because you wouldn't be a member of parliament. Just as I wouldn't be alive if I'd bothered myself about the Sermon on the Mount. All that is for saints, and you're not a saint, Neil Moray. But now is the time to find out just what you are.

He said cheerfully, 'Don't worry. You can wriggle out of it, I expect.' Neil winced. Cope went on, conjuring up a picture of the kind of politician most abhorrent to Moray, 'Make an honest confession that you were mistaken. Be manly about it, don't beat your breast. It may take a bit of time to live it down, but if the scheme doesn't catch on, you may yet be heralded as the man who saved the town. And time is on your side. People have short memories.'

The telephone rang, which was a good thing as he was beginning to run out of clichés. Cope answered it so that Moray might have time to reflect, perhaps even to see himself as a political cartoonist might portray him. Ridicule would come hard to one of Moray's sensibilities.

'Speaking. . . .' Cope was perched on the edge of the table, now he eased round slightly, his back to Moray. 'I'm sorry, this must be a very bad line. *Who* did you say?' He screwed his face up and pressed the receiver to his ear. 'Yes, I did hear, but it *is* a bad line. . . . Well, that wouldn't really be the answer, because I'm engaged at the moment. . . . Yes, if you like. You know the number, don't you? Nice to hear you. 'Bye.' He put the receiver down delicately, as though it was made of cut glass.

Moray said, 'Whatever pressures may be brought to bear,' he looked at Cope coldly, 'I can't commit myself to this unless I am satisfied that it would be right for the scheme to go forward.'

Cope shrugged his shoulders. 'Let it ride awhile. There's a long way to go, it may founder quite naturally.'

71

'No.' Moray shook his head. 'The further I go, the harder it will be to turn back.'

'Look, you're not the only person involved in this!' Cope laughed. 'You didn't launch the project and you weren't responsible for selling it to people in the first place; and as for the final decision, that rests with the Borough Council, the Department of the Environment. . . .'

'From my point of view I am the only person involved.'

'You don't mind if I say that sounds a trifle priggish?'

Moray said levelly, 'Perhaps I am a prig.'

What have we here? Cope wondered. A bloody martyr? Moray's face had a bilious hue. Cope watched him collecting papers together; he didn't look as if he would enjoy gathering his own faggots. Better let him alone for a time, a night or two examining what details of the scheme were available might do more than anything else to moderate his idealism. He said, 'Shall I give you my own papers? They are probably out of date, these schemes change so rapidly, the last drafts I had were numbered eighteen!'

Moray said stiffly, 'If you would.'

He waited, holding to the shreds of his dignity, while Cope searched in the filing cabinet for something that would really give him a fright. He made a practice of keeping even the most incriminating documents in the office so that Moray would never be able to plead ignorance.

Cope had quite forgotten about the telephone call by the time he returned to his basement room in the evening. He had bought fish and chips on the way and he was just emptying them out of the greasy paper when the telephone rang. He picked up the overflowing plate and carried it to the instrument. It was Pauline Ormerod.

'You're still around, then?' he said. Either she could take it that he thought she had been the one to cool off, or that he was supremely indifferent, it didn't matter which.

'Yes. But you've got what you wanted, haven't you?'

'If I say "no", you'll be offended; if I say, "you always

gave me what I wanted", you won't like that, either.' He took a chip and wished he had had time to put salt on the plate.

She said, 'If I say you *took* what you wanted, you won't think I'm talking sex, will you?'

He put the plate down on a chair beside him and said, 'Just at the moment, I'm rather at a loss, so you keep talking and I'll tag along.'

'I'm accusing you of burglary.'

He laughed. 'What am I supposed to be after? That bead curtain you wear for a necklace, or the sheepskin coat with the mange on the shoulder?'

'The papers about Geoffrey's dealings with Mario Vicente.'

'Well, well,' he said softly. 'And you sound quite sober, too.'

There wasn't much steam rising from the fish now, a few more moments and the meal would be quite uneatable; the sight of the food slowly congealing on the plate filled him with revulsion.

'. . . typed it on the typewriter in Geoffrey's study . . .' she was saying.

'Look, Pauline, if you want to work something out of your system, that's all right, go ahead. Talk to me as much as you like, but don't make a fool of yourself in public, will you, love?'

'I've told someone already.'

'You are trying, as they say, to arrest my attention.'

'William Lomax.'

'Yes?'

'Don't worry. He didn't believe me, at least, I don't think he did. . . .' Her voice trailed away, for the first time she sounded very much the person he knew, he could imagine her mind back-tracking over the interview. . . . My God! She *had* told Lomax!

'Perhaps we should talk about this before we both end up in court?' he suggested idly.

'Nothing you could say—or do—would change my mind.'

'As you please. But you're not going to help Geoffrey by

getting yourself involved in a slander action, are you? I don't suppose he wants all the muck dredged up again.'

'It would finish Moray.'

'Pauline, be sensible! Of what are you going to accuse me? Making off with your husband's private papers while I was having an affair with you? Do you think anyone would believe it was necessary for me to resort to burglary?'

'I told you the combination of the safe.'

'Good grief! I don't remember us having that kind of conversation.'

'You said you were getting one for the office, it had to be a small one because there wasn't much room, and the combination had to be simple because your secretary was a simple girl.'

'And you reeled off the combination of your safe, did you?'

'I was reeling anyway that night.'

'But your memory is now sharp and clear.'

'I knew I shouldn't have done it at the time. I was sick the next morning.'

He pushed the plate away from him. The smell was beginning to fill the room, he hadn't had time to open a window.

'Well, now, what are we going to do about this? Do I go to my solicitor in the morning? Or would you like to hear about my alibi first? It's up to you, only hurry, because I have to get something out to the dustbin.'

'Maybe you hired someone else to break in.'

'Maybe, maybe. Which story are you going to settle for?' He wondered which story she had told Lomax.

'You won't talk me out of this,' she muttered.

'Look, Pauline, I don't give a damn what you say about me. But I can't land Moray in this. If you believe I would go so far as to steal those papers in order to get him elected, you can't think I won't fight this.'

'Oh, what the hell. . . .' She sounded completely flat. Her energy had always died suddenly.

'Suppose we talk about it tomorrow evening?' He didn't

sound enthusiastic. 'I must go now. This room smells like a fried fish bar—cold fried fish.'

'Did I interrupt your meal?'

'Not really. I hadn't started.'

'Where shall I meet you, then?'

'Same place? Or do you feel it will be haunted by our former selves?'

'I don't think I'd have much trouble laying those ghosts.' She put the receiver down. She hadn't specified a time; he would have to get there early in the evening and wait. He got up and went across to open the window; the air wasn't all that sweet, Mrs. Simpkins' cat had seen to that. He carried the plate outside, the sight of it filled him with blinding fury; he threw the plate and contents into the dustbin. A puny gesture for so large a rage.

He went back to his room and lay on the bed, looking up at the cobwebs in the corners and around the lampshade. Moray, Pauline, Lomax. . . . He saw them all like figures on a chessboard. Pauline's move had been badly timed. 'What's to do?' he said aloud. His stomach gave him the answer. He went out and had a good meal. First things first; feed the inner man and the rest will take care of itself. But it wasn't as simple as that. As he walked back through the streets, cool after the bright day, he felt energy beginning to build up within him. By the time he got back to his room, his pulse was thudding and when he lay on the bed every nerve in his body twitched; he twisted and turned all night, his mind racing. He was on a train; through the window he could see the telegraph poles striding by in the other direction. He began to count them, his eyelids twitching as they went faster and faster.

8

'I SHOULDN'T have come,' Hannah said, as she studied the menu. Whether the remark was occasioned by the price column, the weight of the menu itself, or a revaluation of her acceptance, was not clear.

She had met Lomax at the week-end. The encounter had not taken place on the seafront on Sunday, but on Saturday at the exhibition of Surrealist painting in the municipal art gallery. Lomax had been sitting on the floor. It was extremely hot in the gallery, which had only very high windows, all of which seemed to be not only closed but securely bolted. Seats were only provided for the attendants. Lomax looked very small and brittle, a twig of a man. After making one or two comments to him about the paintings, Hannah began to feel rather foolish standing over him, so she joined him on the floor. She still felt foolish, but she was more comfortable physically.

'I can see that this must be a psychologist's paradise,' he said. 'Or his hell, perhaps—but then I always feel that both hell and paradise are pleasing to the psychologist, don't you? Hell more so, probably, it gives him more work.' He was sitting with his chin on his knees gazing up at a bland still-life of bread, cheese, wine bottle, grapes, and a human torso which had had either gravy or dark brown blood poured over it. 'But I can't say it appeals to me very much.' He looked, she thought, as incongruous as some of the paintings.

One or two people edged round them, pretending they weren't there; others walked over them as though they really weren't there.

'No wonder dogs look so anxious in a crowd,' Hannah said.

'It's not really a crowd. I doubt if they will make much money out of it. The weather forecast is good for the rest of the month.' He sounded indifferent, both to the prospect of good weather and the financial problems of the art gallery.

Hannah watched people standing in front of the pictures; some looked amused as though they shared a private joke with the painter, some frowned angrily, a few were frankly puzzled. Close by, a young woman furtively eased a frock clammily clinging to her back while she listened to a long dissertation from her heavily bearded companion, and an elderly woman fanned herself with a guidebook. Hannah felt happy, like a child at a party who has won the treasure hunt and can relax, assured of reward, while the other contestants rush round seeking clues. She took off her shoes and put them in her lap.

'Did you lie on the floor of the Sistine Chapel?' she asked.

'But of course. Didn't you?'

'No. I wanted to, but I didn't. I thought I should look ridiculous.' And here she was sitting on the floor of the municipal art gallery with a middle-aged man of no great presence, both of them dressed quite formally!

'You mustn't worry about what people think,' Lomax said.

'It's too late to stop.' Usually, she would not have admitted this; but she seemed to have relaxed her mind along with her posture. 'My life has been one long attempt to convince myself that I don't care what other people think, while at the same time I am worrying about the sort of impression I make.'

Lomax picked up one of her shoes and studied it. 'But we are all inconsistent, aren't we?' He stroked the side of the shoe gently.

'Most people have settled for being one kind of person by the time they are my age.'

'You think so?' He twirled the shoe round. Now it compelled her attention as well as his. 'You must have a very small foot.'

'Size three.'

'Really? You take a size three?' He gazed at the shoe and then at Hannah, astonished and amused, as though the discovery that she took size three shoes revealed more of interest than her attempts at self-analysis. 'Do you find it difficult to get shoes?'

'Not in sales.' Hannah put out her hand and fingered the tip of the shoe. 'It's difficult at other times, but they always bring the small sizes out in sales.'

'Why ever do they do that, do you imagine?' The mysteries of shoe salesmanship now captivated them both and they stared expectantly at the shoe as though it might suddenly move and write words on the air. Hannah's fingers still rested on the toe of the shoe; she felt a prickling sensation in them which travelled right up her arm.

'Perhaps the assistants can't be bothered at other times,' she suggested, after a longish pause. 'And then at the sales they find all these size three shoes lying around. Do you think that might be it?'

He considered this, his face intent, almost austere; then he handed the shoe back to her, thrusting it out of the way as though it irritated him.

'Look, we really have to fix this lunch date!' He sounded angry.

In between this meeting and the day of their lunch date, Hannah made certain discoveries. For one thing, she realised that there was always going to be Hannah, and there was always going to be Joyce, and she would have to make room for both of them in her life. From this moment, they ceased to worry her and she hardly gave them another thought. But instead of finding herself more at peace, a whole new area of unrest seemed to have been opened up.

A relationship was undoubtedly developing between herself and Lomax, and she was not sure whether this pleased her or not. If only one could say to a person 'Hold it!' just as the photographer does when he thinks he has caught the personality of the sitter, how much more straightforward this would make the business of loving! There had been a time, when she first knew Lomax, when she thought she had got the measure of his personality. But now, as he came closer to her, it was apparent that he was a much less predictable person than she had imagined. Hannah was a little afraid of the unpredictable. Although she had rebelled against the suburban image of life, she had not managed to construct anything to take its place, and this failure was reflected in her attitude to men. Her mother had often said, 'Your father and I have a happy marriage,' as though this was something that happened at the outset and could never subsequently be altered. Hannah's own experience tended to indicate that nothing about loving is easy; and she suspected that there was more of conflict than tranquillity in marriage. Nevertheless, she still hankered after the superficial comfort which had seemed to cocoon her parents. She did not think that Lomax would offer that kind of comfort.

Then there was the immediate problem of his motives. Undoubtedly, he was attracted to her. But was that all? Might not this be a convenient blending of inclination with professional interest? She was, after all, secretary to Neil Moray, and there was no doubt that the editor of the *Gazette* was increasingly concerned with Moray's affairs.

Her doubts were not put to rest when she discovered that he was taking her to lunch, not, as she had anticipated, at *The Greyhound*, but at *Sustra's*, of all places.

'I like to think it is my company that has prompted this extravagance,' she murmured as she studied the menu.

Lomax was nonplussed. It seemed to him quite legitimate to take Hannah Mason to lunch because he was attracted by her, and at the same time gratefully accept any scraps of information which she might let fall about such matters as contributions to Moray's campaign fund. He had no wish to appear unscrupulous, however, so he said, 'I assure you, I had no other thought.'

'Really?' She turned her attention from the *table d'hôte* to the *à la carte*. 'Then we shan't need to talk shop at all, shall we?'

Lomax realised it was going to be an expensive meal; she was already talking about smoked salmon on which she seemed to be something of an authority. He moved his chair slightly. The sun was in his eyes. They had a table by the window. It was very hot and there was a fan whirring somewhere near; it stirred Hannah's hair lightly, but did not seem to make the room any cooler. Outside, the promenade glinted grittily. The sea was a long way out, the crinkled sand looked hot and dry. It was all too fierce for Lomax's taste. He ordered grapefruit cocktail and a beef salad for himself.

'I expect you come here often?' he said to Hannah.

'No. It smells of money.' She tilted her chin and looked round the room with the casual unconcern of a duchess tolerantly contemplating the antics of social climbers.

'But you like good food?' Lomax asked. Her order had convinced him that she had an excellent appetite. They talked about food until the waiter came with smoked salmon for Hannah and grapefruit cocktail for Lomax. The waiter poured wine in their glasses and departed.

Hannah and Lomax talked about the weather. Lomax said he did not like the heat and Hannah said she could not have too much of it.

'Even at this hour?' Lomax hated the white-hot midday sun.

'At any hour,' she assured him.

Beyond the window, the promenade was almost deserted; most people were at lunch, but a few stragglers were huddled on the beach, crowded into the scant shade afforded by the breakwaters. There was one person standing by the flag-pole, bare-headed in the full glare of the sun. He was motionless as a lone soldier standing to attention on a vast parade ground. Even Hannah found herself flinching at the thought of how his neck and shoulders must burn. Then she realised that the man was Rodney Cope. He had spent some time in the Near East, so perhaps he didn't feel the sun like most English people.

'It would be June all the year round if I had my way,' she said, turning back to Lomax.

The sun was undoubtedly kind to her; her face was pleasantly brown, peppered with freckles across the bridge of her nose and beneath the eyes. It was not a pretty face, but the eyes were good-humoured and the mouth suggested a generous disposition. A dispassionate observer might also have seen hints of stubbornness that might have warned him that once Hannah and sense parted company, it would be difficult to bring them together again. But Lomax saw her in a glow of sunlight, healthy and with abundant vitality; he thought there was something Amazonian about her and he found this intensely exciting. While she told him about a holiday in Istria, he revised his plans for the afternoon. Lomax was abstemious, and it was unusual for him to drink at lunchtime. As the meal continued, the people at other tables blurred and their chatter was reduced to a murmur unintelligible as the surge of the sea; the atmosphere between himself and Hannah became more intimate.

'Tell me. . . .' He hunched forward, looking invitingly at Hannah. She smiled at him; she, too, seemed relaxed by the wine. He thought of all the things he wanted to be told; where had she spent her childhood? did she come from a big family? why was she content to work as a secretary? why hadn't she married . . .? So many questions, it was difficult to decide which to ask first. He said, 'I should like to sleep with you *so* much. I do hope you don't mind my saying this. . . .'

At this moment, like a great bat diving down, fluttering over empty plates and glasses, the waiter came to ask whether the food had been to their liking, whether they wanted a sweet, cheese, coffee, liqueurs . . .? His questions were endless. By the time they were alone again, intimacy had been destroyed. Hannah looked flushed; perhaps she didn't usually drink at lunchtime either, or perhaps she was amused, or annoyed. Lomax mumbled, 'I hope I haven't said the wrong thing.'

'Well, I did ask you not to talk shop.' She made this allowance graciously enough and then reverted to the subject of the ceilings in the Sistine Chapel.

They parted company at half-past two. On the promenade, it was still bright and shadowless, like an open-air torture chamber. A nerve in Lomax's temple twanged at every step. His mouth was dry.

'If I had my way,' he said to Todd when he entered his

81

office, 'it would be September all the time, and not a month earlier.'

Todd was too taken up with his own researches to pay attention to Lomax's condition. He had plans spread out on the table. Through the glass partition, Lomax could see Allinson with an expression of disgust on his plump face. Allinson thought too much time and energy was being expended on this. Lomax, at this moment, was inclined to agree with him.

'Like a gigantic spider's web, isn't it?' Todd was full of energy. 'You can see Heffernan squatting in the centre, spinning out more and more arched roads and terraces.'

The plans were numbered fourteen, they were an older set than those being studied by Moray, but it had been difficult enough to obtain them; Todd had winkled them out of a girl who worked in the printing room at the Town Hall.

'It didn't even get to the planning committee,' he told Lomax. 'The chairman nearly had a baby when he saw it.'

'Do you think Moray has seen these?' Lomax was becoming interested in spite of his throbbing head.

'He may have done by now, but I doubt if he saw them before the election.' Todd had been doing a lot of work on this. 'They only came to the planning department a week before he was elected. The original scheme was for something rather on the lines of the harbour arrangement on the other side of the town.'

'But that's a natural development which has taken place over centuries.'

'We do things quicker nowadays. And being Heffernan, he'd have to improve on Nature, wouldn't he? His hill is going to be man-made, and it will have to dwarf every natural hill around it.'

Lomax pushed the detailed plans to one side, he was in no condition to go into finer points of detail. In any case, it was the broad outline of the scheme with which he was concerned. He looked at the site plan.

'What was Moray talking about—a development which would bring new life to the town, solve housing and labour problems? This won't solve any human problems, it will create them.'

'It's likely to spread, too,' Todd said with relish. He was thinking of the Downs, one of the few unspoilt regions in the South-East, and Heffernan, sitting like a monster in his new creation, his tentacles reaching out to them. 'Mario has been content with half a mile,' he said. 'Heffernan will end up King of the South Downs.'

'I hope you've got that written down somewhere,' Lomax said drily.

'Talking of Mario,' Todd suddenly sounded disgruntled. 'He wanted to see you. He said perhaps you'd like to dine with him at home.' He looked disapprovingly at Lomax. Todd liked people to be all of a piece, and it puzzled him that a man of Lomax's undoubted integrity could accept hospitality from a man like Mario Vicente.

Lomax said, 'Not tonight, I hope. I don't think my digestion would stand it.'

'He said any night this week.'

Lomax nodded his head and turned away; then a thought struck him, and he turned to Todd again. 'There's one thing that has occurred to me. Ronald Singleton. He wasn't very happy about Cope pushing him into the background, as I recall. In fact, he was quite a nuisance, couldn't stop him talking. Wish I hadn't tried, now. You might manage to run into him sometime. Buy him a pint; it's all he'll need to start him off.'

'He won't know much,' Todd objected. 'He dropped out of the campaign early on.'

'If you're disgruntled about something, you're never alone,' Lomax said. 'I guarantee that by now anyone who has a tale to tell which does Rodney Cope no credit, will have told it to Ronald Singleton.'

9

I<small>T</small> had been a bright day, too bright. Now storms were forecast. People on their way from offices looked up at the bruised sky and said, 'I knew it was too good to last,' and 'we've had our summer.'

Pauline had been up early. Today she was meeting Rodney Cope. She was no longer lethargic; she sprang out of bed like Jack released from his box. She had a bath and opened the windows. Then she went out and walked round the town, which looked fresh and bright and full of promise. She stopped and had coffee at one of the hotels along the front where you sat on a balcony and watched people coming and going beneath. She felt young again, driven by that sense of urgency which demands that the most must be made of every minute.

The coffee made her feel even more excited. She wanted to talk to the waiter, but other people arrived and demanded his attention. She wanted to talk to someone; not about anything in particular, just to exchange gay, unfettered words. There were no fetters any more. Wasn't it delightful? She felt delightful herself. She wanted someone else to think 'You are delightful', to read the message in their eyes. She had seen it often enough before she married Geoffrey and was expected to become one of the fittings about his expensive house, neither dreary nor delightful, just useful. Geoffrey had grown up in the Utility era, however much money he spent he was utility orientated at heart. Her mind was beginning to get in that old, resentful groove. She poured more coffee; it was black and strong and she felt excited again.

She left the hotel and walked along the front. The tide was going out. The sand was littered with sun-worshippers from seven to seventy. But she couldn't stretch out like them; she must do something. She felt like a character in one of those antique Hollywood musicals who suddenly goes into a dance routine, climbing lamp-posts and banging dustbin lids. She raised her arms above her head and stretched until her fingers scratched the sky. A bronzed young man looked at her and laughed. He understood! Ah, these brief encounters, how much more of pure understanding there was in one of them than the whole of matrimony! 'I wasn't meant for marriage,' she said to herself. 'I was meant for brief, ecstatic moments. From now on I must make a collection of them, a string of glittering moments for my life.' She walked to the end of the West promenade and turned; perhaps she would go to the East end now. But she did not want to invade Mario's territory.

The hands of a clock outside a kiosk pointed to twelve. *Martini* time! Or was *Martini* time some other time? It didn't matter. There was a bar farther down the promenade with tables outside under tangerine parasols with tassels. She made her way there, it looked so gay. She had *Cinzano*—just in case it wasn't *Martini* time—with ice and soda and lemon, not because she liked it but because it went with the day. The sun was climbing steeply now. Noon. High noon. A girl in a bikini strolled by, body smooth as a shelled almond. She felt a little drag of envy.

The light sparking up from the pavement was beginning to try her unprotected eyes; a headache was starting. She fumbled for sun glasses and found she hadn't brought them. Once she had noticed the sun sparking like that she could think of nothing else. All the nerves around eyes and mouth were becoming taut, the muscles pulled and pinched. She was still very excited and restless, but not enjoying it so much. She did not finish the *Cinzano* before she moved off in search of food. Not that she was hungry. She hadn't had an appetite for many years. But she wanted to be there, where it was all happening. And between twelve-thirty and two in the afternoon, it was all happening in dining places. She went to *Sustra's*. The waiter said it was a long time since he had seen her, as though every day she hadn't come had been a loss in his life. She had scampi. William Lomax was there with the woman who had been at *Guiseppe's* that wretched Sunday, a pleasant woman in a lime green dress. There was a gallantry about the woman which Pauline recognised and saluted; she was making a fight of life. The woman and Lomax were having an odd, disjointed sort of conversation, dullish with little scatters of brilliance. Something was happening between them, only a sliver at the moment, but Pauline felt the pricking in her finger tips. She wondered if they knew, or whether she should tell them so that they didn't waste a lot of time. They weren't like the girl in the bikini, they didn't have time to waste. She wished them well, if they could find something, even if it was only a little something, it was better than nothing. The world was a little place. She could feel it closing in around her. The sun was very hot on the glass and there was a metal band closing over the sky.

Lomax and the woman went past her. She's older than me, Pauline thought. Nice hair, though, thick and springy still. She thought of going after them to tell Lomax that she was seeing Rodney Cope tonight. She didn't do it, but the impulse to tell Lomax was very strong.

She went back to her room. Her head was hammering. The clothes strewn over the bedroom floor moved as though they had a life of their own and something was rolling about in the bath. The wind was up; the bathroom curtains had blown a talcum powder tin into the bath. The bedroom curtains ballooned out, too. There was plenty of air everywhere. She lay down on the bed. Her nerves were jumping still. It was in her blood, the storm. She hoped it would break soon and lower the pressure. The thought of the evening filled her with apprehension; she smoked endless cigarettes and watched with dismay the day passing out of her grasp. Through the window came the sounds of the town, voices, traffic, car doors slamming; she had a glimpse of trees tossed in the wind and a grey sky with a plume of purple. The afternoon went by in this fashion. Once, she actually dialled Rodney's office to say she would not meet him; that creep Moray answered and said that Rodney was out. She did not leave a message. Just before the afternoon was quite gone, she went out again, snatching what was left of it. She walked through Gloucester Park and on up to the Downs. The wind came tearing down to meet her. She had to lean against it. There was a distant rumble of thunder, and sheet lightning away over Brighton. She had a moment up there when she wondered whether she should strike out along the South Downs Way and not bother about Rodney. But where would that get her? Hampshire. Better Rodney. She came down again, made tea and had another bath. God, she was clean!

She dressed and went out. And came back again. 'Be honest,' a voice said. 'You're not doing this for Geoffrey. You have forgotten more about him than you ever knew.' Here, the voice ran out of inspiration, or courage. But it had spoken the truth. Should she stay here? Close the doors and the windows, build up a nice fug, turn on telly, light a cigarette, pour a drink. Be safe?

She went out.

It was foolish; more than that, it was irresponsible. Geoffrey had told her once that she did irresponsible things deliberately, it was some kind of aggression she was working out. Perhaps he was right. At least when you were aggressive you knew you were alive. She felt aggressive now.

She went down to the garage. She hoped she had enough petrol. She switched on the engine. The indicator on the petrol gauge flickered weakly and managed to raise itself to a point just above the E. They always say you have half a gallon in reserve, don't they, those people who know everything about cars? Or is it a full gallon? Perhaps it was only a quarter, because the car gave up just short of Picton's Quay. She didn't mind. She was glad of the walk.

The river was full and running fast, it wasn't blue but pearl grey, flecked with silver, which she found much more exciting; a blue river is just a reflection of the sky, but now the river was itself. On the opposite bank, the fields and distant hills were dark green and static in contrast to the life that was within the river. Weren't there people who believed the river was a god? It seemed as good an idea of God as any other. She would be happy to give her soul to the river; if only she could be sure that the thing one referred to as 'oneself' would go with it, that there would be nothing left inside this frame of bone still struggling to get out.

The river curved out of sight of Picton's Quay, she could see a few cattle in the fields, a barn. The river curved again and the barn was gone. There was a line of pylons and nothing else. She was suddenly desperately tired and her soul, which a moment ago had seemed so much larger than her body, had shrivelled to the size of a walnut which was lodged somewhere in the region of her chest, hard and indigestible. She flopped down on the bank and rested her head on her knees. The air was still now and she was sweating. She'd done too much today. She hunched there, trying to gather herself together. After a while, someone came and sat beside her.

'I thought we said we'd meet at the cottage.' His voice was strangely unclear, as though his tongue had come up against an impediment.

She said, without raising her head, 'My car broke down.'

He did not answer. Quite what she had expected, she didn't know—a blow, perhaps, her shoulders had certainly been braced. Now, as she raised her head, she saw that he was not even looking at her. He was staring at the hurrying river, as remote as the figurehead of a Viking ship, its force unhampered by any civilising restraint. There had been other moments like this, when she had had to wait for him to come back to her. She had always found him frightening; this had been his hold over her. Now, his isolation seemed so complete that she had to try to break it. She put up a hand and ran a teasing finger down his spine. 'Why are you so angry, then? Didn't everything go as you planned?'

His body twitched as though she had pared flesh from the nerve. 'I never plan.'

She ran her finger up the back of his neck, fascinated by this newly discovered power to torment. He jerked away from her.

'Don't touch me!'

The storm had circled away to the north and a steady rain was beginning to fall.

'We'll get wet. And I thought something tremendous was going to happen.' She eased up against him, wary, but very excited. 'I thought we would have a terrible, rending fight, there would be thunder and lightning. . . .' She had been rubbing her cheek against his shoulder, now she jerked away, crouching in front of him, looking at him with a different expression. 'You're soaking wet already.' She put out a hand and touched his chest. 'What's the matter? Aren't you well?' Her voice became sharp. She grabbed him by the shoulders, they were rigid as though he had cramp. 'You can talk, can't you?' she shouted. 'Talk! Talk! For God's sake, you can't be ill here. . . .

'No! No, I don't want that. . . . No, no, not now, not here. . . .' She lost her balance and slid part of the way down the bank, pulling at the grass with her fingers, trying to get a hold on something. The world tilted over and he was on top of her. Grey sky above. Seagull flying low. She screamed to the seagull. Then hands were round her throat. She drew up her knees and fought to let the power that was in her flow out through her lungs, but it was dammed up inside her and hurting terribly; the greyness was torn aside by brilliant needles of light which seared a way through flesh and bone, and following the path of the needles came the river, a great roaring crimson torrent which grew louder and louder, and louder beyond all belief, pushing at the walls of the skull until the whole universe was inside her head.

The rain, which had been falling steadily, now began to come down much more heavily. The visibility was reduced; the Downs became first of all a grey smudge above the fields, and then dissolved in mist; the mist moved insidiously forward, dissolving everything except one pylon which remained rising forlorn on the far side of the river. The rain drummed on hard ground, and then, as time went on, it fell with less impact on sodden ground. The river rose perceptibly, only the tops of the reeds showed above it. The man and the woman lay still, side by side, she on her back, her head tilted acutely so that her hair began to trail in the slime at the river's edge, he on his face, his hands limp at his sides, palms upward. The darkness came early. There was no light and no sound except the rain and the river running fast.

Rodney Cope had no idea what time it was when he came to himself. His body was heavy and he seemed to have no strength to move it; his head felt light and sore inside, as though someone had rubbed salt into it. His first thought was that he had had a bad nose bleed. He rolled over to one side and looked at his watch. The illuminated dial said eight o'clock, which couldn't be right; he held it to one ear, the rain seemed to have made him rather deaf, but he thought it had stopped. Above his arched wrist, he saw Pauline lying on the ground. It was so dark, he had to hunch down beside her to see properly, but even before he did this something about the angle of the head told him she was dead. The tide was running out, but because of the rain the river was still high; he put his hands beneath her body and eased her gently into the water, steering her clear of the tangle of reeds.

When he tried to get up the bank, he nearly fell. He was very weak and guessed he had a high temperature. His mind was working very sharply, however, although it could only cope with essentials, such as car, home, and bed. He stumbled and fell, and stumbled and crawled, until he came to the cottage at the back of which he had left his car. The hood was down. At first, he thought the engine was not going to fire, but at last it started. By the time he reached the main road, he wasn't sure if he was driving a car or an aeroplane; he nearly landed in a ditch twice. He reached the outskirts of Scotney in the early hours of the morning, which was probably a good thing; there weren't any people about to see him weaving along the road. There had been a flood under the railway arches and the police were occupied with that. He weaved his way to his garage which was just round the corner from Cadogan Crescent. There was a shoe repairer's to one side and the yard of the Downland Dairy to the other; the nearest residential accommodation was a few hundred yards away and only one small window to the side of the house faced in his direction. Even so, he cut off his lights and tried to make as little noise as possible.

It was getting back to his room which was really difficult. He had to hold onto the railings in the Crescent as he went along; twice he sank down on the pavement. Fortunately, his room was entered by a separate door, and Mrs. Simpkins slept on the first floor; it was unlikely that she would hear him. His fingers were as awkward as a bunch of bananas, but at last he managed to open the door.

He wasn't finished yet. He had on a cotton shirt and drill trousers. He washed them and his socks and underclothes, and hung them with other clothes on the rack in the bathroom. He had to sit on the floor with his head in his hands at intervals while he was doing the washing, and once he passed out for a time. But he got it done at last. He couldn't cope with his shoes, they would have to be dealt with later. He put them in an old suitcase. Then he lay down on the bed and let the fever take him.

10

MARIO VICENTE lived in a terraced house in a road which climbed steep and straight up the hill from the harbour. The house was nearly at the top of the hill. It had no splendid view since from the front it looked onto the houses on the opposite side of the street and at the back it was hemmed in by the Baptist Chapel and a private hotel called *The Larboard Light*. Mario's house, like all the others in the road, consisted of three living areas placed one above the other; what was made of this space depended on the ingenuity of the occupants, and the way they wanted to live their lives. Mario had accepted his house much as it had been during the two centuries since it was built. The front door opened into the living-room and the stairs went up from the living-room; somewhere in the regions above a bath and lavatory had been installed, but few other structural alterations had been made. The back window of the living-room opened onto a narrow paved courtyard where Signora Vicente had been successful, in spite of little sunlight, with a creeper, and plants which trailed from tubs and an iron bucket. Lomax imagined it to be much the same as the house in which Mario had grown up in Naples, except that there were three people living here (since Mario's son now lived over the restaurant in Pelham Square), instead of twelve.

Lomax liked Mario for this. He was aware that the fact that Mario chose to live in this way did not mean that he possessed the sterling qualities which are sometimes naïvely assumed to go with a simple style of living. Lomax liked him just the same. It was hard to explain why; but he was at pains to try to do so because this liking for Mario had revealed a part of himself of which he had not previously been aware. Lomax was not one of those people who coast through life only half-alive, aware of things within themselves which must never be released, a dark self locked away in the east wing of personality. So he gave some thought to his reasons for liking Mario.

Lomax was frightened by violence; but sometimes he suspected that he admired Mario because of the violence in his life and not in spite of it. Violence was a part of the life of Scotney, but most people pretended that it was something that happened in another part of the town. Not so Mario. Mario's dealings were direct and uncomplicated; his empire was not spread far and he still lived in a world where a man must face the people who have wronged him, or whom he has wronged. Not for him the immunity of a Heffernan, isolated from the more unpleasant consequences of his acts.

There was corruption as well as violence in Mario's life. Lomax hated corruption. But he was aware that a certain austerity in his own nature, combined with a lack of respect for material possessions, meant that it would be as hard for him to be corrupt as for Mario to accept his standards of honesty. When they sat talking on the rare occasions when they met, Mario would tell stories of his youth in Naples. Listening to these accounts of a life so completely alien to his own, Lomax could understand that Mario would have had to evolve a totally different set of values. This was one of the differences between Mario and a man like Heffernan. If Heffernan had stolen as a child, it would have been to gain attention. Mario had stolen because he was hungry. It was a way of life and well understood by those around him; he belonged to a gang which had laws and customs, he knew his world and had his place in it. He had not grown up in a jungle. There was a solidity about Mario and about his house; in spite of the peeling plaster, the missing tiles on the roof, the house would not easily be shaken. Mario was a Roman Catholic, and in his religious observances appeared to be devout; sometimes on weekdays he could be seen kneeling in the church at lunchtime. This was a source of considerable amusement to many Protestants whose vices were less primitive.

93

Mario, if asked about this strange friendship, would have given a simpler answer. He would have said that he found Lomax 'sympathetic'. Mario was a man who loved and hated, and had very little idea of what went on in the no-man's-land in between in which so many people live their lives.

On the evening when he was due to dine with Mario, Lomax left his car at the bottom of the hill. He did this partly because he liked to stop every now and again to look at the view over the harbour. Also, he wanted time to think. When he and Mario met it was not usually because Lomax looked for news or Mario for co-operation. Tonight, whether they liked it or not, things would be different. Lomax was sorry about this; but as Hannah had had reason to suspect, he was not one to let sentiment govern his behaviour on such an occasion. And neither was Mario.

After dinner, Signora Vicente went into the kitchen where she would occupy herself for the rest of the evening. The window over the courtyard was open and from time to time she appeared, shaking out a cloth, putting bottles in the dustbin, unpegging clothes from the line. Mario poured brandy and made his opening move.

'Why does your paper wait so long to attack Heffernan?'

Lomax shivered. It had been a hot day and now the first breeze of evening, light though it was, caught one unprepared.

'We're not attacking Heffernan,' he said. 'Just asking questions about the West Front development.'

'But what makes you begin now?' Mario persisted.

Lomax looked into his glass. From the Baptist Chapel came the sound of people singing with lusty unconcern, *Brief life is here our portion, Brief sorrow, short-lived care....* Lomax said, 'Information has gradually been coming into the office.' But he knew, now that the question had been put, that his own suspicions had been aroused when Pauline Ormerod walked into his office on the night of the election.

Mario, too, looked into his glass. Whether he was content with the answer or not, he did not pursue the matter. He said,

'Who is this Heffernan?' He could be naïve; Scotney was the whole of England to him.

'A property developer among other things,' Lomax said. 'He owns a chain of hotels and one or two big stores. I believe he started in footwear.'

'Who handles the deal for him here?'

'Officially, you mean? He owns one of the firms of estate agents—Randalls.'

'And unofficially?'

Lomax thought it was Mario's turn to put a little information into the pool. He said, 'I thought you were going to tell me that.'

Mario sipped his brandy. The Baptists had got as far as the *sweet and blessed country, the home of God's elect.* Signora Vicente hurled something into the courtyard, there was a lot of spitting and snarling followed by the clatter of a dustbin lid. When the vibrations had died away, Mario said, 'Heffernan put money into this Neil Moray's campaign. You know that?

'I had begun to wonder about it.' Lomax was cautious.

'I KNOW. He is behind the Whittaker Enterprises.'

Whittaker Enterprises was a wealthy outfit which invested in industrial projects which showed promise but needed help in getting off the ground.

'I would hardly have thought Moray's enterprise would qualify for help from them.' This was not the first time that Lomax had heard of this, but he was interested to know how much Mario had found out. 'We can look into it, of course: but these things are complicated and they take time. . . .'

'No, no.' Mario shook his head and smiled with the weary patience of the professional for the laborious efforts of the amateur. 'There is nothing complicated at all. If you do not understand something, you just ask. Ask and it shall be given to you.' He sighed, suddenly melancholy at the ease with which these things could be done.

'Can I have facts and figures?' Lomax asked briskly.

'Ah, no, no. I give you the information. You find the sort of facts and figures you need. That is fair, yes?' He offered

Lomax a cigar and took one himself. As he lit his cigar, he said, 'Another thing. A large contribution from a small business—Cosgrove's Travel.'

Signora Vicente, who was sweeping the courtyard, began to sing *Santa Lucia* in competition with the Baptists. Lomax let her get through the first verse before he said:

'Do you know anything about Cope?'

'No.' Mario dismissed Cope and the match with a flick of the hand. 'He must work for Heffernan, though. No one works for nothing.'

Lomax was inclined to agree with this.

Mario eased himself more comfortably into the wicker chair which creaked beneath his weight. 'I want to open one restaurant at the West end of the town.' He was becoming expansive. There would be no more exchange of information. 'One restaurant! And they will not give me permission. They say it is residential. It is important to keep some part of the seafront residential. I have the trattoria at the corner of Pelham Square, the *Aubergine* in The Strand, the *Della Conti* on The Avenue, and do they harm the residential area? Since I open the trattoria, you see how Pelham Square has improved. Do any places do badly where I have a restaurant? But no. Here, they say, is too grand, too beautiful. I must not come here. I will bring the harbour atmosphere to this end of the town. And this new development is not one restaurant, is a whole new town.' He enunciated the words 'whole new town' very clearly, accompanying each word with a jab of the left hand, fingers spread wide. 'Is that just?'

'Hardly,' Lomax acknowledged.

'I do not suffer injustice. If it had been another restaurant, well . . .' He waggled his hand to indicate that this would have been a mere wobble of the scales of justice which he could have tolerated. 'But a whole new town . . . a town on, what you call it, long sticks. . . .'

'Stilts.'

'Is not safe probably.' But he did not look as though he thought Heffernan's hill would be swept away in the first high tide. Sabotage of another kind would be necessary. 'And Scotney is nice place without all this.'

Lomax was not fooled. Mario believed in keeping his enterprises to a small scale because in this way he could control them himself; he had no more concern than Heffernan for Scotney as a town. It was the people without money or power, people like Lomax, who were concerned with preservation.

They sat and smoked in silence for a little while. Signora Vicente put the yard broom against the wall and went into the kitchen, shutting the door and drawing the bolt. The Baptists had fallen silent. The air was cooling, Lomax could smell the earth in the tubs; Signora Vicente had not watered the plants, presumably the earth was still wet after the torrential rain last night. He tapped out his cigar ash carefully and said, 'Do you know Ormerod's wife?'

'I have nothing to do with that one.' Mario was emphatic. 'She is crazy woman. And what is more, she drinks.' The Baptists could scarcely have been more wholehearted in condemnation.

Later, as he walked down the hill, Lomax thought about Mrs. Ormerod. He must have another word with her. He felt uneasy and restless. Some of the things which Mario had said had unsettled him. He never looked forward to a fight; something in his nature always pushed him relentlessly on, but it certainly wasn't a love of conflict. He suffered from a Puritan streak of obstinacy, just as other people have an over-active thyroid. It was eleven o'clock as he drove along the coast road; the moon cast a path of dappled mercury across the dark sea. He stopped for a time and sat with the car window down; the tide was on the ebb, the water dragged softly over the pebble beach. He didn't find it soothing. At half-past eleven, he decided to go into the office.

Todd was already there. Todd's landlady objected to the sound of typing in the night. It had been suggested to Todd that a rubber mat, and a re-positioning of the typewriter away from the wall of the landlady's bedroom would work wonders, but he refused to believe this. Lomax thought he liked to come into the office because it gave him the feeling that he was working on a Fleet Street daily.

'I thought you were going to the Drama Festival.' Lomax could tell from the mass of papers strewn over the table that Todd wasn't working on drama.

'Jenny covered that,' Todd said.

That would mean fewer complaints this year. Todd was never at ease with any creative work until he had found a flaw in it: last month he had spent the greater part of the space allotted to a review of *The Tempest* on a dissertation on 'the maladroit opening with the tedious question and answer session between Miranda and Prospero'.

'I went to the meeting of the Downland Association,' Todd looked glum. It turned out he had failed to find a flaw in Moray's performance. 'You have to hand it to him, he always talks sense. You'd think he'd let up once in a way.' Worse was to come: he nodded his head at the mound of papers on his desk. 'I've been going through his speeches during the election campaign. He was very guarded in what he said about the West Front development. It didn't amount to much more than asking that it should be considered and not condemned out of hand before detailed information was available. The trouble was, of course, that other people took up the cry. In the end some pretty extreme things were being said, but not by Moray.'

'He just kicked the first stone that started the avalanche that did for Ormerod,' Lomax murmured.

'I talked to him for a few minutes before the meeting began,' Todd said. 'He looked exhausted and I wondered how he was going to get through the meeting. But when he started to speak, he wasn't content to coast along; he really went into the problems, examined the conflicting claims of conservation and progress, the individual in relation to his environment, our right to mortgage the future, all that sort of thing.'

'Was this what they expected of him?'

'No doubt they would have settled for a few quotes from Kipling and a promise to stop untreated effluent being pumped into the sea. But I think they rather respected him for giving them a bit more. But what, I ask myself,' Todd stabbed a finger at the pile of papers, 'does Moray hope to get out of all this? How does he see himself? Obviously he doesn't want to become the typical politician. But has he thought what he *does* want to be? If not, it seems a terrible waste of energy.' He looked at Lomax. 'I always feel he holds back something. Doesn't he give you that impression?'

'He is elusive, certainly,' Lomax agreed. He wondered why it was that he was never sure about Moray. The man had a certain charm, and admittedly Lomax did not much care for charming men. But it was more than that. This elusiveness was something other than reserve; it was as though Moray felt a need to keep himself apart. Why? A refusal to risk himself?

Todd was impressed by Moray's elusiveness. It made him feel there was something rather special about Moray; getting to know him would be important, like belonging to an exclusive club. Todd disapproved of exclusive clubs on principle, but felt they could most credibly be belittled after one had attained membership.

'Have you seen Singleton?' Lomax changed the subject.

'Not yet.'

'Well, have a try, will you? Facts are what we need, psychological analysis will get us nowhere.'

He was aware that in Todd's view this statement was akin to blasphemy, but he felt a need for sobering draughts of facts and figures.

'Did Mario have anything to give?' Todd asked.

'He thinks Heffernan is behind Whittaker Enterprises.'

'I'd like to hear Moray explain that one away!'

'I'll like a few more facts before we ask for explanations.'

They went out of the office together. Todd said, 'He must be a schizo.' His voice sounded sad. The streets were empty. It was quiet, but not the quiet of a country town or a village; there was no sense of people sleeping peacefully, only of an uneasy vacancy.

'I see the crime rate has gone down,' Lomax said to Todd as they turned into Exhibition Road.

'It'll go up again in the summer.' Todd sounded defensive, as though he was talking about goal averages.

They came to the junction with Marine Drive. Lomax said, 'I've got my car parked on the front.'

'I never park there,' Todd said severely. 'I have enough trouble with rust as it is.'

They parted company. Lomax walked slowly back to his car; although the tide was going out, it was covered with a film of spray. The air was chill now. Mist formed a cone of shadow from the sea to the moon. He felt an inexplicable sense of failure; not a generalised feeling, but as though there was a specific thing he had left undone.

Ever since his wife left him for a man who was more financially successful, he had had bouts of depression. His wife had been a dark, handsome woman; he had thought her very fierce when he first met her and had imagined they would have an exciting life together. But the magnificent wrapping had concealed a fairly ordinary package. He had made the best of things—or so he had thought. But when she left him, on the grounds that he would never 'amount to anything', he had been violently angry. The anger had taken a long time to drain away. It had left in its wake a feeling of failure, harder to bear.

But that was three years ago, and he did not think about it much now. So why did he feel so bad tonight?

He was dismayed at the realisation that there might be a bitter struggle ahead over this business of the West Front development; but this initial reluctance to do battle was familiar and would pass. There was nothing in all this to explain the feeling of personal failure that amounted almost to panic.

He drove home slowly. He lived in the residential area on the less expensive side of Gloucester Park. His wife had wanted a house in a 'nice' area and this had been the best he could provide. He would have preferred to live in the centre of the town. Now that his wife had gone the house did not seem to belong to anyone. He went into the kitchen, made himself a sandwich and had a glass of hot milk; one or other gave him indigestion and he could not get to sleep.

About two in the morning, the dog next door began to bark; after ten minutes of this, Mrs. Pritchard (or Mr. Pritchard, but somehow Lomax did not think it was Mr. Pritchard) thumped down the polished, uncarpeted stairs. The backdoor bolts were drawn back, minutes passed, then the door shut and the bolts were clumsily put into place again. Footsteps on the uncarpeted stairs, another door slammed, another pause, then the flushing of the closet. Lomax listened to the cistern filling. When it was full, he found himself waiting for the dog to bark again. He turned on the light, found a detective story, and began to read. He dozed off about half-past six, only to be woken by the milkman.

He got up and went to the window. The sky was a delicate egg-shell, with the faintest touch of pearl; in the distance, over the roofs of the houses, he could see the Downs, gradually taking shape as though they had just been created. All very innocent. It was hard to understand why he should have had such dark thoughts during the night.

When he got to the office, he telephoned Pauline Ormerod. There was no answer. He tried again later in the day, but there was still no answer.

II

'I'M sorry. Dr. Kearns has a patient with him at the moment,' the receptionist said.

'That's all right,' Moray said. 'I'll wait.'

'I'm awfully sorry.'

'No, no. I'll wait here.'

'I *am* sorry.'

Someone had to put a stop to it. He sat at the end of the row of chairs by the window. The people on either side watched him covertly.

'I'll tell him as soon as he's free,' the receptionist said.

The woman to Moray's right looked at her watch and sniffed.

Moray said, 'It's quite all right. I should have made an appointment.'

'It's our busy morning, you see.' They were now addressing each other down the length of the room.

This seemed quite the most agonising of all the things which had happened to him recently. It drew attention to him in a situation in which he could not defend himself: he could scarcely treat the receptionist as a heckler.

'Now, if it had been Tuesday . . .' she said.

Of all the things he had done, surely the worst that could be laid at Cope's door was that he had not become ill on a Tuesday.

A woman in the row of chairs flanking the long wall scooped up a small, watery-eyed child and bounced him on her knees. 'It won't be long now,' she said. 'We're next.' She kept her eyes fixed on the board where a light came on beside the doctor's name when he was free. Moray hoped she wasn't waiting for Dr. Kearns. The woman next to Moray said to the man on her right, 'It isn't much better now they've got the appointment system, is it?'

A buzzer rang. All eyes turned to the board. The receptionist said, 'Mrs. Franklin, will you go to Dr. Mays now. The woman with the child got up; she gave Moray a look of triumph as she went towards the inner door. The receptionist followed her out of the room. In a moment or two she returned and looked towards Moray, but before she could speak the telephone rang and she turned to answer it. Moray thought that if Dr. Kearns' light came on now he would not have the nerve to thrust himself forward without her support. The light came on as he was thinking this. A man with a heavy grey scarf round his neck got up; the receptionist put one hand over the mouthpiece and said, 'This gentleman is before you, Mr. Spiers.' Mr. Spiers, who was old and had a defeated look, sat down again. Moray found this acceptance of the inequalities of life more distressing than any outburst of righteous indignation. He said to Mr. Spiers, 'I do apologise. I'm afraid this is something of an emergency.'

'It's all right,' Mr. Spiers said philosophically. 'Might as well sit here as anywhere else.'

'I hope I shan't be long.'

'No hurry. It's only my chest.'

Moray went into the hall. There were several doors leading off it and he was afraid of going into the wrong room. It was like a school medical. His heart was thudding by the time he located the door with the plaque which bore Dr. Kearns' name.

Dr. Kearns rose to greet him. 'I'm sorry I couldn't see you before.' He sounded irritated rather than sorry. He was a short, red-faced man with a toothbrush moustache and he talked very loudly as though Moray was deaf. He leant across the table to shake hands; he had a short arm and the effort nearly took him off his feet.

'Sit down, sit down.'

'Your receptionist explained. . . . ?' Moray said tentatively.

'She said you'd been to see this fellow . . . what's his name, Cope?'

'Yes. I went this morning. I only learnt that he was ill this morning. I didn't expect to find him so bad.'

'He's got pneumonia, you know,' the little man barked. 'You don't feel all that fit with pneumonia.'

'Is he all right where he is?'

'Well, I don't know. I was only called in yesterday evening by his landlady. I didn't think it would be a good idea to move him then. I'll have another look at him when I've finished here.'

'Perhaps I should have waited....'

'No. It's perfectly all right, perfectly all right,' Kearns assured him fiercely. 'I'm glad to see you. There were one or two things I wasn't happy about.'

He looked down at his short, stubby hands clasped on the blotting pad. Moray was afraid he wasn't going to say any more. Kearns took one thumb and examined it minutely as though it had only come to his attention this morning.

'Some odd features,' he said. 'I won't bother you with a lot of medical jargon; that wouldn't mean anything to you anyway. Doesn't always mean much to us, either, half the time. Tell me, as far as you know, has he ever suffered from fits, or anything like that?'

'Good Heavens, no!' Moray's reaction expressed his own dismay at the question rather than a thoughtful attempt to answer it. He realised this and added, 'At least, I say that, but...'

'Well, say what you mean, say what you mean.'

'I've only known him for just under two years.' Moray was finding it difficult to marshal his thoughts. 'But in that time he has always struck me as being remarkably healthy?'

'What makes you decide someone is remarkably healthy?'

'I realise, of course, that I'm not qualified....'

'No, no no! I'm not asking you for a medical opinion. That's my job. But you probably see him in a different way. What made you feel there was something so remarkable about his health?'

'For one thing, he looked physically strong to me. He had a youthful ... no, that's not quite it ... his face was unmarked,

104

no lines of worry or tension, and his eyes were very bright and clear . . . I don't know why I'm talking about him in the past tense like this. . . .'

'Don't worry about tenses. Just tell me.'

'He was inexhaustible. He worked at a tremendous pace and it seemed to have absolutely no effect on him. I know for a fact he sometimes worked twenty-four hours at a stretch, and the next day he would seem as fresh as if he'd slept for ten hours. . . .'

'People don't look fresh after ten hours' sleep, they look doped.'

'That was one thing Cope never looked. Quite the opposite, he was almost abrasively wide-awake.'

'It didn't occur to you that he might keep himself going on drugs?'

'No, it didn't. It seemed to me his natural pace was just that much faster than most other people's.'

'Hmmh. You could be right about that.' He screwed up his face and squinted as though he was threading a needle somewhere between Moray's eyes. 'But he's gone down as though he had no resistance at all. Do you realise that? No resistance at all.'

'He was in the army.' This had been much in Moray's mind ever since he saw Cope. Not that being in the army offered any explanation of Cope's condition; it was only a reminder of how little he knew about the man. 'I believe he had a fairly adventurous career.'

'What do you mean by a fairly adventurous career? That could cover anything from the sort of nonsense medical students indulge in to James Bond activities.'

'I don't know much myself.' Moray's mind flinched from the nastier aspects of James Bond. 'It wasn't that he ever bragged about it, but his comments on some of the ones who do, led me to suppose he had been through stranger experiences.'

'I see.' Dr. Kearns frowned down at his thumb again. 'Well, I don't know anything about all this.'

'I suppose the army might help.'

105

'Ever know them to? And even if they wanted to, they probably couldn't. Most army doctors wouldn't recognise measles if they saw it. What do you want me to do?'

Moray, who had come with the intention of asking Dr. Kearns this question, now felt as defeated as the old man in the grey scarf. He said, 'Perhaps I could meet you at Cope's place? You said you would be seeing him later this morning.'

'Yes, all right. That's up to you.'

Moray arrived first. The landlady let him in with a manner which would have ensured her a job as a mortuary attendant. Standing in the stuffy room, Moray understood why he had referred to Cope in the past tense. Nothing that he had said now seemed applicable to the man on the bed.

'Did the doctor tell you to close the windows?' he asked.

'He said to keep him warm.'

'I see.' He could feel the sweat breaking out in his arm-pits, at the backs of his knees, down his spine. 'Well, I don't suppose the doctor will be long now.'

'Would you like a cup of tea? I'm making some for myself.'

He said, 'That would be very nice' to get rid of her. When she had gone, he pulled up a chair and stationed himself by Cope's bed. Sickness had always aroused a physical revulsion in him, and because of this he thought that it was essential to touch people who were ill, that to fail to do so was to abandon them. Cope was moving restlessly, his head turning from side to side; his breathing was irregular and every now and again he emitted a strange jumble of sounds which although they made no sense still conveyed a disturbing impression of urgency. One arm was twisted beneath his body, the other hand plucked at the sheet. Moray lifted the hand away from the sheets and held the wrist; the pulse was hammering, there was something very unpleasant about this thing that jerked beneath the flesh. Moray transferred his grip to the hand; immediately Cope's fingers began to pluck at Moray's hand, just as they had plucked at the sheet. It seemed even hotter in the room. If this went on much longer, he was going

106

to faint. Moray released Cope's hand and moved his chair farther from the bed. It wasn't just the physical nearness that bothered him; he felt he needed space between himself and Cope.

Something had gone badly wrong. Quite why he felt this, or even what he meant by it, he did not know; but the sense of it was terribly strong in this room. He felt the cold sweat of sickness like slime on his face. He concentrated on the low brick wall outside the window, counting each brick from left to right, fighting down the nausea. He wasn't sick, but the nausea stayed with him. When the doctor arrived Moray made this an excuse for going outside; he sat on the steps leading down to the basement and drank the tea the landlady provided.

'You look nearly as bad as him,' she told him.

The doctor said, when he called him into the room, 'Been overdoing it, have you?'

'Electioneering is a tiring business.'

'So I imagine. Can't understand why anyone does it.'

Moray sat down on the chair, his back to Cope. 'How is he?'

'No worse.'

'Are you going to get him into hospital?' Moray wanted Cope in hospital; he wanted the whiteness, the antiseptic smell, the fever charted on graph paper.

The doctor didn't want Cope moved at present. 'Hospitals are the most draughty places on this earth,' he was saying. Moray was about to plead the landlady's case when the health visitor arrived; she looked so formidably capable that he did not dare to argue.

'I shan't be in Westminster until next week,' he said. 'If there is anything I can do, please let me know.'

The landlady was in the hall, making a show of polishing the front door knob. He handed her the empty cup and refused a refill. 'Have you any idea what happened?' he asked her.

'He was out Wednesday night,' she said. 'I went to bed at ten o'clock and he wasn't in then. Perhaps his car broke down and he had to walk in all that rain. Enough to give anyone pneumonia. I've got his garage keys. He'd left them on the chest of drawers. I thought I'd get my husband to go along and see everything was all right.'

Moray offered to do this and she gave him directions to the garage. The car was there, parked crookedly, the hood down. Even after a lapse of some thirty-six hours, the inside was still very wet; there was mud on the floor. Moray poked around and found a washleather; he mopped the car down carefully, it seemed the least he could do.

He returned to his office and told Hannah that Cope had pneumonia. She said, 'But he seemed quite all right on Tuesday.' She obviously found it difficult to accept the idea of Cope being seriously ill and seemed to think a little argument might bring about a more reasonable state of affairs.

'He's not all right now.' Moray did not want to talk about it. His terseness only made matters seem more serious.

'But how did he manage to get pneumonia?

'How does one get pneumonia? *I* don't know. It's no use asking me.' She was not attacking him, yet for some reason he adopted a defensive attitude. He said, to forestall more questions, 'Would there be any coffee?'

While she waited for the kettle to boil, Hannah said, 'Will you be going away this week-end? I could work tomorrow if that would help.'

He had meant to stay with Lucy, but that arrangement had been made ten days ago; Lucy seemed as though she was part of another existence. He said, 'I'll work at my flat. There are one or two things I must sort out. Nothing you can help with.'

'Don't *you* overdo it and get ill.'

It was apparent she felt that things were becoming too much for him. He looked at her round, pleasant face and thought she had about as much sensitivity as an apple dumpling. Usually, he viewed his fellows through a filter which removed such glaring antagonism and left him with an amused acceptance of inadequacies. But there seemed to be nothing between himself and Hannah Mason at this moment, her

108

personality made direct contact with his nerves and his nerves were raw. 'Don't try to soothe me, Hannah,' he said. 'All I need is a few moments' peace to collect my thoughts.'

'Yes. All right.' She made the coffee and returned to her typewriter. She did not raise her eyes from her notebook, but he felt that every time he swallowed it registered with her. He decided to work at the flat for the rest of the day.

At the flat, he had another coffee, but it did not revive him; it was like pouring liquid down a well. There was a letter from Lucy. Usually, she wrote on a single sheet of paper, but this was a bulky package. He couldn't cope with Lucy, he hadn't any emotion to spare. He put the letter on the table unopened.

He looked at the files strewn about the room. He had been through them so many times now his head began to ache the moment he picked one up and he no longer took in any of the words. But the questions went on endlessly. He couldn't have done any more during the campaign, surely he couldn't have done any more? There had been times when he felt as though one extra fact to remember would destroy the whole balance of his brain. He couldn't have gone into the financial side of it; even if he had tried, he simply couldn't have absorbed it. Cope had said, 'You fight the election. I'll pay the bills.' It had seemed fair enough, the right use of time. But now, when there was more time, it was not so easy to understand why he hadn't asked more questions. Where *had* the money come from? Cope had all the details, and he had shown Moray the list of contributions. Had anything struck him as odd? Moray wondered. He hadn't been looking for anything odd, though, just praying there would be enough money. But was that quite true? What was it that Hannah had said? Something about one of the firms that had contributed. . . . He sat with his head in his hands, trying to remember. When no words came, he tried to visualise her when she had said it. What kind of day had it been? Raining, sunny, the wind rattling the window pane. . . . Suddenly he saw her, standing in a dust-speckled beam of sunlight; she was by the filing cabinet, a drawer half-open, and a file resting on it.

He heard her voice quite clearly. 'The miserable devils! I know someone who works for them. They pay her twelve pounds a week, believe it or not. And they've got this sort of money to play around with!' It had irritated him that she had referred to the contribution as 'playing around'. She got under his skin when she made it apparent that to her politics was some kind of game played by men who haven't yet grown up. If his supporters adopted that attitude, how could he expect anyone else to take him seriously? It had been a particularly gruelling day. He had gone out of the office because he couldn't trust himself to keep his temper.

He couldn't remember the contributor, probably he had never known to whom she was referring. Why had he left so much to Cope?

He could hear voices: 'We must have this by tomorrow morning at the latest . . .' and when he had protested, they said, 'It will be too late after that, Ormerod is giving a press conference . . . the socialists are on to it already . . . ten-minute broadcast after *In and around Scotney* . . . the *Gazette* goes to press tonight . . . the Council meets tomorrow . . .' People waited for him outside houses as he walked down a street. 'Do you know how long that house has been empty? Four years, and the one on the other side of the road. . .'. 'No one gets our vote until something is done about those Continental lorries; do you see that gable up there. . . .' It was inexorable, he was on a moving staircase and it was going faster and faster.

And then, the Ormerod scandal broke. It happened and it had to be used. He had campaigned about corruption, how could he evade dealing with this evidence of it? At the time, he had felt he was doing something hard and dangerous, he had not expected to come through unscathed. He had not expected Ormerod to crumple like that.

But *after* the campaign. . . . He should have made a stand immediately after that meeting with Hefferman, as soon as he began to have doubts about the West Front development. But while he was trying to find out more about the development, the rumours about the financing of his campaign started; and now, when he turned his attention to that, *this* happened, this illness of Cope's which seemed so much worse than anything else.

The situation changed so bewilderingly. During the campaign, to have called Cope to account would have been unwarrantable interference, a psychological blunder which would have affected all the other workers. Today, his failure to do so was an inexplicable omission. He was caught in a nightmare where one situation dissolved and he found himself in a different situation, and then another layer was removed and yet another situation was revealed, and each getting worse. He couldn't keep up, the ground shifted so fast, he couldn't find a firm foothold, and without any intention of doing so, he found himself gradually retreating. So little time had passed, and yet already the accusations of delay which he would have to face were formidable. 'Why, as soon as you realised, didn't you . . .?' 'But I had to be sure, and as soon as I started to investigate this, there was that. . . .'

No! It MUST stop here. There were two things: two things which he could and must do. He must publicly express his dissatisfaction with the information now available about the West Front development; and as soon as Cope was better he must demand particulars about the financial arrangements for his campaign. But already, that wasn't enough. There were other, more fundamental questions he must ask Cope; and further, stretching beyond them, were questions he could not even formulate in his mind.

He *must* do something. He rang the office, Hannah answered. 'Do you remember that firm your friend worked with, the one which contributed to my expenses?'

'Yes,' she said at once. 'Cosgrove's Travel. Why?'

'You have a very good memory,' he said acidly. 'I was just testing it.'

'Oh, bugger you!' she said when she had put down the receiver.

But she was sorry that things were becoming too much for him. She worked late. Her brother Colin and his wife and mother-in-law were coming to dinner. It was odd how, whenever they came to dinner, Hannah always found it necessary to work late so that she had a rush before they arrived and the meal was late which upset Nancy's mother who liked to eat early because of her digestion.

Hannah typed all the letters, although they would have to wait until Monday to be signed. Until recently, she had signed letters on Neil's behalf, but he had suddenly become insistent on signing everything personally. He had taken a lot of the files to his flat, too. She hoped he wasn't going to try to do other people's work as well as his own. She was rather surprised at this development because hitherto there had been things he didn't want to know, and these were the very things he was fussing about now.

There were several telephone calls. Councillors, constituents, the chairman of the Chamber of Commerce; they all realised that Moray was busy but thought that they qualified for special treatment. It was a quarter to seven by the time she left, later than she had intended. She became flustered and couldn't think what to do first when she reached the flat. She had never been able to relax with her nearest and dearest, she was too aware of their disapproval. She was a reasonably good cook, but never excelled herself when Nancy was present. The sensible thing would have been to avoid anything complicated. This evening she had chosen to do one of the more testing recipes. There was no doubt about it, she invited trouble whenever they came to see her.

They had not been in the flat a minute before Nancy said, 'Hannah, darling, you've been to a lot of trouble, I can tell that.' She herself had been to the hairdresser, her flaxen hair fluffed like a powder puff around her small, pink face.

Hannah took their coats before they could make the usual joke about 'which of all your rooms do these go in?'

'Colin, will you pour drinks?' she said. 'Do eat the bits and pieces, won't you? I'm afraid dinner isn't ready yet. I was late at the office.'

She waited for Nancy to say that she was always late at *that* office, but Nancy had more important matters to broach.

'I will have you know, Hannah,' she said, accepting a gin and tonic, 'that I went to the meeting of the Downland Association.'

'Was Neil all right?' Hannah asked.

'He was terribly good. I said to Colin, "you really should have come", didn't I, darling? Of course, I was very fond of Tubby Ackroyd, he was a dear old boy, but he was getting a little past it, bless him. No one could say that of your Mr. Moray, could they?'

'I met him recently,' Colin said. 'At the cocktail party at Major Brophy's. He came in briefly. I must say he's one of the few men I've met whom women find attractive and men don't want to kick in the pants.'

'I don't know what that is supposed to mean,' Nancy said irritably.

'It means I quite liked him.'

'Well, then, why can't you say so, instead of always sounding as though you're trying to get at someone.'

'I still can't understand why people vote for him,' Colin went on imperviously. 'What do they expect to gain by it? Will Lomax was saying that he thought they were like those sick people who go to the chemist and take a lucky dip into the drugs that aren't on prescription.'

'Not *our* chemist,' Nancy's mother said. 'He'd tell you to go to the doctor. But then, he's one of the old school.'

'I think that is unkind of Will Lomax,' Nancy said. 'He hasn't been the same since his wife left him.' It was the first time Hannah had ever heard her mention Lomax, but she sounded as though she knew his whole life history.

'Did she go off with another man?' Nancy's mother asked.

'Yes, and he consoled himself with Connie Fairbrother, that's how I know about it.'

Hannah gazed into her drink. If she betrayed the slightest interest in Lomax, Nancy would be on to it like a ferret after a rabbit. Fortunately, however, Nancy had not yet finished with Neil.

'I should think he has a lot to offer, politically.' Nancy knew very little about politics, but this did not prevent her from expressing her views with great firmness. 'We need a change, and we need it soon. I'm convinced of that. But as to his being attractive to women, *I'd* be a little wary of him. He's the type of man who'd never be any good to a woman.' She sounded sad, as though it caused her pain to break this news.

Colin said, 'Oh, come! You don't know anything about the man.'

'He'd string a woman along.' Nancy was shrewd about this sort of thing, which was why Hannah was afraid of her. 'He'll have a lot of affairs, of course; but he'll run away from responsibility. Immature, perhaps. . . .' She went on talking. Will Lomax escaped unscathed, except for Connie Fair-brother.

Hannah went into the kitchen. Nancy's mother said, 'You've upset Hannah. She's got her eye on Neil Moray.'

'These things have to be said, Mother.' Nancy lowered her voice marginally. 'Hannah is unrealistic about men. It's the dull ones that make the good husbands.'

Colin said, 'Thank you, my pet.'

'You'll never convince Hannah of that,' Nancy's mother said. 'She'll never be contented, like you and me. She'll always be wanting something she can't have.'

Hannah said, 'You'll be glad to know we can eat now.'

As he sprinkled ginger on the melon, Colin announced, 'We've had a bit of excitement at Picton's Quay.'

'Don't go into all the gory details, please!' Nancy turned to Hannah before Colin had a chance to say any more. 'They've found a body in the river.'

'And the police have been around, knocking on doors and making inquiries, and all the housewives of Picton's Quay are barricading themselves indoors tonight!'

'Colin, what nonsense you do talk,' Nancy spoke sharply. 'They only wanted to know if anyone had seen a stranger in the village last Wednesday evening. No one had, of course, not in that terrible cloudburst.'

'Do they know who it was?' Hannah asked.

Nancy looked forbiddingly at her husband. When Hannah

went out to the kitchen, Colin followed her and whispered, 'They've been dredging. The body got mixed up with one of the machines.'

At the table, Nancy's mother was saying, 'Well, you would go and live out there.'

'But Mother, you love it, you always say how much you love it.'

'I've never liked being near the river, Nancy. Never!'

'That was because you didn't think it was healthy, not because you expected bodies to come floating up on every tide,' Colin said as he put down the casserole.

'The body was found two or three miles from Picton's Quay.' Nancy was on the defensive. 'And now we will talk about something else, please. Hannah wants you to pour the wine, don't you, Hannah?' As he turned away to do this, she said gaily, 'I don't know where Hannah gets these wonderful recipes from!'

'Gordon Blue,' Colin said.

Nancy said, 'What *would* you do with him?'

Nancy's mother poked at the food fastidiously. 'It's not nice, that sort of thing happening where you live. And Picton's Quay is a long way from anywhere if anything was to go wrong. . . .'

'Whatever could go wrong!' Nancy laughed.

'They've closed the railway, and there's no bus after six. . . .'

'Darling, we have a car! Hannah! This is quite superb. Some nice man somewhere is just waiting for you. You have so much to offer. We've just been saying, Mother and I, how much you have to offer.'

She was usually a little more subtle than this. Hannah wondered why she was so disturbed. Later, she found out. While they were stacking dishes, Nancy said, 'Mother doesn't know about this, but it's just possible we might have to make a move, something to do with Colin's job. This wretched business has come just at the wrong time for us. People are so funny, you never know what's going to put them off buying property.'

115

Colin came out and said, 'Is this private or can anyone join in?'

'I was just having a word with Hannah.'

'Well, when you've finished, I think your Mama is rather anxious to depart. She's afraid Jack the Ripper will be stalking the streets of Picton's Quay if we leave it any longer.'

Hannah thought of what Nancy had said about Neil while she did the washing-up. When she first went to work for him, Hannah had found him very attractive, but as she saw more of him he had lost some of his appeal for her. Perhaps Nancy was right about his being immature, but it was his vanity which had marred him in Hannah's eyes. His reaction to some of her jokes had gradually made her aware of his vanity: one had to be careful when one joked with Neil, familiarity was not permitted. Even his modesty was a form of vanity. He would never thrust himself forward, others must come to him; but they musn't venture too close, that would be familiar. Once his spell had been broken, however, far from being safe, she had begun to feel more involved with him; just as in the fairy stories, there was a penalty for seeing too much. She had a responsibility for him. She had felt this very strongly today. Cope's illness had distressed him more than seemed reasonable. How much did he depend on Cope? Was it possible he was in love with him? It would not have surprised her to discover that Moray was a little ambivalent sexually; but she could not fit Rodney Cope into this picture. These, and other speculations, helped to relieve the tedium of washing-up. When she had finished, and had tidied the sitting-room, she went into her bedroom and opened the window.

It was a warm night; the air was still and petrol fumes hung on it. She could hear men shouting outside a nearby pub, a heavy vehicle changing gear on Station Hill, the caterwauling of a police siren. She thought about Lomax. He had seemed a gentle, thoughtful person when she first knew him, but he had not attracted her sexually. Now that she was becoming aroused by him, she was no longer sure that he was gentle; in fact, she was not sure of anything about him. As always, loving was a step in the dark. She was not too dismayed by the prospect.

In his flat, Neil Moray was writing. He was feeling better. There is no surer cure for despair than action. '. . . at the time when I made these statements, I was unaware. . . .' In ten days' time he was to address the Chamber of Commerce, and he had decided to make this the occasion for a full statement of his position with regard to the West Front development. It was going to be hard for him, this was an audience which would not applaud what he had to say, and some harsh judgements would be made. But he needed to do something hard.

He did not finish until three in the morning, but he slept more peacefully after that than at any time since his interview with Heffernan. It was almost as though, at that interview, Heffernan had taken possession of a part of him. Now, he had freed himself.

12

IT was obvious from the pathologist's report that the inquest would be adjourned. Enough had been said by then to convince most of the people in the village hall that Pauline Ormerod was a 'load of old rubbish'—words actually used by the woman sitting next to William Lomax. One of the people who had helped to create this impression was the neighbour who had given information as to how Pauline spent her last few days.

'In bed, with a bottle of whisky, no doubt.'

'This isn't an occasion for speculation,' the coroner rebuked her.

'I had to go into her house on the Tuesday. We are having North Sea Gas installed, and the equipment for my stove was left at her house by mistake. She was in her nightdress when she opened the front door, and reeking of whisky. That was three in the afternoon. I don't know if you call that speculation.' She was a lady of the old Imperial school with a crisp, commanding voice and assured bearing. Although she had no time for Pauline Ormerod, she was not malicious; she was simply speaking the truth and saw no reason why she should soften it. The coroner was not quite sure how to handle her.

'You were not on good terms with Mrs. Ormerod?' he asked.

'No,' she agreed. 'I was not. Geoffrey Ormerod is a friend of mine.' Her tone made it clear that no one who was friendly with Geoffrey Ormerod could do other than deplore his wife.

A similar impression, no less damaging for being conveyed with a show of reticence, was given by the Ormerods' doctor. He acknowledged that Mrs. Ormerod was a patient of his with brisk disdain. She suffered from bouts of depression and he had prescribed anti-depressants. She had not been to him recently. He could not comment on her drinking habits.

Identification was made by Mrs. Ormerod's brother. He had not seen much of his sister over the past few years and was unable to give any information about her activities. It was three months since they had last met and on that occasion they had had a disagreement over money. He did not seem to approve of her any more than her husband's friends had done.

The only person who appeared to be upset was the man in charge of the dredger who had discovered the body. He kept saying that it was a terrible thing to have happened; although the coroner pointed out that Mrs. Ormerod had undoubtedly been dead for some time before her remains came in contact with the machine, this did not comfort him. It was plain that he irritated the coroner. Lomax thought he was the only witness to display any human feeling.

The police evidence was mainly negative. No information was as yet available to explain why Mrs. Ormerod had gone to Picton's Quay that night. The house had been searched and had revealed a state of affairs which, while it had shocked the impeccable young constable who gave evidence (clothes strewn around, dirty bath, a number of half-empty spirit bottles in the bedroom and six full bottles of milk in the porch) had thrown no light on Pauline Ormerod's plans for the evening. Her car had been found on the outskirts of Picton's Quay on the morning of Thursday, 19th June; the tank was empty. No one in the village had seen her or noticed the car. The rain had caused a lot of damage and for once in a way the villagers were absorbed in their own affairs to the exclusion of all else.

The pathologist gave evidence that death was due to strangulation.

'A woman like that asks to be killed,' the woman sitting next to Lomax said when it was all over.

'Did you know her?' he asked.

'I know *of* her. Lord Piers Plummer's daughter, she was.' She spoke as though the name itself was sufficient proof of

119

depravity. 'My sister used to be in service with Lord Piers Plummer. She said for all her lovely face, that girl never washed her neck, you could see the tide mark.'

On his way out, Lomax encountered the Ormerods' solicitor. Harold Slater took him by the arm. 'Now what brings you here, Will?' It was more than a casual inquiry.

'I have a personal interest.'

Slater gave the high-pitched laugh which was his invariable way of expressing exasperation. 'What a provoking person you are! How could you possibly have a personal interest in Pauline Ormerod? Now, look here, Will. . . .' They had come out into the village street; Slater halted Lomax, pushing him back against the rough stone wall surrounding the church, rather in the manner of a bad man giving the sheriff a warning, Lomax thought, except that neither was built for violent action. 'I hope you aren't going to make a lot of this. Ormerod has been pilloried enough by you fellows as it is.'

'I haven't pilloried Ormerod. Why wasn't he here, by the way?'

'His doctor advised that the strain might be too much for him. He's had a bad time, so leave him alone, like a good chap, will you?'

Lomax rested his arm on the wall which was already hot from the sun. 'Pauline Ormerod came to see me on the night of the election. . . .'

'She was always going to see people,' Slater interrupted. 'She wasn't in control of herself. She came to see me a week or so ago. She'd been drinking, I had to ask her to leave. I hope you had the sense to do the same thing.'

'She had some story. . . .'

'For goodness sake, Will! You fellows are quite unprincipled. The woman was a complete neurotic, you know that as well as I do; but for the sake of a story you'd take the word of a raving lunatic as the sober truth! The trouble with journalists is that they have no code of conduct. You won't mind my saying it, I know.' He gave Lomax a glassy smile. 'We've known each other a long time.'

'We have indeed,' Lomax said indifferently. 'Pauline

Ormerod came to me to tell me something about that
burglary. . . .'

'Burglary!' Slater laughed more shrilly than ever; his
eyes were unwinking as those of a china doll. 'Come now,
you're not as naïve as that!'

'Are you suggesting. . . .'

'I'm not suggesting anything at all. And if you're wise, you
won't make any suggestions either. One way to land yourself
in real trouble would be to follow up anything that woman
may have said. I wouldn't like to see you in trouble, Will.
Aaah!' He suddenly stretched out a hand and stood on tip-
toe; Lomax wondered whether he was going to levitate, but
it turned out he was attracting the attention of Inspector
Braithwaite, who was about to enter *The White Hart*. The
inspector waited without any show of enthusiasm while Slater
scampered across the road to join him.

Lomax remained by the church wall, feeling tired and uncertain whether to return to the office or have a drink at *The
White Hart*. The decision seemed to be one of great importance, it weighed him down. He went into the church to
wrestle with it.

All his life he had been unduly moved by defeat. Automatically, and often unreasonably, he was on the side of the
country over which battles must be fought for the greater
good of the greater number, on the side of the villagers who
must leave their homes so that the long-needed reservoir can
be provided, on the side of those who choose to sleep under
the arches or on the beaches, on the side of the squatter, the
gypsy, the prisoner at the bar. There was nothing necessarily
good or even praiseworthy in this attitude, the world would
not be a better place because there were a few like him who
lined up with the losers. But he was as he was, and in his way
he had been true to himself.

Fine, fine! Good rousing journalism, Todd would be proud
of him! And what did it amount to in practical terms? What
was his reaction when he was presented with one human
being in trouble? He had not raised a finger to help her.
Why? Well, he had just heard why, hadn't he? The

neighbour, the doctor, the woman who sat next to him, had expressed it clearly and unequivocally. She was neurotic and she had been drinking. What was more, she had been biting her nails. No one had thought to mention *that* to the coroner.

The vicar came out of the vestry and said apologetically as he hurried down the aisle, 'Don't let me disturb you, please; you are welcome to stay.' He gave Lomax a rather hunted look, as though afraid he might want something more positive than a few moments' peace. Lomax recalled that he was a keen bird-watcher, people said he preferred birds to people.

The vicar opened the door quietly and made his escape. It was dark and peaceful again. The church was small and smelt of old age; it was a good place in which to meditate. Lomax meditated, not on God, but on his servant William Lomax. Ever since his wife had left him he had been living well within his limits, emotionally and intellectually. Discretion does more than age to dim our senses. He said, 'God deliver me from discretion.' He could not think of anything else to say, so he left the church, pausing at the door to put ten pence in the box labelled 'repairs to the fabric'.

By the time he got back to Scotney it was nearly two o'clock and he was hungry. He parked his car near the clock tower, and went into the nearest eating place, which was a snack bar with dark mock-leather seats and the dull pink lighting he associated with the heyday of the cinema; piped music did little to enliven the atmosphere. Inspector Braithwaite was sitting alone at a table by the window.

'I thought you were lunching with Slater,' Lomax said as he sat opposite the inspector.

'You can't have thought anything as silly as that. I had a half-pint and told him I had to get back to the station in a hurry.' Braithwaite probed suspiciously at a hamburger and stretched for a bottle of tomato ketchup. 'What did you say to upset him so much?'

'I told him that Pauline Ormerod came to see me on the night of the election.'

122

'I wish people would attend to their own jobs and leave me to do mine.' Braithwaite's superior was suspended, there was a rumour that other officers might be implicated, Braithwaite had had his fill of scandal; the only kind of job he would be happy with at present was looking for stolen bicycles. But having so recently decided to eschew discretion, Lomax could not consider Braithwaite's feelings. He said:

'She told me that she had had an affair with Moray's campaign manager, Rodney Cope, and that he had been responsible for the break-in when those documents were taken.'

Braithwaite smeared tomato ketchup liberally over the remainder of the chips and said, 'And you believed her?'

'I can't be sure.' The waitress came and Lomax ordered cheddar cheese and French bread. When she had gone, he went on, 'I believed she had had an affair with Rodney Cope. I wasn't sure about the burglary.'

'Been drinking, had she?' Braithwaite's face was expressionless, not for nothing was he known as Stonewall Jack.

'She knew what she was saying.'

'She went around the place saying things and making scenes according to Slater; he said he had to throw her out of his place only ten days ago.'

'You'll have to steel yourself to collect some evidence, won't you?' Lomax asked mildly.

Braithwaite pushed his plate to one side and ladled sugar into his coffee. 'This is evidence you're offering me, is it?'

'I am offering a statement made to me by the deceased which seems at least as relevant as anything said at the inquest today.'

'Taken you a long time to do anything about it, hasn't it?'

'I'm afraid it has. But I didn't know she was going to be killed.'

'Now wait a minute, wait a minute!' Braithwaite slopped coffee onto the table and screwed up a paper napkin to dab at it before it trickled off the edge onto his trousers. 'What's got into you, man? Are you trying to run a new scandal every month? You got circulation problems, or something?'

The waitress came with a thin paring of cheese and sliced bread. Braithwaite stirred his coffee more cautiously. 'I've got enough trouble with the Ormerod affair still rumbling on. Now you want to start something that's going to upset all the people who kept clear of that! It's all very well for you to play around; but Moray and Ormerod have powerful people behind them, and if I make a false move and fall on my face, you won't be there to give me a helping hand. You'll be the first to put the boot in.'

'Who is the powerful person behind Moray?' Lomax asked.

'You know the talk as well as I do.'

Lomax ate a piece of bread; he was saving the cheese until last. 'Why do you think Mrs. Ormerod went to Picton's Quay?'

'You never give up, do you?'

'She must have had a reason for going. It's not the kind of place one gets a sudden urge to visit on a wet night!'

'Maybe she did have a reason. We've got reports of a fellow who was hanging about the area in the last few days. . . .'

'Long hair and a beard?'

'Look, Will, anyone mentions long hair and a beard and I'm automatically suspicious, particularly if they've been sleeping rough and are of no fixed abode. Right? While you automatically assume innocence. Right?'

'I'd want a bit more information before I assumed anything.'

'So would I, so would I. But I guarantee I'd be proved right more often than you. I take a good look at people; you just look at your navel and think about your principles.' Obviously recognising a good exit line, he hailed the waitress as she passed and demanded his bill. 'As for what you've told me, I'll look into it. But I'll need something more to go on than Mrs. Ormerod's unsupported statements. You heard what people thought about her at the inquest, and those were people who knew her. But if you come up with any real evidence, you know where to find me.'

Lomax wondered what Slater had said to him over their drink at *The White Hart*. It was rumoured that other influential people beside Ormerod had been holding their breath at the time the disclosures were made. If there was one thing all parties seemed agreed on, it was that, for better or worse, the Ormerod file should now be closed.

When he had paid his bill, Lomax walked along the promenade before going into his office. The tide was on the ebb, there was a smell of damp sand and seaweed; under the pier, children were waiting for donkey rides. The heat was beginning to build up; Archie Maxwell, Scotney's amateur weather man, said it was going to be a record summer.

13

SOMEWHERE up above a bird was singing, a thrush, a black-bird? He wasn't good on bird song, but it was very nice and he hoped the wretched cat wasn't about. He was not sure of the time, the clock on the table had stopped; there had been a rattle of milk bottles a couple of hours ago, but milkmen, according to his landlady, weren't as reliable as in former years and this one could come at any time from eight until twelve noon. The postman was a better guide, but he hadn't been this morning. The feet in the street? More stopping and starting now, he could imagine women shifting shopping bags from one arm to the other as they exchanged the little currency of their daily lives; the nine-till-five workers had moved briskly off at least an hour ago. Ah, now this was something – the thud of bottles in wooden crates, quite a different sound to the cheerful cacophony of milk bottles, and quite a lot of crates. A delivery was being made to *The Three Trumpeters*, and that usually took place just after ten o'clock. He looked at the brick wall beyond the window, it was not easy to tell the time by the sun in a basement room; once the sun came down the steps, he knew it was getting towards evening, but that was no help in the morning. But something about the air told him it was not much later than ten o'clock; there was a little freshness left, not much, but a little.

So it was ten o'clock. In the next hour three things could happen: the doctor could call, the landlady would certainly come with a cup of coffee and one of those biscuits with dried flies embedded in it, Neil or Hannah would call to see whether there was anything he needed. The excitement of waiting to see who would be first scarcely bore contemplating. But he did contemplate it and decided to put his money on Mrs. Simpkins; since he had begun to improve, the doctor called on his way back to the surgery at lunchtime, Hannah would go to the office because it was Friday and Neil would probably be down from Westminster (didn't they ever work on a Friday at Westminster, or was it just Neil who didn't?); they would go through the urgent mail before deciding which of them should visit him. His callers would, therefore, be Mrs. Simpkins, then Neil or Hannah, then the doctor. He hoped they wouldn't all come at once, he couldn't have all his little joys concentrated like that.

That was his morning settled, the only thing left to decide was whether it would be Neil or Hannah who came; and that would depend on the amount of soul-searching Neil had done during the week and whether he had found his soul. Cope rather expected Neil to avoid him.

In between these wandering thoughts, he lay quietly, listening to the bird singing. He was at that stage of recovery where the body needs rest and the mind is prepared to let it rest. Soon his body would begin to ache with inaction and his mind would leap ahead of his strength; but now he felt as though he was stretched out in a hammock slung some little distance above earth's sad and lowly plains, like the angels who came upon the midnight clear. He could not have believed that there could be such peace in being thus suspended, nor, for that matter, that he could ever find satisfaction in peace. It was something that had been missing from his life. Should he have been a monk? He had left it a little late for that. Nevertheless, it was good to think that there was a whole world as yet unexplored, indeed, scarcely imagined, a Shangri La, perched just above the lamps in Scotney Square.

A breeze blew the curtains back and fluttered the sheets of newspaper lying on the bed. It didn't worry him that Pauline Ormerod should intrude into his thoughts. She had had no place in them alive, but she fitted easily enough into them now that he had killed her. There was no disharmony. He didn't believe that she had resented her death nearly as much as the people who would read the account of the inquest in *The Scotney Gazette.* In any case, it was over and done with. He didn't remember much about it. There were times when his thoughts whirled round and round, faster and faster until they concertinaed and there was an explosion. He did not think this would be an acceptable defence. To defend oneself, one must study the system; in the eyes of the law, the truth is an irrelevance. The truth, in any case, was between himself and Pauline Ormerod.

Neil came first, carrying the cup of coffee which he had taken from Mrs. Simpkins thus depriving Cope of her morning news bulletin. Cope eased up on the pillows and then rested against them, feeling a delicious weakness after the exertion; he had come to recognise this weakness as being, in fact, the hidden strength which heaved him up into that hammock. He was well up in it this morning. He could view Neil in much the same way as a pilot flying over a cornfield will see the lines of a Roman encampment, all that intricate plumbing beneath the golden surface.

'The doctor says you have made a remarkable recovery.' Neil was making his excuses because he had something unpleasant to say and couldn't wait much longer.

Cope sipped his coffee, and nibbled a bit of the biscuit.

'You *are* feeling better?' Neil asked anxiously; he had made his plans and didn't want a hitch in them now.

'I feel that "I have slipped the surly bonds of earth",' Cope said. 'Can you remember where that comes from? I've been trying to think all morning.' Neil studied his fingernails, he wasn't trying to remember the poem. Cope went on, 'Something about putting out one's hand and touching the face of God.' He finished the biscuit. Neil allowed a short period of silence before turning from the sacred to the profane.

'I'm afraid there are one or two things I must ask you,' he said eventually. His eyes had the unwavering determination of the man who is quite inflexible where his own interests are at stake. 'In the first place, I'm not happy about the West Front development. At the beginning of next week

128

I have to speak at the Chamber of Commerce dinner and I think I must make my position clear then.'

Cope finished the coffee and put the cup down on the table, then he folded his hands across his chest, like a crusader, and said, 'Go on talking. I am listening, but I find this rests my eyes.'

There was a pause. Neil had been prepared to override resistance but was at a loss as to how to deal with lack of resistance. He wants a fight, Cope thought, a gentle skirmish to give that final stiffening to his moral fibre. 'What are you going to tell them?' he asked sleepily.

'I am going to tell them that now that more details of the scheme have become available, it is not one which I could support. I will admit that some of these details may well have been available during the campaign, but that there were other more important matters to which I had to attend then, and so I merely entered a plea that the scheme should be given careful consideration. I shall remind them that at no time did I commit myself to the scheme. . . .' Perhaps it had sounded devastating stuff the first time it was said, but the words now fell as flat as pancakes. Wisely, he broke off. 'Exactly what I say is not of importance now. But I must know the extent to which you have been involved with Heffernan.'

'I saw him once or twice.' Cope opened his eyes and gazed up at the ceiling. 'Three times, I think . . . yes, three times. What a pity you didn't come, too; we might have sorted all this out.'

Neil said, 'I don't think you understand my question.' His voice sounded strained. Cope turned his head slowly and looked at him. Neil's face was strained, too; personal combat at close quarters was something Neil didn't enjoy.

Cope said, 'I'm sorry. Could you spell it out for me?'

'Did you have a business deal with Heffernan?'

'With Heffernan? I'm not in his league.'

'You had no business transactions with him at all? He didn't ever pay you money?' Neil spoke the word 'money'

129

without flinching; all emotion had been levelled from his voice, he might have been asking a doctor whether he had cancer.

Cope said, 'You know, if you are going to make this kind of accusation, it's Heffernan you should see, not me; because it is him you will have to reckon with. He's fairly formidable. I think you'd be advised to see him before you make any public statement.' He closed his eyes again; he was genuinely very tired now, he wished Neil would go. 'I'm sorry, Neil. I'm not being very helpful. But just at the moment I don't feel I have the stamina to take on Heffernan *and* Mario Vicente–and you've already made an enemy of one of them.'

There was silence in the room. The bird was singing again, it must be a thrush, mustn't it? Blackbirds sing in the evening. He heard Neil get up and go to the window.

'Is that a thrush singing?' he asked.

'No. It's a blackbird.' Neil sounded very sure.

'Can you see him?'

'I don't need to. I was brought up in the country. It's a lovely call, isn't it? Lovelier than the nightingale's, I always think.'

Cope opened his eyes and looked at him. He was really listening to that bird.

'What are you going to do?' He was intrigued by the possibility that Neil might do something interesting.

'Do?' Neil sounded as though their conversation was a long way behind him.

'About the Chamber of Commerce speech.'

'I shall tell them that I can't commit myself to the development and why. But don't worry, I won't bring you into it.' There was no bitterness in his voice; he sounded gentle and considerate. 'You get some rest. I shouldn't have come bothering you like this. Would you like more coffee? I could place an order on my way out.' He smiled; he wasn't a person who smiled if he didn't feel like it. Whatever else Cope had expected, it wasn't that Neil would seem so serene, just as

130

though he had found his own Shangri-La. Something would have to be done about this.

After Neil had gone, Cope lay listening to the blackbird which was still singing at noon. Regretfully, he stretched out an arm for the clock. It was surprising how much effort he had to put into winding that clock.

14

On the Saturday, Major Brophy gave a party for Moray.

It was a warm evening. Hannah had all the windows in the flat open, but the leaves of the plants on the window ledge were still. The town seemed hushed, as though no one was in a hurry.

The air in the flat was moist and smelt of talcum powder and pine bath oil. Hannah was drying herself leisurely; she felt a delighted incredulity as though she was performing all these simple, intimate actions for the first time. When she had finished, she sat for some moments on the edge of the bath, her eyes closed, enjoying all the pleasurable sensations that come simply from breathing. She had said she would go to Lomax's house for a drink before they went to the party. In her bedroom, the wardrobe door was open and her summer skirts and dresses, bunched close together, orange, lime, cinnamon, plum, looked bright as fruit on a stall. It took her some time to decide what to wear. Her mind wasn't very active, consciousness seemed centred in her stomach; it fluttered at every movement and when she tugged a brush through her hair it set up a series of sharp quivers that spread through her body.

She dressed slowly, shivering as the silk blouse touched her flesh. Out in the street, the air was gentle and a little warmer than it had been in the flat; it seemed dense, she felt it under her arms and between her breasts. It was the first time this year she had been out in the evening without a wrap of any kind. She felt as if she had shed a skin. The streets had been crowded at lunch-time and she had had to leave her car in a cul-de-sac off Scotney Square. The strap of one of her sandals was tight and this slight discomfort had the effect of sharpening her awareness. There were people sitting

132

on benches on the square, sweating lightly in the shadow of the plane trees; they were relaxed and quiet, making no demands on one another, yet briefly belonging together. Children frisked about the fountain in the centre of the square and shouted shrilly when the water touched their sunburnt flesh. In one of the houses, someone was playing a piano; the notes trilled up and down Hannah's spine.

It was an hour later that Moray set out from his flat. By this time the garden at the back of Lomax's house was mostly in shadow. It was a sad garden which spoke of a stand having been made against chaos and little more; Hannah appeared momentarily at a bedroom window, paused, a hand to her blouse, and smiled with dazed tenderness at a tub in which wallflowers fought a losing battle with weeds. The clock of St. Barnabas Church struck the quarter hour. It was always ten minutes fast; but Moray, who did not know Scotney well enough to be aware of this, wondered if he had set out too soon.

He decided to walk. There would be plenty to drink at the Brophys, and he was in a mood to accept all that was offered.

One way and another, things had gone badly for him since the election. He had imagined, rather naïvely, that the very fact of standing as an independent candidate would ensure his independence; but it soon became obvious that to the local councillors, the trade union representatives, the members of the Chamber of Commerce, he was no lonely eminence, he was *their* member of parliament. The possessive *their* disturbed him. On all sides, people snatched at him as he passed, until in the end he began to feel they were tearing bits of him away. His time alone was precious; yet when he shut the door of his flat and took the telephone receiver off the rest, instead of peace descending upon him, he had a feeling in the region of his stomach as though he had severed an umbilical cord. He had to fight down panic at the thought of being alone. He had never worried about being alone before his meeting with Heffernan.

Then came that moment in Cope's room when he had realised that he must break free or be destroyed. As he had

133

stood listening to the blackbird his whole life, and the pattern of events which had made him what he was, had been etched on his mind as clearly as the finest engraving: it had all been there, past, present and future, and because it was incomplete it had resolved all the questions and eliminated the need for answers.

If only he could have gone immediately to face the members of the Chamber of Commerce, he could have accepted his destiny—or whatever it was that had been vouchsafed to him in that meaningful moment. Unfortunately, as the days went by, it became increasingly difficult to hold on to the experience. The beautiful precision was lost; the pattern became blurred, and he began to feel insecure, even a little giddy, as though Cope had pushed him over the edge, out into space.

This disorientated feeling had been even worse this morning. The heat didn't agree with him. It was still very warm now. Everywhere, windows were open and music blared into the streets; people spilled out of pubs and stood drinking and laughing on the pavements. A young couple strolled in front of him, the tips of their fingers touching; this roused more erotic sensations in him than if they had been mauling each other. The girl wore a long brown dress which looked dowdy and old-fashioned. Moray didn't like brown. But he admired the style of her boy friend who wore a purple corduroy suit. He had thought of buying a purple suit himself, but had decided that this wasn't what Scotney expected of its member of parliament. Only a few days ago, he had seen a vision of himself fearlessly flouting the members of the Chamber of Commerce, and here he was fretting because he couldn't wear a purple suit! It was the heat; he had never been able to think coherently in the heat. He was glad when he reached the tree-lined streets on the edge of the town.

Major Brophy lived in a baronial style mansion which had been completely refurbished by his wife after their marriage in a style more suited to a cinema foyer than a private house. All the reception rooms had enormous plush sofas and there were velvet curtains looped on either side of french windows so that one half-expected to see engraved on the glass the censor's certificate that the entertainment which was to follow had been given a 'U' certificate. The carpets were thick pile in shades of pale blue and pink and there were enormous vases of flowers in alcoves with coloured pink lights above them. Moray found all this rather exciting. As a child he had studied the films advertised on hoardings outside cinemas, and had made laughing comments in the hope that he would be taken to one of the films. His mother had always said, 'You don't want to see *that*, do you?' and he had been too ashamed to say 'yes'.

The Brophys themselves were quite unreal to Moray. Major Brophy still had a bewildered look as though he had gone on reconnaissance one night into unfamiliar territory and had never been able to get back to base; but he was devoted to the lady who had taken him captive and who was always dressed in a froth of some material which Moray imagined to be either voile or chiffon. Moray's parents had been quite different from the Brophys. He had no idea, for one thing, whether his father had loved his mother, although undoubtedly he had respected her; demonstrations of affection were unknown in the Moray household where physical contact was limited to helping one another off with Wellington boots and the conversation was devoted almost exclusively to intellectual topics, even a reference to the next door neighbour's cat being invariably followed by a quotation from T. S. Eliot.

Tonight, he needed the world of illusion, and as he walked towards Major Brophy's house he felt like a character in one of those films in which the hero staggers down a long, straight road towards the iron gates of an embassy, once inside which nothing can touch him. As he came up the drive, he heard music through an open window, a big band record, very smooth, a vocalist with one of those effortlessly sad voices, singing, *For all we know/We may never met again/Before you go/Make this moment sweet again. . . .*

The front door opened and Major Brophy stood in a square of light, hands extended, as though inviting him to step through the silver screen. Major Brophy wore a mulberry-coloured velvet jacket which toned well with the mushroom pink walls of hall and staircase; he had a waxed moustache and thick eyebrows which jerked up and down, giving to even the simplest remark a suggestion of the risqué.

'Your secretary has yet to arrive.' His eyebrows did double duty.

Neil, at a loss, said, 'The last shall be first.'

Major Brophy chuckled, 'Eh, eh? Don't like the sound of that at all!' Conversation with him was unnervingly disconnected. He cried, 'Onward, onward!' and pushed Neil through an archway. 'The conquering hero!' he shouted in a parade ground voice.

The long lounge, with its ornate chandeliers, was full of people, unfamiliar in evening dress: the style of the house inhibited the casual and most people had, for better or worse, made an effort. Someone cheered and Mrs. Brophy started *For he's a jolly good fellow* in a tremulous soprano. Major Brophy handed Neil a dry martini. Feeling rather foolish, Neil raised the glass in the general direction of the people on the dance floor. When they stopped singing, he said, 'There'll be no speeches tonight, folk. So carry on dancing.'

Mrs. Brophy came up to him. She insisted that he must call her Fay. 'You know, Neil, I was so delighted by your success. I can't tell you how much it meant to me.' In spite of her doll-like prettiness, she had anxious eyes. 'You seem to stand for things that. . . .' She looked at him vaguely, perhaps hoping he would put into words some unease she had about life for which he had the cure. 'The world is a maggoty place now,' she said with unexpected bitterness.

'There's certainly a lot that needs to be done.' Moray felt inadequate to bear the burden of such a conversation on one dry martini. He took an olive from a bowl on the table beside him and chewed it, feeling rather guilty. Fay Brophy had an unwholesome flair for rousing guilt feelings.

She said, 'You stand for something. . . . It makes a difference.'

'A fellow must stand for something.' Major Brophy took

up the theme as he returned to the table carrying two glasses. 'These young Liberals, now! Lying down on tennis courts, stopping tours by rugger teams! But they'd queue for tickets for the Russian ballet! I say to these young men, "We've heard what you're against. Now let's hear what you are for!" What you are *for*, see! That's what is important to me.' He clasped Moray's shoulder. Moray tried to think of something he was for; it was rather embarrassing, like being asked if one was saved.

'Do have one of these.' Mrs. Brophy produced a plate of sausage rolls. 'But they are rather greasy; I'll get you a napkin.'

'I was telling Neil how important it is to stand for something.' Major Brophy turned to William Lomax who had arrived at the same time as Hannah.

'Such as parliament, or the county council?' Lomax looked bemused, as though he had come in half-way through a film and couldn't make out whether it was supposed to be comic or serious.

'I don't know about the county council. Tell me, what do you make of this. . . .' Major Brophy began to tell Lomax about an incident at a meeting he had attended recently.

Moray and Hannah were left alone. Hannah said, 'I'm hungry. We haven't missed the food, have we?'

'I'm not hungry. The heat, I suppose.'

'I'm desperately hungry.'

'Why do you think these people voted for me?' he asked her. He looked at the people who were dancing. There must be someone who had a clearer idea than the Brophys of why they had voted for him. There were two school teachers within earshot, talking about capitation allowances; they sounded very decisive, he could not imagine they would ever perform an act of such social significance without knowing exactly why they were doing it.

'Perhaps they didn't all vote for you,' Hannah said. She seemed to find the possibility amusing.

Moray turned away and left her to search for food, which

137

was obviously her main concern. The music had stopped. Fay Brophy thought people would like a respite. Now that everyone was talking the volume of noise was much louder. Moray moved into the centre of the room, with a feeling of putting himself in peril, like a swimmer leaving the shore behind. He talked to as many people as possible. 'I know this isn't an appropriate time, but I so seldom have a chance to talk to you. . . .' He gave each person his slow, diffident smile, and asked what reform they most wanted to see brought forward. The replies varied alarmingly, even allowing for the amount of liquor which had been consumed. 'Get us out of the Common Market', 'Get rid of the national health service', 'Repeal the abortion Act', 'Equal rights for men' (from a very drunk young man who wanted to stay at home and look after the baby), 'Get us out of Ireland', 'Abolish the Race Relations Board' and 'Take over all private housing'. One girl said, 'Oh, what the hell!' And it seemed to Moray that she was summing up what all the others really felt. They didn't expect that any particular reform would make much difference to the world in which they lived; they had lost their belief in government. But they did believe in him. They looked at him with an expectancy which he found at once pathetic and daunting. Hadn't Yeats once said something to the effect that one should never define one's symbol? Was he a symbol to these people? Did they value him because they felt they knew what he stood for, or because they could interpret him in a way which most satisfied their needs? He had never been unconscious of his magnetism and had not found it unpleasing to see its effect on other people; but in the past it had required little effort on his part, whereas now it seemed that the charm must be put to work. He didn't like the idea of that.

As the evening wore on, the gin began to produce melancholy reflections. They had paid for him, all these people had paid for him with their vote; he was more of a gigolo than a member of parliament.

A girl in a tight-fitting tangerine dress came up to him. He could not remember where he had met her, but she saved him from embarrassment by saying to the young man who was with her, 'I always thought Neil was an old world gentleman until that night when we went round to Jimmy Hearn's after the meeting in Gloucester Park. Some of the stories he told then!' Her reference to that particular evening helped him to place her; she was the Brophys' daughter, Arlene. 'I've got a story for you, lover boy.' She swayed towards him and laid a thin, brown hand on his arm; where her dress parted he could see the bones in her chest and her small, firm breasts. He wondered whether she would come back to his flat with him if she could get rid of the boy friend. Vincent Strick, who was Chairman of the Chamber of Commerce, joined them. They were still countering one another's stories when the centre light was switched off for a record of Hildegarde singing *Love's last word is spoken, cheri*. In the dim light, Arlene Brophy's skin looked very dark and Neil was reminded of Lucy whose letter was on the mantelpiece in his flat, still unopened.

He moved away in search of another drink. Major Brophy also seemed dispirited. 'I could dance all night when I was a young man,' he said. 'Now I get tired soon after eleven.' He poured stiff drinks for himself and Moray. The two men stood side by side, not talking. Nearby, Hannah and Lomax were standing by the french windows looking into the night. She was saying, '. . . maddening to be born in the wrong hemisphere. . . .' She didn't look very deprived; in fact, as she talked about the Southern Cross something happened to her face which surprised Moray. Hannah was a cheerful person; but happiness is something quite different, something for people set apart, not a thing to radiate from the faces of the homely. He experienced a sense of harm having been done to him, as though there wasn't enough happiness to go round and it was inconceivable that some should have been allocated to Hannah Mason. He hadn't had this feeling (which shocked him since it put him in direct competition with others) since a boy at his school, who wasn't supposed to be as clever as he, had been awarded a Cambridge scholarship.

Major Brophy had also been watching Hannah. He said, 'Nice of her to take him in hand like that. Funny fellow, Lomax. Not good socially and doesn't drink much. Thought journalists had to drink, condition of employment. . . .'

The wind rustled the curtains, puffing warm air into the room. It seemed to act as a signal for which they had all been waiting; there was a drift towards the door.

Moray stayed until most people had departed because he felt this was required of him as guest of honour. When eventually he left he was surprised to see Lomax, who had apparently returned after taking Hannah back to her flat. Lomax explained that he had left something behind; he sounded rather vague, as though he had already forgotten what it was that he had left behind. They went down the drive together. Moray said, 'I can't remember a warmer night in years.'

Lomax said, 'The heat doesn't agree with me. I suppose one shouldn't be ungrateful.'

They turned into the avenue which was lined with tall, dark trees which seemed to hang heavy as velvet over them.

'It's the humidity that makes it so unbearable,' Moray said. He was beginning to feel sick.

Lomax said, 'A pity Cope couldn't be here tonight. How is he, by the way?'

'He has made a remarkable recovery.'

'A remarkable man.' They paused under a street lamp, where their paths separated. Lomax, standing with his head a little to one side, looked up at Moray like an alert bird examining with disinterested curiosity a creature of another species. 'I heard a remarkable story about Cope.'

'Really? He's that kind of man.'

'You think these stories are true?'

'Some of them, no doubt.'

'This one was told me by Pauline Ormerod. She said that Cope had an affair with her, and that it was he who was responsible for stealing those documents.'

'She must be a mad woman.' Moray had momentarily forgotten that she was dead.

140

'Somebody's mad,' Lomax agreed. 'Anyway, I thought you should know about it. I go this way. Good night.'

Moray watched him go with a disturbing, almost superstitious feeling that he ought to run after him; when the small figure was lost in the shadow of the trees, he remained listening until the footsteps had died away.

When Moray got back to his flat he made strong black coffee. He sat in the sitting-room, drinking the coffee and looking at the files strewn around. There were too many files; it would take weeks to sort out the contents. When he had finished the coffee, he lay down on his bed without undressing. His heart pounded, his head ached, and he felt sick; but he was beyond caring. He tried not to think of what Lomax had said. Too much had happened, he couldn't take in any more.

He stayed in bed the whole of Sunday thinking about what Lomax had said.

He did not go to London on Monday morning. He knew that he should have gone; but he lay in bed, watching the hands of the clock informing him that he had missed the ten to eight, the ten to nine, the ten to ten. . . . At ten he got up, had breakfast, washed and shaved, and went to the office.

'I didn't feel well,' he said to Hannah.

'I had a bit of a jolt this morning,' she said.

Why, he wondered, is there this one-up-manship where misfortune is concerned? If you have a bad cold, you can be sure that everyone you speak to will have had an even worse cold. Now that he didn't feel well, Hannah must needs have a jolt.

This morning she had read her Sunday newspaper which contained a brief account of the inquest on Pauline Ormerod. It had recalled to her mind an incident which she had witnessed in Mario Vicente's restaurant at the harbour. She recounted the incident in minute detail.

'Do you think I should go to the police?' she asked.

'Perhaps you should,' he said listlessly.

141

'I'm not anxious to inform on Mario!' She made a joke of it, but she was obviously worried.

'Don't go to the police, then.'

In the end, she went; she had one of those sturdy Puritan consciences.

'Did they rush out and arrest Vicente?' Moray asked when she returned.

She laughed. 'I saw a nice fatherly sergeant who took a note of all I said. He made me feel silly, in the nicest possible way. He said very soothingly, "You know, Madam, I expect there are quite a few restaurants in Scotney where they don't serve coffee on its own at lunchtime." Reduced to that, it all sounded quite harmless.' Moray could see she was relieved that her story had not been taken more seriously.

'When you have finished dwelling on your clash with the Mafia, perhaps we could look at the post,' he said. 'I've got to catch the two-thirty to London.'

'Is it worth going now? You're speaking at the Chamber of Commerce dinner tonight.'

'I may not be able to make it. I must be in the House for the debate on immigration, and if it goes on into the evening I shan't get away.'

'What a pity. It's your first big engagement here.' She made it sound like a vaudeville act.

He stayed in London all that week. He was barely aware of what went on in the House, it was all happening so far away. Out in the street, in the little cafés around Westminster, along the Embankment, on Westminster Bridge, it was just the same; it was all rushing away from him, getting smaller and smaller. How absurd it was, this business called life!

He had taken a room in a house off Sloane Square. He went back to the room every night intending to think this thing through; but the trouble was he was not quite sure what was the thing he had to think through. The words were meaningless, like the words which echoed round the House all day. Usually, he ended up thinking about himself. He had always taken great trouble to preserve this thing that

142

was himself. He had built a wall around it. But now it seemed as though he was on the outside of the wall, and there didn't seem to be any way in. What was happening to the person inside, the himself he had guarded so faithfully all these years? If himself was trying to get out, surely he ought to know. There must be some means of communication between them, a tapping on the wall. He began to listen, but he couldn't hear anything. If there wasn't anyone inside, then he was in a bad way; because there wasn't much left outside.

15

Todd met Ronald Singleton one evening when they were both drinking at *The Crossed Keys*. Singleton had dropped out of Moray's campaign early on, but Lomax had been right in suggesting he would have plenty to say on the subject.

'The trouble with Moray is he has no more idea where he is going than have any of his followers.' Singleton's thin, sallow face was bitter as he gazed into the mug of beer Todd had just put down in front of him. 'Look at his record! Formed a community housing association with a group of architects when he came down from Oxford, the idea was to buy up slum property and modernise it in co-operation with the tenants—no capital, and they didn't speak the same language as the tenants, so that didn't last long.' Singleton ticked off Moray's failures with satisfaction. 'After that, he was appointed as community relations officer to one of the local authorities in the Midlands that has a big immigrant problem. In that kind of job, for every inch you gain you lose two—it wasn't his idea of progress. Then he did a three-year stint with the Flaxman Prisoners' Aid Society. He'd been arrested once or twice at various demos and used to say there were better men in prison than you ever met outside, but once he got down to the grind of trying to help some of the less "better" ones his enthusiasm waned fairly rapidly. The Scotney by-election cropped up just about the time he packed it in with Flaxman.'

'And you jumped at him,' Todd reminded him.

'I don't deny it.' Singleton looked out of the porthole window at the boats bobbing about in the harbour in a sunset glow of saffron, rose and emerald; the sight appeared to give him little pleasure. 'He has what you fellows call charisma. But there's nothing behind it; no vitality, no stamina.'

'But he won the election.'

'Oh, he polled the votes.' Singleton spoke as if this was the least part of an election campaign. 'But Cope had more to do with that than Moray. It's the organisation that counts in the long run.'

'Cope hadn't much experience, though,' Todd said. 'I was surprised you let him take over the running of the campaign.'

'Let him!' Singleton gave a little bark of contempt. For a moment, it seemed as though he wasn't going to say any more. It was very hot, the door was open; there were people standing in the porch and sitting on the benches outside. The sunset was breaking up, charred remnants were still scattered about the western sky, but the evening star was up. Singleton said, 'I wasn't given any option.'

'You mean Cope pushed you out?'

'He poured red paint over me.'

Todd put the mug down on the table carefully and held the beer in his mouth for several seconds before he managed to swallow it. He looked at Singleton. The man wasn't laughing. He was looking out of the porthole again. A lantern had been lit on the wall to his right; in its amber light his face looked tired and defeated, the bitter mouth sucked in slightly as though his gums were receding along with his hopes.

Todd said, 'How come?'

'You remember all those slogans which appeared in fluorescent paint?'

'I remember one on that dump near the Dominion Cinema. "This site has been empty for three years. Why? Neil Moray is the man who will get an answer to this question." Or words to that effect.'

'Cope painted those slogans. It stirred up a lot of feeling; but it's not the way to go about things, you make enemies of people you're going to need as your friends if you win. I caught up with him one night when he was doing it. It was in Jakes Yard; the Council had a compulsory purchase order on five of the cottages and they'd been left to rot for years.

Cope was up a ladder, painting on one of the walls. I started to argue with him and he said, quite amiably, 'Bugger off and leave me to handle this.' I put my hand on the ladder and rocked it. I suppose I meant to give him a bit of a fright for talking to me like that. He stared down at me and laughed. He said, 'That was a silly thing to do.' He looked absolutely delighted, as if I had given him a present. Then he picked up the tin of paint and poured it over my head. I had to walk home; it was dark, but that made it worse, the paint being fluorescent. Some people screamed and others laughed, but no one offered to help. I remember a man calling out "What happened to the other fellow?" I could have sued Cope, I suppose. But he would have said I upset the paint when I rocked the ladder. No one would have believed me. Even my wife said I'd been fooling about. She wouldn't speak to me for a week afterwards, it gave her such a fright.'

'Did you tell Moray?'

'No. I didn't want any more to do with any of them. It shook me up.' He put down his empty mug. 'I'd better be getting home. The wife gets a bit touchy if I'm out late.'

Todd watched him elbowing his way to the door and thought, 'Must have looked like Count Dracula.' This struck him as very funny. He began to laugh. Todd did not often laugh, and perhaps because of this he had never learnt to regulate his laughter; once it started it got out of control and he snorted, neighed and hooped helplessly, while his stomach ached so painfully it was almost unbearable. When people turned to stare at him in one of these paroxysms, he became panic-stricken and this made the laughter worse. He had not been taken so badly since a garden fête at which he had accidentally knocked a woman's hat into a bowl of trifle. It took him some time to calm himself. He was still having a few convulsions as he wiped his streaming eyes, but the worst of the attack was over, and the realisation that someone had joined him at the table had a final sobering effect. He looked up into the face of Rodney Cope.

Cope said, 'You should be more careful of the company you keep.'

Todd tried frantically to collect his thoughts to deal with what his brain told him was a coincidence and his stomach recorded as an emergency.

'Or,' Cope said, 'you will find yourself in trouble.'

Todd's glasses had misted over. He polished them on a handkerchief. 'You have a bloody nerve,' he said hoarsely.

'Oh, I have a nerve,' Cope acknowledged. 'Bloody or otherwise.'

Todd cleared his throat and put on his glasses. 'I reserve my right to speak to anyone I choose.'

'What do you mean, you reserve your *right*?' Cope's voice blared out very loud, an explosion of amusement that had in it a hint, not only of contempt, but of threat. The few people at the bar looked at Todd, appraising him to see why he should make such pretentious claims for himself. Cope said, 'Who the hell do you think you are?'

Todd said, 'I am a journalist.' It didn't sound enough.

'And that entitles you to go around talking a lot of irresponsible nonsense about other people?' Cope's voice was still very loud and the loudness appalled Todd more than the actual words, it assaulted him in a violent way like the noise of a discotheque; one or two people had moved in from the porch and were peering round the door to see how Todd was taking this.

'Now, let's have it, to my face, this story of yours,' Cope said.

Todd put his hand out for his mug of beer, his sweaty fingers slipped on the handle and he thought better of lifting it; instead, he regarded the froth on the top with frowning suspicion as though he feared he had been given short measure. 'Get yourself a drink, man, and cool down,' he said. He met Cope's eyes which, always bright, now seemed incandescent; also, perhaps because of his illness, they had become rather protuberant. These strange eyes stared at Todd with delighted incredulity, either applauding Todd's temerity or gleefully snapping at a challenge. The man's reactions and his behaviour were so totally inappropriate to the situation that Todd could not predict what would happen next.

What did happen was that Cope went to the bar and ordered a pint of beer. Todd was filled with misgivings. He looked at the people standing in the doorway; at moments such as this he was very conscious of his weak eyes and receding chin, and he knew that whatever happened no one would have any sympathy for him. Cope returned with the pint of beer, he said 'Salut' and raised the mug. Todd managed not to close his eyes or cringe; it was a considerable effort and he felt foolish when Cope proceeded to drain the mug at one long draught. The people by the door gave a faint cheer. Cope said to Todd, 'Come along ! We can talk this over outside.'

Todd, whose throat seemed to be closing up, left his beer on the table and followed Cope. The people round the door made way for them.

Todd said, 'Now, what is this all about?' He was relieved that nothing had happened, and felt reasonably in control of himself if not of the situation. There were one or two people fishing on the jetty; Cope and Todd strolled along, watching them. Cope said:

'Do you think they catch anything right here in the harbour?'

'They must do,' Todd said. 'They are always here.'

'How unscientifically you arrive at your facts !' Cope laughed. He sounded quite friendly now.

'I observe,' Todd said, 'and then I check my facts very carefully.'

'Well, be careful, you observe that rope . . . careful, I said !'

Todd was never sure whether he tripped over the rope or was pushed. It didn't seem to matter much anyway. He had been threatened. As he lay in bed, with rum and a hot-water bottle provided by his landlady, this was the most significant fact to emerge from the affair. He had always known that one day he would be threatened and had looked forward to the experience as a journalistic coming of age; he believed passionately that it is the business of the press to live dangerously and this included making enemies. So far, there had been little opportunity to live dangerously in Scotney, and the nearest he had come to being threatened was the refusal of the operatic society to provide him with a free ticket because his reviews were so caustic. His reaction to that had been petulant, his present attitude not much better. He had been caught woefully unprepared for his great moment and had behaved with all the staunch intractability of a stranded fish gasping on a beach. The worst thing of all had been sitting shivering on the jetty, trying to get his breath back. How they had laughed, the people in the bar, grateful for any diversion, the children bored with the monotony of fishing; their reaction had been as lacking in reason as Cope's action. He tried to summon anger from somewhere deep inside himself where anger could usually be found; but there wasn't any anger in him tonight.

The next day it was hotter still. In the *Gazette* office, the smell of curry from the Indian restaurant next door was particularly strong.

'It must come up through the floor boards,' Lomax said. He looked pale and listless, but he sharpened considerably when Todd told him his story.

'What an extraordinary thing for him to have done! There was nothing to be gained by giving you a ducking. What do you make of it?'

Todd, who had expected Lomax to register anger at this treatment of one of his reporters, said, 'My trousers are ruined.'

Lomax tapped his front teeth with a forefinger, pondering something unconnected with damage to Todd's trousers. 'I suppose he would regard it as a nice piece of improvisation,' he said eventually.

'Like pouring red paint over Singleton?'

'Yes, that was odd. I wonder why Singleton kept quiet about it.'

'People laugh at you,' Todd said bitterly.

'I'll see if I can speak to Cope.' Lomax reached for the telephone. 'It will be interesting to see what line he takes.'

'He'll say that I fell over a rope.'

'That's all right. We'll say you didn't fall over a rope.' While the telephone was ringing he reverted to his grievance about the smell of curry. 'Allinson got food poisoning from one of their curries, do you remember? I wonder if he'd like to risk it again. We might get the wretched place closed down. . . .'

Todd, who considered singleness of purpose to be essential in matters great and small, was too irritated to reply.

16

BY mid-day the temperature was in the nineties. Hannah went home at lunchtime, had a bath and changed all her clothes. She liked the heat, but, as with most things in life, there were limits. As far as heat was concerned, once her limit was reached, she faded. She was fit for nothing today. This gloomy thought brought Lomax to her mind; he had scarcely been out of it throughout the week. In the past, she had been cautious about committing herself to the business of loving and had avoided casual encounters. Perhaps this was a failing, but might it not be wiser to stick with one's failings instead of trying to emulate the enterprise of others? At least one's failings were one's own, and understood. Had she been too precipitate in starting an affair with Lomax, thereby jeopardising the prospects of a more enduring relationship? During the week she had worried about this, imagining she was an episode in his life. Today, exhausted by the heat, she was not sure that she wanted either the affair or the relationship.

The office was hotter than ever when she returned in the afternoon, and she felt no better for the bath and change of clothing.

At three o'clock Rodney Cope arrived.

'No telephone calls, no furious trumpeting from the press barons?' It was an effective entrance; his attack was formidable.

'I did have a call from the *Gazette* to ask whether you were active among us again,' Hannah said. 'Are you just making a call?'

'What nonsense! I'm back in action.'

'Are you well enough?' He was pale and she thought there

151

was something unusual about him. 'You look as though you've been kept in the shade.'

'How nicely you put things.' He glanced round the room; his energy dwindled momentarily and Hannah was again fleetingly aware of sickness. 'Surely it wasn't always like this? So dusty and drab, and rather dead. What has happened?'

'Nothing has happened.' She passed the tip of one finger across her forehead, following the hairline; she did this very carefully as though she had calculated the exact amount of energy required to give temporary relief without creating more sweat than was actually removed. 'What did you expect?'

'Dynamic government, I suppose.'

She raised one eyebrow, to have raised both would have cost too much effort. He picked up the letters which she had typed and began to read them. The heat had slowed her down considerably, but it seemed to have had no effect on him; perhaps it was this that made him seem a little odd, as though he existed on a different plane. 'Hallo!' He looked up from a letter. 'What's this? Didn't Neil attend the Chamber of Commerce dinner after all?'

She tried to put a file of papers into a foolscap envelope; the envelope split and she went to the waste-paper basket and stood poised above it, too dazed to decide whether to throw away the envelope or the papers. Cope said, 'So the great speech was never made. Why not, do you know?'

Hannah dropped the envelope into the waste-paper basket and took another, larger, envelope out of the cupboard; this show of decisiveness exhausted her so much she could not reply.

'He must have given a reason.' Cope was determined to force the pace. 'How did he make his excuses?'

'He didn't.' She wrote an address on the envelope and fitted the file of papers in successfully. 'He didn't even tell the Chairman that he wouldn't be able to attend and he hasn't written to apologise.'

'Can't you get in touch with him?'

'I've tried. And I've left messages asking him to telephone me.' She stuck down the envelope and reached for Sellotape. 'But I'm leaving early this afternoon, so if he telephones later it will be too bad.'

'Why are you leaving early?'

'Because I can't stand the heat in this room; with the low ceiling and that wretched little window, it's like an oven. And the lavatory smells. And anyway, there is less and less to keep me here. Neil doesn't need a full-time secretary.'

Cope put the letters back on her desk and strolled round the room, giving an exaggerated start as he came to a wire tray on top of the filing cabinet. 'Nothing to keep you here! There's mountains of filing, you can't have done any for weeks.'

'I haven't. The files aren't here. Neil has them in his flat.'

'Poor Hannah! But you must be patient, my love. I suspect one's first year as a member of parliament is rather like marriage. . . .'

'Neil is the one who is out of patience.'

'Why? Did you have one of your sweet-and-sour days?'

She went across to the scales with the envelope and squinted down at a table she had typed and stuck to the base of the scales. 'I suppose this will go letter post.' She put the envelope down on the table and stared at it; her thought processes were sluggish. 'I went to the police about something that happened to Mrs. Ormerod in one of Mario Vicente's restaurants, the one opposite the harbour. It seemed to annoy Neil. He kept making references to my Puritan conscience. I think this will go letter post.'

'Keep to the point. Mrs. Ormerod?'

'Yes. Mrs. Ormerod. You knew her.'

'Did I? What was I supposed to know about her?'

'You tell me.' She was irritated by this barrage of staccato questions. 'I saw you with her once—out at that cottage in the marshes.' She put the parcel down on the scales. The needle swung round, she watched it quivering from one side

153

to the other; when it steadied, everything was still. She might have been alone. She looked at the weight recorded by the needle. It seemed to be the silence she was weighing: it was oppressive. After a few moments, she reached out a hand, without taking her eye off the needle, and groped for a pen. She wrote 27p on the corner of the envelope. 'Well,' she was still looking at the envelope. 'I'll go now.'

'Yes,' Cope said. 'Off you go, Hannah.'

She picked up her handbag and looked down at the envelope again as though the decision to send it letter post was troubling her. Finally, she said, without looking at Cope, 'You can manage?'

He did not reply. At length she was forced to look at him. It was as though neither had a face, only eyes. He said, 'Yes, I can manage.'

Hannah ran down the stairs and walked so rapidly to the post office that the people she passed looked at her in amusement. A man said to his wife, 'Perhaps she's found a letter bomb!' She thrust the package into the letter-box and walked on, towards the promenade.

It was half-past four; the tide had turned and the breeze had died down, the heat was intense. A hard light caught each ripple on the sea and danced along with it. The white buildings dazzled and a hot red band glowed above the door of a café. The pavilion at the end of the pier looked dark and rather dingy, the sun catching a few of its domes but leaving the rest in shadow. The tread of passing feet had lost its sprightliness, no one hurried; it had been a wonderful day, but this was the moment when one felt the gap until drinking time.

Hannah sat in one of the deck-chairs near the Imperial Hotel. After what might have been a few minutes, or an hour, she was conscious of a quiet, hairy young man standing, shirt flapping, ticket machine held at navel-level.

'I only sat here for a moment to rest,' she explained.

'Yes, all right.' He spoke gently, as though she wasn't well. 'I don't think they ought to charge after four, anyway.' He moved on. Behind Hannah, a woman said to a companion,

'That's where the ratepayers' money goes! People sit out here until seven o'clock.'

Hannah sat in the deck-chair until a quarter to seven. It was still very hot and she did not think she could eat much; at the same time, she felt hollow and in need of something. She had a cheese salad in a help-yourself buffet. Then she walked to the Summer Gardens and bought a ticket for a concert by the Bournemouth Symphony Orchestra. The great glass doors at the side of the concert hall were open; instead of going inside, Hannah sat on a deck-chair in the garden. It was a brilliant evening, the stars seemed to be just above the trees. She had no idea what music was played.

It was a quarter-past ten when she came to the corner of Saddlers Row. There was a lot of noise on the promenade; singing from the pavilion on the pier, shouts from the beach where there were several swimmers and even more spectators; from open windows came the sound of voices, music, a television serial of the more violent kind involving endless police sirens. But most of the buildings in Saddlers Row were deserted at night and as Hannah turned the corner the volume of sound diminished considerably. She opened the door to her flat and hesitated, looking up the dark shaft of stairs; she glanced back towards the street. There were two people in the car park opposite; she heard a woman say, 'Leave the doors open a moment or two, Alf; it's like an oven.' Hannah closed the door, bolted it, and went up the stairs to her flat. It was stiflingly hot. She opened all the windows. The man and the woman were still in the car park, she could see the car's headlights.

They had gone by the time she was ready for bed. The car park was empty, save for the few cars which never seemed to be collected. In the distance, there was music from a discotheque; it must have been at least two streets away, but although it did not come very loudly to her ears, it still had that violent quality, the sense of a need to break through the civilisation barrier. There was no relief from the heat; when she leant out of the window it was like breathing in warm cotton wool. A long shadow moved in the car park. She crouched on the bed, to one side of the window, watching. There was no further movement. She listened intently, but each time she had her ear tuned to the silence in the immediate area, there was a grinding noise from the promenade as though all the cars were travelling in second gear. She lay down on the bed and drew a sheet over her body. Gradually, it grew quieter. It became darker, too; she could usually see from her bed a portion of the ruined wall surrounding the car park, thrusting up from the pavement like a fang, but now it merged into the darkness. Everything beyond the window was without form.

Now, she became aware of noises which seemed to come from within the framework of the building. On the other side of her bedroom area, just beyond the head-rest of her bed, was the building where the obscure religious sect met. They occupied one floor. She had never been sure what went on on the other floors. In fact, she knew very little of what went on in the neighbourhood in which she lived. From the sounds which reached her ears tonight, she judged that the next building must be infested with rats; there was a constant scratching and a squeaking of floor boards. How flimsy it was, this little shell in which she lived; a paper house. She looked at the clock on the shelf by her bed; it was not facing her directly, but as far as she could make out the time was five past two. There was a sound as though somewhere a door was swinging on rusty hinges. Why should this happen on an airless night? She lay listening for noises, negotiating them cautiously as if they were stepping stones which would lead her through to the morning. She was having trouble with a sharp click, which sounded more metallic than anything she had yet heard, when she became aware that someone was moving very quietly close to the skirting board on the other side of the wall. Alarm produced a sensation in her head she had had only once before when she bit into something very hot in an Indian restaurant; it fizzed up her nose and exploded in her brain. She put out her hand and switched on the light, banging her elbow against the wall as she did so. The noise stopped; but she knew, as she huddled with her ear to the wall, that there was someone within less than a foot of her on the other side of the wall. She got out of bed and dressed quickly in whatever came first to hand. The floor boards creaked, betraying every step she took; it was as though the flat itself had turned against her. In under three minutes, she was down by the street door. Her car was parked some distance away; there were double yellow lines immediately outside, but at the end of the road there was space for four cars to park. She bent down and eased the bolts back gently. Suppose someone was standing just outside the door? She knelt down on the floor, gently drawing back the door mat, and peered through the crack at the bottom of the door. Nothing but cobwebby blackness. She opened the door and raced up the street. There were six cars parked very close, hers was hemmed in so that it could not be extricated. She walked on.

No one followed her. But this did not bring any relief because now danger seemed to lie ahead, in the doorway of a shuttered shop, in an alleyway, hunched in a telephone kiosk.

As a child, it had been 'you must always come through the well-lit streets'. She made for Scotney Avenue. The hands on the clock in the post office were at a quarter to three when she turned into The Avenue. The wide street, livid in lamplight, was empty. It had the look of a place which is waiting for something to happen. On the opposite side of the street, the church of St Stephen the Martyr rose high above the surrounding buildings, massive and dark, save where the great rose window winked in the moonlight like the eye of a Cyclops. Immediately beside her, a traffic light turned from red to green, and farther on another light responded and passed the signal on, 'something human this way comes'. She crossed the road and began to walk down The Avenue, past food shops with closed notices hanging up, jewellers' with grilled windows and an antique shop with portcullis drawn across its entrance. Nothing stirred behind the barricades; the daytime people had evacuated the area. Whatever might happen, they did not want to know about it.

Something was wrong, perhaps it was herself. The street was so large whereas she was getting smaller with every step she took. A dark road tunnelled off ahead of her. She turned into it. The shops here were no bigger than booths in a fairground. Most of the wares would be out on the pavement in daytime, but now they were inside; Stetsons, studded leather belts, ponchos, kimonos, dresses feathered and fringed, all penned inside until the day's charade began again. Dustbins blocked doorways and it was necessary to walk carefully. Even so, she stumbled over a pile of old newspapers and had an encounter with an angry cat. Farther on, she nearly fell over a pair of old boots. As she paused to get her breath back, the boots drew away from her and tucked themselves beneath a shapeless bundle of clothes lying between a dustbin and the door of one of the shops. Hannah walked away, avoiding pity like a snare.

The buildings grew more dilapidated. Through one window she saw a rent in the roof and a jagged piece of sky beyond. She regretted taking short cuts but dared not turn back. Now, she was in a no-man's-land of vacant sites cordoned off by wire mesh fencing. On a wall at the side of one of these sites a slogan had been painted, the words no longer decipherable. The pavement had dwindled to an asphalt path which even at this hour sweated in the heat; she felt it give slightly beneath her heels. To her right, there was a long, low corrugated iron structure which looked as though it might be a relic of war-time occupation. As she walked towards this apparently derelict place, something stirred on the other side of the wire mesh. It was delicately done; she was aware only of two eyes which bobbed forward to wait for her to come abreast of the gate leading to the site. The gate was heavily padlocked. As she came to it, the guardian of this mystery snuffled to show that he had picked up the scent of her fear. For a time, he paced beside her. When she moved out of his territory, she could hear him grumbling in his throat.

She came to another main road, livid and empty as Scotney Avenue, save for a police car in a bus bay. The two policemen encapsulated in the car watched her speculatively as she crossed the road. She turned into a street lined with squat, semi-detached houses. She was committed to the dark streets now. In front of her, a tattered creature, unidentifiable as man or woman, proceeded jerkily down the street, one foot in the gutter and one on the pavement; it was engaged in a tirade of abuse which rose to a shriek whenever the uneven method of perambulation resulted in a more than unusually severe jolt. As Hannah edged by, the creature caught its foot on an uneven paving stone and lurched against her. Terror and guilt, the combined product of a lifetime of such misadventures, found vent in an accusation–so set about with profanities it was barely understandable–that Hannah had tried to shove past. A touch of a hand in the dark, a friendly word, might have made an end to the scene; but Hannah walked away. Behind her, the voice rose in unexpectedly lucid comment on this uncharitable behaviour. 'You're the devil! You pretend to be so fine, but you're the devil. Don't think I don't know you're the devil. . . .' She hurried on and was soon out of ear-shot; but a rank smell had got into her nostrils and remained with her.

Ahead, there were lights and intermittent traffic sounds. She was near the main road which circled Gloucester Park. She could see the trees in the park stretched against the sky and a moon thin as the Cheshire cat's grin. She began to run past parking meters rearing up like caterpillars. Lomax could get little sense out of her when she arrived at his house.

She was too confused to find a beginning at which she could start her story. If she could have done that, it wouldn't have been so bad; a cause from which all this unpleasantness derived might have offered the possibility of an eventual restoration of order. But when she tried to tell Lomax what had happened, the thing which came first to her mind was the person next door. A drop-out, a tramp, it didn't matter who he was or why he was there. It was the fact that he *was* there and she had not realised it that was so terrible; they had been living within a foot of each other, night after night, for weeks, perhaps months. And outside? When she leant from her window at night to look at the stars and dream her dreams, it was all down there; the bundle huddled by the dustbin, the guardian of the derelict hut, the tattered creature who knew about the devil. . . .

Lomax gave her brandy, wrapped a blanket round her and let her talk. Many people haven't the patience to wait, if you hesitate they find words for you, not the words you want; he waited for Hannah to find her own words. Eventually, her ramblings brought her to Rodney Cope who had killed Pauline Ormerod. This no longer seemed so important, it was something left on the surface of her mind; she was able to talk about it more rationally than the things which had happened since.

'When I told him I had seen him with Mrs. Ormerod, he didn't say anything and I felt the hairs on the back of my neck begin to rise, as though someone had come up behind me and touched me with the tip of a finger. I didn't know how we were ever going to look at each other again. But we did.' She ran a forefinger lightly round the rim of the brandy glass. 'It wasn't that his eyes were wild, or anything like that. . . . they just accepted that I knew he had killed her. I don't think I would have known, I'd have found a way out of knowing, if only he hadn't looked at me like that.'

Lomax said gently, '*Where* did you see Mrs. Ormerod and Cope?'

'Coming out of a cottage in the marshes near Picton's Quay, months ago, at the end of March. I never mentioned it because it was a special place to me. I thought of it as my territory and I didn't want him to invade it. But I suppose really it was I who invaded his territory.' She leant against Lomax's shoulder, suddenly spent; she had run her race and touched the tape, it was all over as far as she was concerned.

But later, in bed, the other things came back, and most vividly of all, the creature who had recognised her as the devil when she walked away. She could not explain this to Lomax, but her need for comfort communicated itself. There was nothing he could do to drive out the terror because the terror was real and he was as powerless against it as she. And yet, inexplicable as the terror, human warmth worked its miracle, and as he held her close she was gradually eased of fear.

Lomax did not sleep all night. He had suspected that Cope had killed Pauline Ormerod, and yet murder seems so unlikely that one's intelligence continues to protest against the facts. Fear can accomplish more than reason. As he lay beside Hannah, he was convinced beyond all doubt that Rodney Cope was a killer.

'I think you should go straight to the police,' he said the next morning. Hannah was still in bed; he fussed with the breakfast tray to conceal his nervous impatience.

'I'll go if you like, but they won't believe me. I've been before.' She buttered a piece of toast before she explained about the statement she had made regarding the incident in Mario Vicente's restaurant.

'I see.' Lomax thought about this while he poured coffee for himself. 'In that case, they may be sceptical; but the important thing is that the knowledge should be shared.'

'Yes, I see.' She sounded apathetic. While she ate, she looked towards the window. She said, 'Another fine day.' She thought about Rodney Cope and wondered what it must be to have done something so irrevocable, to wake one morning and think 'last night I killed a woman', not to be able to turn over and try for a better dream, to have to drag that into the day with you and all the subsequent days. For a moment, she seemed within a hair's breadth of understanding; but it was too much for her, she couldn't hold on to it. She said, 'I don't feel well. I'd like to stay here.'

'You'll feel better once you're up.'

She looked at him reproachfully and he kissed the tip of her nose. She closed her eyes.

'I don't think I can face everyone.'

'I'll be with you.'

'You won't be at the office.'

161

'The office!' he said sharply. 'You're not going back to that office.'

She did not answer. Her face assumed a vague expression, like that of a deaf person who has switched off the hearing aid. She pulled the clothes back and swung her feet slowly over the side of the bed. 'I'd better wash.'

He began to speak and then thought better of it. She looked very strained, as though she might burst into tears at an unkind word, yet stubborn enough to resist all argument.

When she came downstairs some forty minutes later, she gave him a tentative smile while her eyes pleaded to be spared reproof. She said, 'I'm ready at last.'

He said, 'Hannah, let's try to be sensible about this. . . .'

'I won't go to the office today,' she said quickly. 'I'll wait until I can see Neil; then I'll tell him that there's not enough work to keep me occupied full-time. And anyway the room is too hot. I'll suggest I work at home. I can't come to any harm that way, can I?' She looked at him anxiously, dreading argument in the way a woman does when she has no intention of being persuaded by it.

He turned away and stood by the window, drumming his fingers on the sill. In the last seven hours his feelings for Hannah had changed so much that the woman who had delighted him only a few days ago seemed a stranger. The woman who now stood before him caused only pain, but she was a part of himself. His thoughts about her were confused, his impulses tended to violence; he wanted to shake some sense into her, to shout that she was his, that she had no right to risk something that belonged to him. He was bewildered, ashamed, and a little frightened.

She said meekly, 'Shall we go to the police now?'

'Hannah!' He turned to her, distracted. 'What is the point of this nonsense. What good can it possibly do?'

'I'm not trying to *do* anything,' she muttered wretchedly. Life had seemed a dangerous affair last night, and she had seen that there were some warnings one could not afford to ignore. Now, she didn't see anything very clearly and there was a thinness about life. Sufficient unease remained, however, to hold her to her purpose, if it could properly be called 'her' purpose. Who was she, anyway? She dragged words out of confusion. 'This is going to be a bad time for Neil. I must keep in touch with him. I can't walk away and forget him.' It didn't sound convincing, even to her. She said, 'Don't be angry with me, Will. You must help me.'

'Yes, all right.' He put his hands on her shoulders and they stood close for a moment, thinking their own thoughts. 'All right.' He felt they both needed time for reflection.

On the way to the police station, he asked cautiously, 'How do you feel about sleeping at your flat?'

'Not too good,' she admitted.

'You could stay with me, but I'm often out very late.' He thought it unwise for her to be with him, since he himself might qualify for Cope's attentions.

'I know a married couple in Pelham Square,' she said. 'I could go to them. I'll say the flat gives me claustrophobia in the heat.'

'Won't they think that odd?'

'They've got all sorts of wrinkles in their own personalities, so they accept other people's oddities.'

Braithwaite was not at the police station. They saw the sergeant who had taken Hannah's previous statement; he listened impassively and promised to report to Braithwaite when he returned. Afterwards, Hannah went to see her friends in Pelham Square. When he got to his office, Lomax telephoned Neil Moray's office. Rodney Cope answered the telephone.

'I hear that you were friendly with Mrs. Ormerod,' Lomax said. 'I wonder whether you could fill in one or two details for me?'

Cope said that he had not known Mrs. Ormerod; he added, 'There could be only one source of that little story.' He sounded amused. Not that it mattered how he took it, the important thing was that the risk should be spread.

163

17

'PAULINE ORMEROD, by all accounts, had been somewhat unreliable for a long time. There is a rumour that it was she who despatched those papers to us–did you know that?' Cope stopped the car by a wire fence round a slope of the Downs where bullocks grazed. There were other cars parked up here, scattered about, with people sitting beside them on the grass. To the right and left tracks wound along the ridge of the Downs. Cope and Moray stayed in the car while Cope finished with Pauline Ormerod. 'I've no doubt she told Lomax some story and no doubt that he believed it, journalists are an incredible mixture of *naïveté* and cynicism. You only have to listen to them commenting on political wrangles to realise that–some chap calls another a fanatic or a hypocrite, or some other form of mild abuse, and the press talks about "a fierce attack"! A journalist is the easiest fellow in the world to shock. Shall we stretch our legs?'

To the left a track led up a steep incline and soon joined the South Downs Way; there were people strung out along this route, mostly making for the parking area, it was eight o'clock in the evening. Cope turned onto the path to the right which was deserted.

'You knew there had been developments?' he asked, as he and Moray started up the steep incline.

'No.' It was Thursday evening; Cope had met Moray at the railway station and suggested that they should have a walk and then dine out. He had implied that there were matters which needed to be discussed and Moray had imagined these to be business matters.

'Hannah has suddenly recalled that she saw me with Pauline Ormerod at some place that I wot not of at the end of March–early one morning as the song goes.'

'She had some tale about Mario Vicente when I last saw her.' Neil stopped. His breathing was laboured, and he could taste salt in his mouth. It had been another hot day, and even up here at this hour it was still very warm. 'I'm out of training!' he said fretfully. 'I used to walk for miles. That's what a few weeks in London does for you.'

They started walking again, more slowly. Neil said, 'She went to the police about Vicente.'

'She's been again. And so have I.'

'You?'

'There are times when it is wise to put the record straight without delay. I can't have it getting round that Pauline Ormerod was my style.'

'You knew her?'

'I recall seeing her once or twice, an emaciated woman with her hair in rags.'

They had reached the top of the slope. Moray said, 'Do you mind if we sit down for a moment?' He hunched on the ground, his knees drawn up, his arms folded round them. Cope stretched out with his hands beneath his head, looking up at the darkening blue sky. 'Listen to the larks,' he said.

Moray said, as though he was being led through a difficult lesson step by step. 'But why would Hannah behave like this, it's so unlike her?'

'A woman scorned is a vessel of wrath.'

'I don't know about being scorned. . . .' Moray muttered.

'My dear Neil, Hannah has never been the same since you said thanks for the memory with a bunch of carnations.'

'Oh, what rubbish!'

'Is it? You ask some of the others how she reacted to that little gesture on your part! Think of it from her point of view. She worked damned hard during the campaign, for very little financial reward; she ministered to you like an angel—and you were very glad to be ministered to, you can't deny that. Tea and sympathy at her flat at all hours. What do you think she did it for? Has Hannah ever struck you as being deeply involved in politics?' Moray rested his forehead on his knees. 'And don't say you didn't think about it. You thought about it quite carefully and your message was received and understood.'

Moray said, 'These things happen.'

'But when they happen to an unmarried woman of Hannah's age the results are unpredictable. There's a side to Hannah that isn't all sweetness and light—or haven't you noticed? I explained all this to the police and they understood all right. Policemen know a deal more psychology than they are given credit for.'

Moray raised his head and looked out over the humped hills which stretched away into the blueness of evening seemingly undisturbed by man. He did not think he could go on any longer without something to hold on to. Now, in this lonely place, where there was only the sound of the larks and the wind in the long grass, he saw that one must grasp at something; it was no use waiting, as he had waited, for some kind of inner truth, one must grasp at something. Wasn't that what scientists did? In order to arrive at the truth about something, one postulated a theory: the theory, of course, must be tested, but first you must postulate. . . .

He said, 'Yes, I see what you mean about Hannah.' Hannah was an unmarried woman, nearing forty; he should have taken her out to dinner, told her how much he depended on her, she might have settled for that. If Cope was not telling the truth, then one was left with an alternative that was altogether too bizarre.

He postulated that Cope was telling the truth. And almost immediately, some block in his mind was removed and ideas ran out like a network of little veins drawing inspiration from this central theme. He must trust Cope. It had all started—his candidacy, the campaign—because he had trusted Cope. So now, he must go through with it. If he trusted Cope he would be all right. The reason why things had been going wrong was because he had failed to trust his own judgement: Cope and his judgement were one and the same. There was a kind of logic about it. He took a great gulp of air; the air was cooler now, he felt refreshed for the first time. He seemed, also, to be drawing himself together again, to be firm and whole; he could make affirmations–'Where I put my trust, I am not easily shaken.'

He looked down at Cope and saw that he was still pale and that his face had become rather fine drawn. His body was thin, beneath the taut shirt the ribs were outlined too sharply. The illness had taken its toll of him. Perhaps it had been an effort to come so far? It occurred to him that Cope was one of those men who will push themselves to the far limit of physical endurance and never complain. This idea excited him. How extraordinarily fortunate he had been to be served by this man, and how ill he had rewarded him! He must have felt guilt about Cope for some time, now it stirred heavily within him. He put his hand out and ran it along the grass, close to Cope's body. He wasn't quite sure what he was doing, but a tremendous longing for absolution surged through him. It was the most intense feeling he had ever had; it was so intense that it frightened him and he held back from touching Cope, digging his nails into the earth which was hard and dry, pitted with sharp stones.

Cope said, 'We'll go a little farther.'

'You're not too tired?'

Cope looked surprised at the question as though his physical condition was of no possible interest to anyone, least of all himself. He got up and said, 'The brow of the next hill.'

Moray was breathless and his legs were shaky. The path was stony and he was not wearing suitable shoes; besides him, Cope walked more easily although he still had that strangely exciting look of a man whose resources are severely stretched. They reached the top of the hill and Moray, who had long ago lost his whereabouts, was surprised to see ahead of him the lights of Scotney reflected in a calm, dark sea.

'How far away it seems!' he exclaimed.

'And how ridiculous to suggest that "Heffernan's Hill", as they are calling it, will be anything more than a modernistic Christmas tree! I think it would look rather beautiful, don't you?'

From this bird's eye view, things did indeed seem different;

the lights to the west petered out aimlessly, a scintillating spiral would certainly be more exciting visually.

'I can see it could be made quite attractive,' Moray said cautiously.

'One needs to get things in perspective,' Cope said. 'Heffernan is coming down next week, he means to throw a party at the Imperial Hotel and try to influence people if not win friends. I thought we might bring him up here, impress upon him the importance of making the development compact so that it doesn't straggle onto the Downs and spoil everything—the drama of complete contrast. I think he might go for that.'

'Yes. We shall need to do some hard thinking before we see him, though.' But it was good to have an aim in view. Something *could* be made of the West Front development; it would mean a fight with Heffernan, but surely no large-scale scheme ever got off the ground without considerable amendments having been made to the original plans. The important thing was not to be frightened by the size of the project: thinking small was no less dangerous than thinking big.

As they came down the ridge, it was nearly dark. There were hares leaping in the field ahead of them; they stopped to watch.

'There must be at least six of them,' Cope said softly. He laughed, 'Oh, what joy!' He waited, not wanting to disturb them. A breeze was getting up; it was the first time for weeks Moray had felt cool air brushing against his face and he began to shiver. When they eventually crossed the field, and the hares scattered, Cope said, 'What a bore for them, two of these wretched humans still abroad at this time of the evening!' One of the hares had wandered onto the road and was caught in the headlamps of the car as they drove down the hill; it ran frantically from side to side, dazzled by the light. Cope stopped the car and turned out the lights. He wound down the window. 'There it goes! Look!' The escape of the hare really mattered to him. The cool air now seemed to have penetrated the whole of Moray's body and he could not stop shivering. He began to talk, hoping to distract Cope's attention from the hare which must by now have disappeared.

'What shall I do about Hannah?'

'I shouldn't do anything if I were you.' Cope started the engine again. 'Let her make the action.'

'She's been seeing something of Lomax.'

'So I gathered.'

'I'm not going to feel very easy having her around.'

'Don't do anything heavy-handed. It never looks good, particularly if you're dealing with someone who is a bit off-balance.'

Cope drove into Scotney and along the promenade to the harbour. 'You get better food here than anywhere else,' he said. 'Must give Mario his due.'

It was the kind of gesture which he enjoyed, but which seemed to Moray to be rather foolhardy. Moray's first impressions were unfortunate as he tripped over some obstacle in the narrow foyer; a man who was on his way out and a waiter helped him to his feet. Cope was not there, he had gone into the gents.

'It looks as though they are full,' Moray said to him when he emerged.

'I booked a table. Hullo, been in a fight already?'

Moray glanced at a mirror on the wall; his right cheek was slightly bruised.

'And your hands, man! However did you do that?'

Moray went into the gents to wash his hands. He had torn the finger tips and he whimpered as he bathed them. He could not handle the cutlery very well so they took a long time over each course. The service was slow; Cope did not seem to mind, but Moray was aware that people at other tables were served more expeditiously. The food, however, was good and so was the wine. It was at the coffee stage when Moray realised that he had lost his keys; he was fumbling for a cigarette lighter when he made the discovery.

'Perhaps they dropped out of your pocket when you fell over in the foyer?' Cope suggested.

'It's hardly likely.' But Moray spoke to the waiter, who also thought it unlikely, although he departed to make a search. A few moments later, he returned, smiling triumphantly. 'Under the umbrella stand, sir,' he said, as he handed the keys to Moray.

'The files were everywhere, left open, on table and chairs,' the young man told Mario Vicente resentfully; he was something of an expert in his field and felt that his talents had been wasted, it was like calling in a surgeon to stop a nose bleed. 'He even had some of the interesting bits marked with scraps of paper.'

'You photographed everything we needed?' Mario asked sharply. 'Not just the bits he thought were important.'

'I got everything. It was too easy. Oh, there was one thing.' He brightened at the recollection. 'A letter on the shelf over the fire; it hadn't been opened and it was postmarked over two weeks ago! Can you imagine that?' This way of managing one's affairs had shocked him.

Mario said, 'I cannot imagine what it was if you do not tell me.'

'It was from a woman. You never saw anything like it! Pages and pages, saying things like how much she loved him, and how he had changed her life, and how proud she was of knowing him, and how she wished she could be worthy of him. . . .'

'And how she has found another man?' Mario showed a brief flicker of interest, and the young man laughed delightedly and nodded.

'I never saw anything like it,' he said. 'What kind of man is this Moray?'

Mario spread his hands out and gave a little shrug. 'Obviously, a very worthy man. . . .'

'And Cope?' the young man said persuasively. 'I think we need to talk to Cope.'

'No. You leave Cope alone.'

He didn't want to become entangled with Cope. He had

seen men like him, not many, but one or two, who did not
conform to any pattern of behaviour which he could understand. If he was going to have a confrontation with a man,
he had to understand him. He was no longer a gambler; he
took calculated risks, but he didn't gamble any longer. It
made him sad because it was a sign he was growing old. But
age had its compensations, you learnt to wait. You would
get nothing out of a man like Cope by inflicting pain on him,
as this energetic young man so longed to do; but leave him
to his own devices and eventually he would destroy himself.
That was another lesson you learnt as you grew older: to sit
back and let other people do the hard work for you.

18

HANNAH was frightened when she left her friends' house in Pelham Square on Friday. She walked to the office. A walk would calm her down. 'Now, just what is it that you are making this fuss about?' she asked herself as she waited to cross from the square to Villiers Street. 'You have written Neil a letter saying that you don't feel you can continue to manage the office, but offering to do his personal letters for him. This morning you are going to the office to see how he feels about it. The only really difficult thing will be confronting him and Rodney Cope for what may be no longer than a quarter of an hour.' It was the same argument she had put to herself when she was a child on the way to the dentist. Why is it that one's moments of happiness all seem to take place in time and are whisked away almost before one has noticed them, whereas the black moments are as long as a lifetime?

As she turned into Pont Street, she said to herself, 'Let him do the talking. He will probably have decided that the arrangement won't suit him. In a few minutes, you may be walking out of here completely free of any obligation.' She went up the stairs, trying to summon the courage to walk into the room quietly.

Neil was on the telephone when she entered the room; Cope was standing by the window, looking down. 'Hullo Hannah,' he said. 'Did you see my car down there when you came along? I believe the police have moved it, the bastards!'

'I didn't notice.' She walked across to the window and looked down into the street; she was so close to him her shoulder touched his arm, it was like looking over a precipice. 'You wouldn't be able to see from here anyway, would you? Not if you've parked in the usual place.'

172

Neil put the receiver down. He said, 'Hullo Hannah. Thanks for the letter. Come and sit down and we'll talk about it.' He sounded like a doctor giving a consultation.

Hannah sat on the only spare chair. Cope remained by the window. They had not been so formal with one another since she first came to work for Neil. There was a pause while Neil read through the letter again; she looked down at her dress and followed the pattern which fortunately was quite an intricate one. Now that she had started quietly it began to seem possible that she might keep it up.

'You don't feel there is enough work here to keep you going all the week, is that it?' Neil might have been asking where the pain was.

Hannah said, 'That's it.'

'What had you in mind, then?'

'I thought if I put it in a letter it would give you time to think about it,' she said. 'Aren't you happy about my suggestions?'

Neil frowned down at the letter and turned over a page; he read as though it was written in a foreign language and he was having to translate as he went along. Hannah wished she knew what Rodney Cope was doing, she would have been more comfortable if he had not been behind her back; she visualised him sitting on the window ledge, smiling.

'You will come into the office, whenever I'm here, is that right? Neil said. 'But apart from that, if there is any work you would like to do it at home?'

Hannah said, 'Yes.'

'You don't like the office?' he asked.

'You've got your jacket off, and you still look hot,' she pointed out.

This annoyed him. She sensed that he had expected her to become flustered and apologise for herself. He was not prepared to meet her on equal terms. Behind her, Cope said, 'It's a damned uncomfortable place, Neil. I can hardly stand upright in it. By the middle of the afternoon it must be like an oven. I don't know how Hannah has stood it for so long.'

Hannah was overcome by gratitude at this unexpected intervention; tears came into her eyes. 'We've worked together a long time,' she said. 'I felt I should offer something.'

Neil was somewhat mollified by her distress. He said, 'Yes, of course,' and put the letter aside. 'Well, let's give it a try and see how it works, shall we?'

'There is one thing,' Cope said. 'How about the post? Could you come in and deal with it on days when I shan't be here? When I am here, if there is anything that needs doing I could run it over to you.' He sounded as though he was trying to make things easy for her.

'We could try it that way.' Her voice was husky and she cleared her throat.

Neil said, 'Don't be upset about it, Hannah. We've been thinking that we can't keep this place on much longer. After next month when the lease expires, I shall probably run things from my flat until we've got the organisation sorted out.'

'What about coffee?' Cope suggested. 'Are we allowed to ask for that under the new regime?'

He injected that little bit of raillery into his voice that was needed to lighten the atmosphere. Hannah got up to fetch the kettle, but Cope said, 'I'll fill it for you.' He went out of the room with the kettle. Neil and Hannah were left alone. Hannah said, 'I'm sorry about this, Neil.'

'You must do as you think fit, Hannah.' He picked up a letter from the tray on the table and began to read it, his face stiff with resentment.

'Would you prefer to call it a day, now?' she asked.

'No. We'll give it a try.' He spoke as though he was reluctantly agreeing to a tiresome arrangement which was entirely for her benefit. 'I can't say I'm very impressed with the way you have gone about it.' Before she could reply, Cope came in with the kettle. His eyes met Hannah's, and for a moment it was as though they were allies, people who had played their parts sensibly only to be badly let down by a third party.

'Don't be such a miserable bugger, Neil!' It was the first

time Hannah had ever heard anyone speak so tersely to Neil. The result was unexpected; Neil's anger evaporated and his attitude became almost fawning. She turned away to get out coffee and cups. Cope continued to make fun of Neil, rather savage fun which included a few home-truths about behaving as though he was god–'a little prep. school god'. Neil was giggling nervously, almost as though he enjoyed it. Hannah waited impatiently for the kettle to boil.

Neil said, 'You must be right about this room, Hannah. It has a bad effect on all of us. Perhaps we should close down for the summer. I could dictate to you on the beach. It would probably be good for the citizens to actually see their Member at work. What do you think, Rodney?'

Cope said, 'I think I'd like coffee now.' His voice was flat and tired.

When Hannah gave Neil his cup of coffee he said to her in a bantering tone which was not natural to him, 'What are your plans for this morning? Do they include a little note-taking?'

'That's why I'm here. Do you want to start now, or drink your coffee?' She had never expected to speak to him so brusquely.

Cope said, 'That's my girl!'

Hannah took notes and it was agreed she would type at home and let Moray have the letters at his flat early on Monday morning. She did not say she was staying with friends in Pelham Square.

When she left, her footsteps flagged as she walked down Villiers Street. There had been little drama of any kind; but an association had come to an end and her reactions were inexplicable and unreasonable. There was no doubt which of the two men she should hate, and which she should pity; but she found she did not hate either of them, and pity was not reserved for Neil alone. Indeed, she seemed to have moved further from Neil, whereas a relationship which was by no means a hostile one had been established with Rodney Cope who had shown magnanimity in his dealings with her. She was aware that this was not a socially acceptable attitude.

175

But at the moment she did not see these strange events in relation to society, the need to see justice done, or the upholding of moral values; it was all happening inside her.

She had promised Lomax she would telephone him when she left the office; he was at a civic lunch, but had insisted she should speak to him. 'You will probably interrupt some boring speech.'

She told him what had happened and he asked anxiously, 'How do you feel?'

'Muddled,' she said.

Lomax returned to his office an hour later. He was carrying a daily newspaper which seemed to have put him in a bad mood. ' "A fully paid-up member of the human race!" ' He threw the offending newspaper across the room. 'Sometimes I think I'll give up journalism.' Todd, who had been waiting his return from the civic lunch, had more substantial cause for concern to report. He followed Lomax into his room.

'Allinson wanted to see you, but he's had to go out.' Todd paused, waiting for Lomax's full attention. Lomax perversely began to rummage through the papers on his desk as though something of great importance was buried among them. Todd, satisfied that this was a form of attention, said, 'We've lost Colcott's advertising.'

'What do you mean, we've lost it?' Lomax went on creating chaos among the papers for some moments and then looked up. 'We've *lost* it!' Todd said nothing, allowing time for the shock to register. Lomax sat down. Todd thought how small and frail he looked, hunched there behind the mound of paper. Then Lomax said, 'Well, well. That's interesting.' He had completely recovered his good-humour and smiled benevolently at Todd. Todd wondered whether he was insane.

'This will be a loss to Colcott,' Lomax said. 'It's not as though there is another local paper.'

'It will be a loss to us,' Todd said grimly. Colcott owned several businesses in the town and spent a lot of money on advertising. The drop in revenue would be noticeable. Lord Cannock didn't interfere with his editors, but he didn't like to make a loss either.

'If Colcott has done this, there must be someone behind him who means to bring pressure to bear on us.' Lomax rubbed his hands together energetically: Todd didn't think he was washing his hands of the West Front controversy. 'That someone must be getting rather worried, don't you think?'

Todd decided to leave it to Allinson to bring him to a more sober frame of mind.

Major Brophy was in an unusually sober frame of mind as he drove to Moray's flat. All the traffic lights were green, there were no lorries unloading goods, no buses moving out of the bus-bays, no learner drivers stuck on Station Hill. He made the journey in a record ten minutes. He wouldn't have minded a bit of stop-and-start *en route*; he wasn't looking forward to seeing Moray. As he got out of the car, he hoped that Moray was at the House of Commons.

When Moray opened the door of the flat, Brophy said reproachfully, 'Thought you would be in Westminster.'

'I had business to attend to here. I've only just got back from my office.'

'Like a word with you.'

'About what?'

'One or two little things.'

Major Brophy did not feel that it should be necessary to be too specific between gentlemen. So when he said to Moray, 'Look here, let's get one thing clear, no one doubts *your* honour,' he felt he had stated his mission with all the clarity that could be expected of him. Moray greeted the remark with the bemused surprise he might have accorded his bank manager had that gentleman thought it necessary to call on him to tell him that his account was not overdrawn. He allowed Major Brophy to manoeuvre him into the sitting-room.

'Vicente seems to be stirring up a bit of trouble,' Brophy said when he had Moray with his back to the mantelshelf.

'Trouble is his business.' Moray snatched at the phrase.

'They say he claims to have information he will hand over to the police.'

'Everyone goes to the police. Even my secretary. She goes one day about this and the next day about that. You mustn't believe a thing she says.'

'It's Vicente I'm talking about.' Major Brophy was perplexed but dogged. 'There are rumours he is on to something about contributions to your campaign fund. . . .'

Moray waved his hand at the files strewn round the room as though by their very existence they were a proof of innocence. 'He's welcome to look at them if he wants to.'

'Glad to hear you say that. It's the right line to take, absolutely open and above-board. Unfortunately, that's not all. There's a suggestion that . . . well, quite frankly, that Cope is in Heffernan's pay. Don't want to say too much, you understand. Mustn't condemn a fellow untried. Damn good chap in many ways, excellent army record, brave. . . .'

'And audacious.'

'That's it!' Major Brophy wiggled his eyebrows at Moray knowingly. 'Audacity can be a damn nuisance. Believe me, I've had some of these fellows. You can't hold them. Brilliant in their way, some of them; but you know what they say, only a thin line between. . . .'

'Thin red line. . . .'

'Perhaps I'm not making myself clear.' Major Brophy was becoming uneasy. 'People are saying things—lot of nonsense probably, but they are saying things just the same. And Cope's the fellow the finger points at, so to speak.'

Moray said, 'I'm glad you see things this way.' His face was bland as though something very pleasant had been brought to his notice. 'We've been through a lot together. Solidarity is important. I really do appreciate it very much.' He spoke these phrases as though he was trying them out for sound, volume, inflection; he might have been standing in front of a mirror in an empty room. In spite of this lack of contact, his manner towards Brophy became effusive. The major was a tower of strength who had done yeoman service to the organisation; he was also a hewer of wood and a drawer of water; the member of parliament must shoulder a heavy burden and it was comforting to know that things were in good hands on the Scotney front. He was shepherding Brophy into the hall; at the front door, he said that it was particularly comforting to know that Major Brophy was ready to stand up and be counted.

Major Brophy made a last-ditch stand. He said, 'I hope you will think over what I have said about Cope.'

They stood eyeball to eyeball on the doorstep, there was little room to do otherwise. Moray said, 'Cope has my complete confidence.' He made this statement without emphasis, as though it was a religious truth which was not subject to the normal process of reasoning.

As he got into his car, Major Brophy said, 'Mission accomplished,' although he wasn't any too sure of it.

Moray was pleased that the visit had taken place. He saw it as something inevitable which, by its very inevitability, was a proof that all was well, as reassuring as the continuing habit of night to follow day. He saw every development as a good sign. Even unpleasant suggestions were as welcome as if he were making a collection of them. The more varied the collection the better. He was like a person with a terminal illness who, when it attacks another part of the body, says with relief, 'This is something new: perhaps the diagnosis was wrong.'

19

'THE drama of complete contrast. That's what I'm after,' Heffernan said.

Councillor Cray said, 'Ah, yes, yes.' He nodded his head slowly, so that Heffernan could see that here was a man capable of envisaging such a concept. He repeated, 'The drama of complete contrast.'

'Well, you try putting that across to the planning committee, Sid!' Alderman Bakewell, who was a crude, unimaginative little man, knocked back his gin and vermouth and looked round hopefully. Heffernan pursued him with more gin.

'I find it hard to know just what it is that your planning committee does want,' he said. 'I get the feeling, I may be wrong, of course, but I get the feeling that the only development it would be likely to approve is a bungalow estate.'

'God forbid!' Bakewell was shocked. 'Scotney has never gone in for bungalows.'

'That's why I'm so disappointed,' Heffernan said. 'Most of the coastal towns only come alive during the summer months; for the rest of the year they are ghost towns. But not Scotney. Scotney is a town in its own right, full of life and vigour, *and* a bit of honest vulgarity. . . .'

'Oh, it's vulgar enough,' Bakewell acknowledged with affection.

'But over this development,' Heffernan pursued his advantage, 'you'd think the town was a retreat for retired gentlefolk. Just what are the objections? Come along, you tell me.' He fixed Bakewell with his bright, unwinking eyes. 'Seems to me you're the one chap who doesn't mince his words, and that's the kind of person I like to deal with. I never take offence, never. I've been in business too long to take offence at anything! The harder a man hits, the better I like it.'

Bakewell searched around in his mind for something offensive to say, but for once inspiration failed him. 'It's not the development itself, so much,' he said, 'it's the people it would bring here.'

'Don't you want people to come here?'

'They do come here.' Bakewell warmed to the issue. 'They come because the town's got a lot to offer as it is; just as you said, it's alive. What we're afraid of is that your development wouldn't be part of the town, it would take people away from it.'

'All right, then, all right!' Heffernan stabbed a forefinger like the muzzle of a gun aimed between Bakewell's eyes. 'Now, we're getting down to it. I came to listen to objections, and when I listen to an objection I don't just dismiss it, I think about it. The opinions of the people who live in a place have got to be considered, and I'll tell you why.' He poked the finger at Bakewell's breastbone. '*Not* because I don't like hurting people's feelings, because I'm not squeamish about people's feelings. *But,*' he prodded Bakewell again, 'I KNOW there's a good chance that the chap who lives in a place may have thought of one or two things that haven't occurred to me. Now! You don't want Scotney to become a dead town. And I don't, either. If I wanted to destroy life and vigour I'd go to Hinton or Seacombe Bay or some place where the work's been done for me. So, it seems we've got a lot in common. Right? Then shouldn't we get together about this? You're saying my scheme is too comprehensive, too all-inclusive. That *is* what you're saying, isn't it?'

'Something of the sort.' Bakewell was hypnotised.

'All right, then! Maybe that wants looking at; maybe we need to look at it together and strike a balance.'

He had appalling energy, Lomax thought, as he watched the performance from the window alcove where he had taken refuge with a glass of tomato juice. It wasn't what he said, but the extraordinary force which he put into each word which was so impressive; and he had that utter lack of

181

sensitivity which can get a man over hurdles insuperable to other men. One felt helpless with him, in the grip of an obscene monster against whom neither right nor reason can prevail. Beside Heffernan, Bakewell, himself no mean performer, seemed totally ineffective.

'Didn't imagine Bakewell could take such a clobbering, did you?' Rodney Cope had appeared at Lomax's side; he was carrying a tray loaded with empty glasses and bottles. 'Mind if I join you?' He sat down with the tray on his lap. 'What an appalling creature that is! Like a frog in a particularly nasty fairy story.' He was looking at Heffernan. 'It makes one wonder whether he has the mentality to envisage anything beyond a high-rise block of flats.'

'Your interest in the scheme doesn't extend to a high-rise block of flats?' Lomax scarcely expected an answer other than a denial of any interest, but Cope replied without hesitation.

'I thought the scheme would be exciting. An aerial city. But nowadays we have so many guardians of mediocrity you couldn't hope to get away with a concept like that.'

'Nevertheless,' Lomax pursued his mundane way, 'you will find it financially rewarding?'

'Oh that, yes,' Cope shrugged. 'Juggling with such vast sums of money has a certain excitement.'

"Ask and it shall be given to you," Mario had said: as far as Cope was concerned, this appeared to be true. Perhaps later he would deny ever having had this conversation, but even so there was something extraordinarily reckless about the man's behaviour which Lomax found disturbing.

'Do you think all tycoons are dreary?' This was not said in Cope's usual derisory tone. His dissatisfaction went deeper than Heffernan's failure to hold his interest. His face, though filmed with sweat, was very pale and the lips were chafed and bloodless; he gave the impression of someone suffering from a severe cold rather than heat. It seemed to Lomax that Cope had reached a stage when life, like Heffernan's scheme, seemed to be shrinking and growing daily less notable.

Behind them, a man was trying to open one of the windows. 'The bloody fans aren't working,' he grumbled.

Cope pulled himself back from whatever bleak prospect he had been contemplating. 'Have a drink,' he said to Lomax. 'Whatever *is* that you've got there?'

'Tomato juice.'

'Oh well, have a trip on this!' He extracted a bottle of Worcester sauce from the miscellany on his tray and shook it liberally over Lomax's glass. 'And may God bless all who sail in her.' He eased his shoulders against the wall and closed his eyes.

Heffernan went past with Alderman Bakewell and the mayor in tow.

' "The drama of complete contrast"!' Lomax repeated disdainfully. 'Contrast between life and death, do you suppose he means? The international set coming to Scotney for a blood transfusion.'

'There speaks a true provincial.'

'And why not? Scotney is a provincial town, the only one with any character on the whole of the South coast.'

'Brighton?'

'Too big.'

'Perhaps you're right. But shouldn't you learn discretion? You aren't built to be a giant killer.' Cope eyed Lomax provocatively, reminding him that between them there was a question of killing. 'As it is, Heffernan regards you as an enemy.'

'Indeed?'

'Yes, indeed, and verily, verily! From the way he talked about you, you'd think the one thing he regretted about Scotney was the passing of the harbour gangs with their handy ways with a razor blade.'

In spite of evident fatigue, words spilled out lightly and effortlessly, it was difficult to tell what was nonsense and what was meant more seriously. Or was he ever serious in the way that most of us attempt to be serious? It seemed to Lomax that this man existed almost entirely without forethought, taking each moment as it came and making what

183

he could out of it. This impromptu attitude to the business of living no doubt explained some of the apparent inconsistencies in his behaviour.

'How very composed you are!' Cope laughed. 'You sit there, looking prim and a trifle superior, as though the prospect of being carved up was not of the slightest concern to you.'

'If the harbour gangs still existed, and I was likely to be involved with them, I should be very concerned,' Lomax assured him, and added severely, 'As would any normal person.'

'You disappoint me,' Cope said. 'There are times when you seem far from normal.'

Lomax sipped his tomato juice and spluttered. Cope laughed. 'Serves you right! That will liven up your normal life.'

Neil Moray came towards them; he seemed displeased to see them talking so freely together. 'Do you know where Major Brophy is?' he asked Cope.

'He hasn't come.'

'Oh.' Moray's mouth dropped. He said sulkily, 'Why are you sitting over here?'

Cope got up. 'Let me get rid of this tray, then I'll join you.'

When he had gone, Moray stood on the fringe of the crowd, looking disconsolate as a lost child waiting to be collected. Councillor Cray came up and spoke to him. Lomax watched the two men. Moray responded with a reluctant interest which was oddly effective, giving an impression that Cray was gradually extracting something that, without his skill and ingenuity, would not have been brought to light. Cray would come out of this exchange with the pride of the miner who has struck a rich vein where others have failed. Whereas in reality, he had himself provided the treasure because there was nothing in Moray, it was all a conjuring trick. Lomax was having some very strange thoughts; he was on the verge of something important to do with Moray, so much on the verge it made him giddy. He wished the fans would come on again. He looked out of the window. The sky had darkened to violet and the waves were white-crested. An elderly man and woman were standing in a shelter putting on raincoats, people were collecting children and deck chairs; it must already be raining, although as yet the pavements did not look wet. He felt an imperative need to be out there in the rain.

A woman had now come to stand beside Moray, one hand resting lightly, but minatorily, on his arm. She had a face of singular sweetness, and yet one felt that had Councillor Cray dropped dead she would have continued her conversation with Moray over his prone body.

'Is the editor of the *Gazette* here?' she asked Moray. 'I very much want to meet him. Will you introduce me, please.'

'You're standing in front of him,' Moray said.

'Oh, don't get up !' She laid a restraining hand on Lomax's arm as though he was much older than herself, which was not the case. She sat beside him. 'It is so hot in here, isn't it?' She looked concerned. Lomax was reminded of the way his infant school teacher had looked at him once when he was sick in class. The woman reminded him of the teacher, same severe hair style and clothes, same implacably gentle manner . . . many similarities in situation . . . feeling sick at present time. . . .

'I have read your paper with such pleasure, Mr Lomax, I felt I must congratulate you.' They had not been introduced and she did not make good the omission, but Lomax remembered that she was Heffernan's secretary. 'My father edited the *Church Chronicle* for many years, and although it was a comparatively humble periodical, it was beautifully presented. I noticed at once the care . . . indeed, the love I think I would call it . . . which had gone into the format of the *Gazette.*'

One or two people were leaving, perhaps affected by the change in the weather. The rain was coming down heavily now and the greyness of the evening made one imagine it was much later than half-past seven. Moray eased his way towards the door where Hannah was talking to the chairman of the Chamber of Commerce. She smiled at Moray, but went on talking. Hannah was playing life very straight just now. Yet, because she was not glittering so much, there seemed to be more substance to her; she had begun to draw the threads of her personality together and was becoming someone to be reckoned with. When at last she freed herself from her companion, Moray said with mock humility, 'May I approach you now?'

'If you are quick about it. I see Mr. Quinton making his way towards me.'

'I wonder if you would mind running over to my flat? I've left some papers there that I need. Heffernan wants to have a talk with me before he goes back to London.'

'You'd like me to go now, would you?'

'If you don't mind.'

She consented willingly enough, but without that bubbling air of being glad to be of service which he had at one time found irritating. He explained where she would find the papers. 'There's one other thing. Could you come to the office tomorrow? I'll have a lot to do after this talk with Heffernan.'

'When will you be there?' she asked.

'Not until the afternoon, I've got a meeting in the morning. But if you could help Rodney. . . .'

'I'll come in the afternoon. What time will you be there?'

'Really, Hannah, you're not still. . . .'

'Two o'clock?'

'I shall be there at half-past one,' he snapped. 'I don't suppose I'll have time for lunch.'

'I'll be there at two.'

'You disobliging bitch!' Although he did not say this aloud, he felt as though he had shouted it at her and was surprised that she did not respond; he turned uneasily to see whether anyone was standing near by. There was only Quinton, who was making some kind of signal to Bakewell. Moray watched Hannah walk towards the door; under his breath he muttered every filthy term of abuse he had ever heard spoken of womankind. Other people were moving

186

towards the door now. Some of them stopped to exchange a few words with him. As he answered, he was afraid that something obscene would slip out instead of the expected civil banalities.

The room was almost empty. Cope was shepherding Bakewell and Cray towards the door, collecting a few other stragglers on the way. Heffernan was standing by the window with his secretary and Lomax.

'*She* may like your paper, but I can't say I'm impressed. Lacks any spark. Ideas are narrow, provincial, no vision. And the writing is just that bit dull. All right for maiden ladies, I daresay.' He was talking loudly; this was the kind of offensiveness which is intended for public display. The secretary, standing a little to one side, stared at Lomax, forehead creased and eyes narrowed in distress at what was happening to him. Her attitude had the effect of reinforcing Heffernan's attack; it was as though she was gently insisting, 'You do realise, don't you, how badly you are being mauled?'

'A few home truths won't do that little bugger any harm,' Bakewell said.

'He looks a bit under the weather,' Cray observed. They passed through the door together.

Heffernan said, 'To really succeed with a newspaper you've got to have attack, a certain toughness. . . .'

Lomax said, 'Is that why you have taken away your advertising?'

'Advertising! I don't need to advertise. What the devil do you mean by that?'

Lomax closed his eyes and tried to think what he had meant. Heffernan turned to his secretary and said, 'The man's drunk.' He looked at her angrily, as though she was responsible for this.

Moray, who had overheard this exchange, said to Cope, 'What does he mean about the advertising?'

'Nothing. He's a bit drunk by the look of him.'

'But he must have meant something.'

Cope said, 'You worry too much. I think I'll push off now.

The blasted English drizzle wakes the fever in my bones. And anyway, Heffernan will expect to talk to you on your own.'

'I don't care what he expects. I want you to be there.'

But Cope had already gone.

It was ten minutes later that Lomax came down to the car park. He walked to his car as though treading a tight-rope and then leant against it, his head down. He was sweating, but felt very cold. After a moment, he tried to pull himself upright, but this produced a wave of dizziness and he had the greatest difficulty in keeping on his feet. Like many men who are not physically strong, he was reluctant to give way to weakness and believed that will-power is sufficient to conquer most temporary indispositions and many more serious disorders as well. This particular indisposition did not appear to be responding very well to the dictates of will; and had not Rodney Cope appeared beside him at this moment, he would probably have had to sit on the ground. 'Which would have been unpleasant,' he said cheerfully to Cope, imagining the intention had already been stated, 'seeing how much water has collected.'

Cope said, 'Let's have your car keys.'

He eased Lomax into the passenger seat, from which he then flopped out, like a Jack-in-the-Box which has lost its spring. 'I shall be all right,' he assured Cope unconvincingly as he was again propped into an upright position.

'Nonsense ! I'm going to drive you home.'

'I might be sick,' Lomax fretted. 'So unpleasant for you . . . please don't. . . .'

Cope righted him once again and slammed the door. He walked round the back of the car, glancing about him as he did so. The rain was heavy and the car park was deserted. He opened the door and got into the driver's seat. 'Now, which is the reverse . . . ah, I see. . . .'

Lomax said, 'So very sorry about this.'

The few people walking along the promenade had their heads bent to avoid the driving rain.

Lomax was still apologising faintly when they stopped. He squinted out of the window and saw hills, and far below, down a green slope, a coastguard's cottage and the sea beyond . . . at least, this is what he would have seen had he felt better, but in fact it is doubtful whether he saw anything at all. When Cope opened the driver's door, Lomax moaned gratefully as the damp air cooled his face.

'We'll move you over,' Cope said, and he did this quite gently. Lomax, who hated being a nuisance to anyone, did his best to be helpful. When he was in position, he muttered, 'Thank you so much. Leave me now, I shall be all right.' He rested his head against the driving wheel. Cope raised his head and put a bottle to his lips. At this, Lomax showed signs of protest, but this time Cope was firm rather than gentle. 'Come along, drink, it will do you good. . . . Oh yes, it will!' He forced Lomax's head back. 'Come on, you can take some more. . . .' When he was satisfied, he put the bottle in his pocket. Then he took a duster from the side-pocket of the car and wiped it carefully over the seat, doors, the keys, and the driving wheel; he held the duster in his hands as he started the engine and released the hand brake. The car, which was on an incline, began to move slowly forward. Cope shut the door, still holding the duster.

It was eight o'clock, the visibility was poor, but it was not yet dark and the rain had stopped; some insatiable dog-walkers might still be abroad. In any case, the main point of the exercise was to discredit Lomax, and as he did not dislike the man he was content to leave it to fate to decide whether he should be killed or convicted for driving under the influence of drink. So he did not wait to see what happened to the car after it passed out of his line of vision. Nor did he subsequently give much thought to the incident; his mind darted from one point to another leaving no time for reflection on past events.

What happened, in fact, was not as dramatic as he might have envisaged since the car, now bumping along at a fair speed, first hit a hedge which surrounded a disused concrete gun-emplacement and then rammed the concrete itself. At the impact with the hedge, the door swung open and Lomax was thrown out, which meant that he cut his head and did

189

very painful damage to his right shoulder. The front of the car was so badly buckled, however, that there was no doubt that had he remained at the wheel he would have been seriously injured. Shock and pain brought him back to consciousness and for a few moments he imagined that he was dying. 'If I'm dying, there's not much I can do about it,' he thought. 'Whereas if I'm not dying, there is a lot I ought to be doing.' This led him to the conviction that he should attempt a few simple movements designed to discover how much of him was broken. It was quite obvious, without moving at all, that something was badly wrong with his right shoulder, but a series of careful jerks and wriggles led him to the hopeful conclusion that elsewhere he was only bruised. There was his head, of course: if he had fractured his skull it was important not to move. After a little cautious prodding, he decided he would have to assume he had not fractured his skull. This examination had been exhausting, and for a few minutes he lay staring through the large rent in the hedge which the car had made. Gulls wheeled overhead, but that did not mean anything, because they often came quite far inland; ahead of him, however, the ground rose steeply to a ridge which had the appearance of having been amateurishly snipped all along the edge with giant pinking scissors, frayed edges of chalk were visible. He was somewhere on the Seven Sisters stretch of coastline. There would be a farm, a coastguard's cottage, something, it didn't matter what, the important thing was to have an objective.

He had always maintained that until the time comes for us to die, there is always going to be a way to live. On a less dramatic level, during his many walks on downs and fells, he had argued, to the irritation of various companions, that however incapacitated one might be by a fall it would be possible to drag oneself to safety. Now seemed a good time to put these theories to the test. He raised himself gingerly on his undamaged arm and tried to sit up; immediately, the sky wheeled over and the hills came down on top of him. It was apparent that there could be no question of attempting to walk, some kind of crawl stroke using only one arm seemed

190

to be the answer. He started towards the gap in the hedge. The pain in his shoulder was intense. He soon realised that compromise would be needed—such as a short crawl and a long rest. It took him five combined crawl-and-rest periods to get through the gap in the hedge. But really, he told himself as he lay sobbing in a clump of wet ferns, he was remarkably fortunate in that he knew where he was and where he was going. The coastguard's house, which he saw clearly now, was only half-a-mile away. He moved towards it feeling like a wounded caterpillar. After what seemed like an hour, but was probably only ten minutes, the coastguard's house had not moved appreciably nearer. He must look on this as a long-term project, he decided as he rested, shivering and sick. 'You have had a remarkably fortunate life,' he reminded himself severely. 'This is the first time you have ever had to put up with such agonising pain; think of what people suffer in war, prison, car accidents, incurable disease. . . .' At this point, he fainted. When he came to, he decided to substitute encouragement for severity. 'Tomorrow, you will be laughing about this and boring anyone who will listen to you with the recounting of your exploits. . . .' Mental effort was too exhausting. He crawled: thought blanked out. When he was actually crawling, it wasn't so bad because the pain took over and he became a tongue of fire curling on the grass. It was only when faintness made it necessary to rest, which was increasingly often, that he became a human person with limited resources and failing strength inching his way across a vast continent. The coastguard's house was becoming more and more like a mirage: he lay with his face in the grass and did not look at it when he rested. He told himself he would not look at it for what he judged to be half an hour, by which time he might be pleasantly surprised.

In fact, he was surprised after twenty minutes. It was then that he found another face very close to his, large, deeply furrowed with worry, and canine. It was a wise creature and stood at some distance from him after the first shock of encounter. Then it put its noble head back and barked; it had a deep, imperative bark, the bark of a dog who is accustomed to note being taken of its utterances. Lomax closed his eyes and left the rest to the dog.

After a time, a man came up and said, 'What have you got there, Samson?' and Samson proudly displayed his find.

20

I⊤ soon became apparent that the constable by his bedside
was not primarily concerned with his welfare. At first, when
he woke to the hospital's more strident version of the dawn
chorus, Lomax was not interested in the constable. He felt
very ill and seemed to have lost the tenacity which had carried him through the misadventures of the previous evening.
Clarity of thought and feeling had blurred. He had escaped
from hell into limbo: hell was preferable. In spite of the
dawn chorus, he drifted away from the hospital on an abor-
tive journey which he had been making all through the night:
he was journeying on the four sides of a square which he
could see drawn quite clearly on a sheet of paper; as he
journeyed, he kept muttering a formula of which he was
very much aware although he could not translate it into
words in the normal way. From time to time he jerked close
to consciousness, and on each occasion the formula was still
there, agitating his mind more than ever, but before it could
issue forth in words, he drifted off again and began his
journey down one side of the square.

This process of alternate journeying and hovering close to
consciousness continued until about ten in the morning, by
which time the near-conscious periods occurred so often that
he never got beyond a right angle turn of his square. At a
quarter past ten he opened his eyes and said clearly to the
constable, 'Hannah Mason. Must find Hannah Mason.' The
constable was not impressed. Persuasion would be necessary.
Lomax had neither the strength nor the time to be persuasive;
he said to the constable, 'I must talk to Braithwaite. I won't
talk to anyone else.'

The constable appeared to be under the impression that
he wished to see his solicitor.

193

'Where am I?' Lomax asked.

The constable told him he was in hospital.

'In what town?'

'Eastbourne.'

'Eastbourne!' Scotney seemed as far away as China and as inaccessible as Patagonia. He could have cried with weakness and despair; but as this would achieve nothing, he lay quietly trying to compose as lurid a piece of journalism as he had ever deplored. 'Mass murder in Scotney, homicidal lunatic at large, Inspector Braithwaite in charge of case.' The constable's countenance remained unperturbed. It was just as Lomax had always contended, people had learnt to live with sensationalism just as germs learn to adapt to antibiotics. He said, 'The chief constable is a friend of mine. If you don't get Inspector Braithwaite from Scotney at once I shouldn't fancy your chances of promotion.'

The constable was prepared to gamble on mass murder, but not on his promotion chances. He left the room immediately. His place was taken by a cheerful ginger-haired nurse who smiled at Lomax as though she was on his side whatever he had done. Lomax hoped the constable had gone to find Braithwaite and not to verify his statement with regard to the chief constable with whom he had never enjoyed a harmonious relationship let alone friendship.

'What am I suffering from?' he asked the nurse. There was bound to be an interval before he could speak to Braithwaite; it was important to make use of this time.

The nurse told him he had a broken arm, abrasions to head and ribs, and was suffering from shock.

'Well, that's not much, is it?' he said.

She giggled: she was very young.

'I'm sure you've got a lot else to do besides sitting with me,' he suggested.

She became uneasy. He did not want to get her into trouble, and doubted whether he had the energy to do so.

'Could you get someone to make a telephone call to *The Scotney Gazette*?' he appealed, and lied 'We go to press today.'

She agreed to arrange for a message to be sent, the communications media having made her aware of the vital importance of deadlines. Lomax hoped that either Allinson or Todd would come quickly and would have the sense to bring clothes.

He must get to Hannah. 'Act,' he said to himself. 'Act, now!' He got up and sat on the edge of the bed while the ceiling dipped like the veering wing of an aeroplane. 'Act,' he said to himself. 'Do something, anything. . . .' When the ceiling had righted itself, he got to his feet and began to walk round the bed; waves of nausea alternated with faintness but he fought these back by resolutely concentrating his mind on *The Ballad of East and West* which was the longest poem he knew. The pain in his arm was bad, but did not present a problem since it did not incapacitate him. He walked round the bed several times and then had a rest; then he walked round the bed again. He was beginning to get the trick of walking—if Braithwaite didn't come to him, then he would be able to go to Braithwaite. Something must have delayed the nurse. He had twenty minutes bed-walking before the constable returned. He started *The Ballad of East and West* for the third time and had reached the Tongue of Jagai by the time the constable came into the room.

'What do you think you are doing?' the constable demanded.

Lomax said, ' "*There was rock to the left and rock to the right, and low lean thorn between/And thrice he heard a breech-bolt snick tho' never a man was seen. . . .*" '

The constable departed in search of the nurse.

Lomax went on walking round the bed. He was saying, ' " ' '*Twas only by favour of mine,' quoth he, 'ye rode so long alive. . . .*' " ' when he heard angry voices in the corridor. Allinson and Todd had arrived. Allinson was very effective, Lomax had never realised that this large, placid man could be so unpleasant; thanks to his hectoring of the constable, Lomax learnt that he had had his 'accident' while driving his car under the influence of drink.

'Knocked back two tomato juices, had he?' Allinson asked. 'Now, listen carefully. . . .'

Lomax said, ' *"If there should follow a thousand swords to carry my bones away. . . ."* ' He wondered how much time had been wasted by now; but he must not think of time, it was an enemy and would undermine resolution. ' *"The thatch of thy byres will serve their fires when all the cattle are slain. . . ."* '

He stopped at the window and looked out. There was a park opposite, neatly laid out with lawns and flower beds brilliant with red, yellow and purple flowers, old people sat on seats in the shade and younger people stretched out on the grass. Higher up the canvas, there was a fuzz of trees and above them a ridge of the Downs, green against a deep blue sky. He thought it was dreadful, so bright and clear, yet totally unreal and quite unrelated to anything which really mattered. He could not think why it had ever convinced him, why he had allowed himself to be taken in by it all these years.

Todd thought Lomax had become formidable, physically he was more frail than ever, but the will had been sharpened to a fine point on which he bore down with all his nerve and spirit. When he demanded, 'Clothes, Braithwaite,' the constable offered no resistance.

Out in the park, two of the old ladies were talking.

'The flower beds are a picture now.'

'My husband says he prefers Kew Gardens.'

'I used to live in Richmond. You can walk from Kew to Richmond along the towpath. I never did it, but you can go all the way.' The sun was eating into the shade. Little beads of sweat pricked through the powder on her face; she patted her cheeks with a handkerchief, and, memory performing one of its somersaults, said, 'My father gave my grandmother one of the dog's cooling powders once, by mistake. She didn't know, of course. But we did laugh.'

A police car went down the road at the side of the park, its siren wailing.

'They do that all the time now, whether they're going

anywhere or not. The little boy next door rides round and round on his tricycle imitating them, "ee-aw, ee-aw", it's all he ever does.'

The sun was within an inch of their feet.

'They're all the same. My nephew has been at university for two years and he doesn't know what he's going to be.'

A fire engine went down the road, followed by an ambulance. There was a fire on the heath and fire brigades from all neighbouring areas had been alerted. Traffic jams had built up and Braithwaite had been delayed on his way to Picton's Quay.

It was a bad morning for Braithwaite; he was finding the vicar of St Mary's, Picton's Quay, a tiresome man.

'I don't spend all my time out bird-watching.' The vicar was so obsessed with this grievance that it was difficult to get through to him. 'No matter what my parishioners may say to the contrary. And, in any case, there isn't a great deal of work here. That was why I came, part-retirement. If I had wanted to work full-time, I shouldn't have come here. . . .'

Braithwaite cut in on his self-justification. 'You never saw Mrs. Ormerod with this man . . .?'

'No, I didn't.' The vicar did not like being interrupted. 'I've already told your sergeant. He showed me one of those identikit photographs of this tramp you're after. I had never seen the man. As I said, I don't spend all my time out bird-watching. . . .'

'And Mrs. Ormerod? You did know her by sight?'

'Of course I knew her,' the vicar said testily. 'She opened the flower show for us last year, and I saw her several times after that with Mr. Cope.'

There was a pause while the vicar scratched with a finger-nail at something encrusted on the lapel of his jacket. Beyond the window, sunlight flashed from a greenhouse. Braithwaite said, *'Where* did you see Mrs. Ormerod and Cope, sir?'

'At the cottage, of course.' Exasperation was tinged with misgiving. 'Should I have mentioned that? It wasn't what your man asked me before. . . .'

'We have been asking people if they saw *anyone* with Mrs. Ormerod ever since. . . .'

'Well, then, I'm sorry!' The vicar decided to be magnanimous. 'Apologies, inspector, unreserved apologies. Only I didn't think it could be important because I saw them so often.'

'What do you call often, sir?'

'Once a week, twice perhaps.'

'Out by the cottage?'

'Yes, yes, where else would I see them at that time in the morning?'

'Did you ever speak to them?'

'Well, of course I didn't! It was bad enough that *they* made a noise; I certainly wasn't going to reveal myself.'

'I shall want a statement from you,' Braithwaite told him.

'I shall be delighted,' the vicar assured him.

It was only when he returned to the police station just after one o'clock that Braithwaite received the message from the Eastbourne police station. 'I'm not going to waste my time with Lomax now,' he said.

By the time Lomax reached Scotney, Braithwaite had already done the thing which Lomax had wished to prevent.

21

HANNAH did some shopping before going into the office. The rain of the night before had broken the vicious spiral of heat. The day was bright, but clear, and streets, houses and distant hills were in sharp focus. She walked up a narrow street; it was very steep and ahead, outside one of the terraced cottages, fuchsias in a hanging basket seemed to decorate the branches of a plane tree at the top of the hill. She allowed the scene its beauty without trying to project herself into it. On a stone wall to her left, a young cat arched its back and made a swaying movement of its limbs as though about to pounce on her, but was distracted at the last moment by the wind in its tail. She laughed and left it to its distractions. Although she was reluctant to go to the office, and the reasons for her reluctance were not pleasant, she nevertheless felt that life was good; its goodness flowed through her from the soles of her feet to the top of her head, and she was released from the need to take possession of the things around her, to look at streets and houses, trying to find in them a sense of being.

She turned into Station Hill and crossed the road to a delicatessen where she knew she could buy curd cheese. The station clock said five to one. The street was bright and starkly shadowless. In his shop near the station, the greengrocer was taking a moment's rest on an up-ended wooden crate. He was elderly and told Hannah that the heat was bad for his heart. The blinds had been drawn in the rooms above the shop.

Outside the station, a ragged group of youngsters gathered round their leader; they were shouting some slogan or other – Heath out, Wilson in? – whatever it was, they seemed vigorously happy. As she came nearer, she heard the leader, a bearded youth with a pleasantly impudent face shout:

'Give me an "S".'

'S!' they shouted.

'Give me a "U".'

'U!' they shouted.

'Give me an "S".'

'S!' they shouted.

'And what does it say?'

'Jesus!' they roared.

A man waiting at a bus stop said to Hannah, 'Summer season. All the clowns are about.'

Hannah hurried by. Will would probably have stayed to talk to them, she could imagine him evincing that bird-like interest, bright, sharp and quite detached. Perhaps he would have got something out of them, found out why they behaved in this embarrassing way. She wondered whether she should turn back and try to be more like him and immediately began to feel anxious. The world was fine until one came across people, people fractured one's feeling of wholeness. She looked at her watch and saw that she was late.

When Rodney Cope arrived at the office, Moray said to him, 'Hannah will be here soon.'

Cope was carrying a rifle. He propped it in a corner by the window. 'I may be doing some shooting,' he said.

Moray knew nothing about weaponry, but to him it looked an efficient piece of equipment and well-maintained. He accepted it as he accepted everything else about Cope now. If asked to explain his attitude to the rifle, he would probably have said that it was too obviously lethal to be intended for any lethal purpose.

He said, 'Hannah said she would only come if I was here all the afternoon.'

'You *will* be here all the afternoon.'

'I think she meant she wouldn't stay here with you. She is carrying this rather far, isn't she?' Moray laughed, but he nevertheless sounded as though he expected an answer. Cope made no answer.

Hannah, who thought people only carried a rifle if they meant to use it, did not see the rifle when she came into the room because it was masked by the filing cabinet.

'Is my car all right?' Cope asked. 'The back wheels are on double yellow lines.' He was standing by the window, looking down.

'I didn't notice. But there's a police car down there, so if you're not happy, perhaps you had better move it.' She said to Moray, 'I'm going to make that Austrian cheese cake we had at the Brophys', the one with curd cheese. Do you remember?'

'It was too rich for me.'

'Do you think this window has been cleaned since we came here?' Cope asked. 'It makes me feel as though I am suffering from a visual defect.'

'You could always open the window,' Hannah said.

'Only one half,' he pointed out, sliding it back. He leant out.

Moray said, 'Does it matter about the window?'

'Just that I'd like to have the whole thing out, that's all. Get a bit of light and air in here.' He began to explore the window frame as if he seriously considered taking it apart.

The constant fiddling with and thumping on the window made Moray uneasy. He felt that he could not concentrate on dictating to Hannah. He was also disturbed by Cope's irritation, which was large for so small a room.

'I'm going to the loo,' Cope said, suddenly turning away in disgust.

'What's wrong with him?' Hannah asked.

'I expect the heat is getting him down,' Moray answered.

When Cope came back, he showed no further interest in the window, but sat on the edge of the table, flicking over the correspondence and laughing about it. He had scattered a lot of grit and dust about as a result of his efforts and Hannah was rubbing a duster over chairs and table.

Moray said, 'Mind those plans for the development, Rodney. I've got to do some notes about them.'

Cope said, 'You can roll up the map of Scotney Supra, it will not be needed in my lifetime—or, all things considered, it might be better to say, in your lifetime.'

Hannah said, 'Let me shake the dust off the plans before you roll them up.'

Moray went to the window, the room wasn't big enough for three of them milling round the table, not in this heat. Cope had scraped some of the paintwork off the frame, Moray ran his finger along the roughened edge. There were two police cars outside now; he could see Inspector Braithwaite getting out of one of them.

Hannah was saying, 'There was a group of people from the Jesus Movement by the station. At least, I suppose that's what it was, they were chanting. . . .'

'What absolute rubbish!' Cope's temper was tinder dry, anything could spark it off. 'Don't tell me you believe in all that nonsense.'

'It's not my way,' she admitted.

'Not your way,' he mimicked. 'Not the way they do things in your chapel? It's all nonsense however it's done. Jesus people, Children of God! We are descended from the ape, didn't you know that, Hannah?'

'Really? I thought you were descended from Henry II.'

Moray could not bear their bickering any more. A feeling of panic surged up in him; he had cramp in his chest, he could not breathe in this room. 'I'm going to the bank,' he said. 'I'll be back soon.'

He was back sooner than that.

'The front door is locked.' He looked incredulously at Cope.

Cope raised his eyebrows and smiled, a rueful, almost apologetic smile. ''Fraid so.' As though motivated by a delicacy which prevented him observing their attempts to come to terms with the situation, he turned away and strolled over to the window.

'Locked?' Hannah repeated.

Moray said, 'Come on, Rodney. Let's have the key.'

'Do you think I should make an announcement or

something, just to start the thing off?' Cope sounded like an anxious host. He picked up the rifle and leant out of the window.

Hannah put her fists to her cheeks and said, 'Oh dear, oh dear, oh dear' very fast and low.

'Good afternoon,' Cope called. 'Just in case you are thinking of breaking down the door, I have two people in here with me.' He turned to Hannah and Moray. 'Would you both mind coming and looking down? You know the kind of thing. It's been done rather a lot lately, I'm afraid, but there it is. Nothing is new under the sun. A little to one side, Neil, so that they can see Hannah. That's it. Lovely! "Hold it"—as the photographer says, or "deep breath" if you prefer to think of it as an X-ray.'

Neil and Hannah looked gravely down and then withdrew. Cope was leaning against the window frame, with the rifle pointed over the sill where it could be clearly seen, the sun glinting on its well-polished metal. He said, 'My landlady warned me they were looking for me. She thought I had been speeding again. How long did the siege of Sidney Street last, can you remember?'

Moray said, 'Give me the key, Rodney. I'll go and cash my cheque now.'

'All your immediate needs are catered for,' Cope said. 'There is coffee, milk and sugar in the cupboard, and Hannah has thoughtfully provided us with curd cheese and apples. Any loaves and fishes tucked away in your basket, Hannah?'

'Only soap.' She was very subdued.

'Oh well, I suppose we may be glad of that. Wait a minute! This is getting quite exciting. There's a man with a loud hailer. I can hear perfectly well without it, but no doubt it adds to the spirit of the thing and the English policeman is nothing if not spirited. Do you suppose we shall have the army and the fire brigade, or would that be too much to hope for?' He wasn't talking blandly, the words were beginning to race.

203

Hannah put her hand over her mouth and doubled up as though she was going to be sick.

'There's one of your friends over there, too, Hannah. He has a placard; it says, "Repent, the day of the Lord is at hand!" There now!'

Moray said, 'Rodney, I must cash my cheque.'

'You aren't very good at accepting the truth of a situation, are you? But then, you never were. Hannah is much better at it. Don't look so glum, Hannah. I bear no malice to any man. There's not a lot I can say for myself that would commend itself to you, but that at least is true.'

'You killed Pauline Ormerod,' she said.

'Yes. But I don't think she minded. Not that I recall it very clearly.'

Moray said, 'Let Hannah go. I'll stay.' It was a ritual offer that had no real significance.

'A woman has a higher value in this particular game than a man, even a member of parliament. Sorry, Hannah.'

Moray put an arm round Hannah's shoulders. It seemed to her an invitation to weakness which she could not afford to accept and she said snappishly, 'I'm all right, Neil.' He remained beside her for a moment, but she was too concerned with the effort of holding herself together to spare any attention for him. She watched Rodney Cope as though he was an actor whose gift might bear her away into another world; every time she relaxed her concentration she experienced a sensation akin to vertigo.

Unable to play the comforter, Moray looked round the room seeking another role and, failing to find it, eventually sat on one of the packing cases. He did not look at Cope.

Cope was talking. He had not stopped talking for the last five minutes. Now, he was saying, 'Of course, I suppose there are times when one should look ahead. In this kind of situation, one must be prepared to bargain. What do you think it would be reasonable for me to ask for? Do you think Braithwaite would give me an aeroplane? I suppose that would be beyond Braithwaite, wouldn't it? It would involve a high-level decision. A walk on the Downs would be a much more local affair. The trouble is, I've done that.

'I ran away from my prep. school. Did I ever tell you about it? Come on, Neil, damn you! We've got to keep one another entertained. Now, DID I EVER TELL YOU ABOUT THE TIME I RAN AWAY FROM MY PREP. SCHOOL?'

Moray, slouched on the packing case, made no reply. Hannah said hoarsely, 'Tell us about the time when you ran away from your prep. school.'

'Thank you, Hannah, thank you!

'I wasn't unhappy. Not in the way that people like you think of children at prep. school being unhappy. I wasn't lonely or homesick, and I certainly wasn't bullied. I was bored. I was so bored I thought I should die of it if I didn't do something. There were one or two others who were bored, too, and they suggested setting light to the school. I knew then they weren't bored in the way I was bored. When you set light to something what does it amount to? Collecting a lot of inflammable stuff together and putting a match to it–then you have to stand back and let other people take over. That wasn't my idea at all. I wasn't going to waste my time lighting fires for other people to put out. So, one afternoon –in September, I think it was–I just walked out. I didn't take anything with me, or make any plans. If you do that kind of thing you are merely ensuring that you carry your world around with you. That was the last thing I wanted. So I took a bus into a country town, and walked up a side street. . . .'

The man with the loud hailer said to Braithwaite, 'No answer, sir.'

'I know that. I'm not deaf.' Braithwaite looked down at a sketch plan which had been made of the office and surrounding buildings. The 'ground floor' consisted of an enclosed passageway with a flight of stairs leading up to the office; there was a lavatory on the half-landing, it was built into what was once a cupboard and had no window. 'It doesn't look

205

as though anything in this outfit is legal,' he muttered. 'Not even the office accommodation.'

'It was supposed to be temporary,' one of the plainclothes men recalled. 'They said they would only be using it for a few weeks.'

'What's at the back?'

'Jake Hacker's Furniture Emporium in Wick Street.'

'So it is. Built like a fortress as far as I can remember. No hope of getting through from the back, then.'

'No, sir.' The plainclothes man's face was blank; but he was aware that Braithwaite did not fancy the idea of cutting a way through a wall, or any caper of that kind, and Braithwaite was aware that he was aware of it.

The baker whose premises were below Moray's office was now giving a guided tour to two constables. He had said he didn't think the walls were very thick, but when the constables returned they reported that the wall between the bakery and the downstairs passage of Moray's office seemed 'pretty solid'.

Braithwaite said, 'I see,' and looked grim, as though he had had to relinquish a much-favoured scheme.

At this moment, the chief constable arrived. 'Now, what do we know about this fellow?' he demanded. 'How does he tick, eh?'

'Unmarried,' Braithwaite told him, 'and I don't think he's the kind who would listen to an appeal from his old mother— even if we knew she was alive, which we don't. But I've got someone on the way here who may know something useful about him. Major Brophy. He was concerned with Cope and Moray in the election campaign. And, of course, Cope was in the army.' He spoke as though the very fact of Cope having been in the army would mean that Major Brophy would read him like an open book.

The chief constable was not impressed by Major Brophy, but agreed that no harm would be done by hearing what he had to say. 'As long as we don't waste much time.' He had publicly criticised the inactivity of the police in other cases of this kind and felt he was committed to action.

'Lomax wants to see you, sir,' a constable, who had been waiting the moment to intervene, said to Braithwaite. 'He says Cope tried to kill him last night.'

They stared at him incredulously. He said, 'There may be something in it, sir. We had a message from Eastbourne and it's true he was in hospital there.'

'Better get him,' the chief constable said.

They were talking in the saloon bar of *The North Star*, the public house opposite to Moray's office, which had been taken over as emergency headquarters. The constable went into the street where other officers were holding back sight-seers and newsmen; he beckoned over the heads of the crowd to the officers who were with Lomax.

'Is that 'im there, that one up at the window?' a small boy asked.

Above, from the window over his jewellery shop, Sebastian Shoemack was entertaining a few favoured customers, one of whom was regarding the scene through a pair of binoculars; the small boys, despairing of information from the police, turned their attention to him. 'What can you see, mister? 'As 'e got them tied up?'

The policemen pushed the boys back as they escorted Lomax through the crowd. He looked white and shaken when he entered the saloon bar of *The North Star* and the chief constable grudgingly offered him a brandy. Lomax, who wanted above all else to keep his head clear, insisted on water. It was not an auspicious beginning and the arrival of Major Brophy did nothing to improve matters.

Outside, an ice-cream van had stopped on the periphery of the crowd, but had attracted no custom; there was a feeling that anything might happen at any moment, even in the few seconds it would take to buy a choc. ice.

'An alternative world,' Cope said. 'Right here in Sussex on the Downs. It was like being born again. There is something in your myth, Hannah. One does need to be born again. But it has dangers. Do they tell you about them? After a few days, my mental processes were affected; ideas had been jettisoned some way back, but now even thoughts didn't string themselves together, in fact, they seemed to be unravelling rather than knitting up. All impressions were visual, undifferentiated and without meaning. I was an unrelated being in an atmosphere in which there was no reason, no pattern, no sequence of events, no cause and effect.

'You know, dogs are much more conditioned to civilisation than man. I begged from farmhouses from time to time; the farm folk thought I was a gypsy boy and no one reported me to the police. But the dogs didn't like me. I didn't fit into their idea of the respectable. Nor yours either, I suppose, Neil. Do you think we might have some coffee, Hannah? See if it will liven him up. I really must try to stimulate a little more audience participation.'

Neil was still sitting on the packing case. His position was unchanged but he had undergone a physical transformation. His body seemed to have shrunk so that his clothes hung on him, while his features had become slack as though the mechanism which controlled them had worked loose. He appeared to be aware of this and from time to time he fumbled with a fold of cloth, examining it with some perturbation; then, this having provided no clue to his condition, he would raise a trembling hand to trace the line of mouth or cheekbone. He looked furtively ashamed. It was plain that Cope's words made no sense to him.

'I kept to the hills most of the time. Occasionally I saw a town in a valley, white and black, or grey and black; I only felt secure when I put a fold of the Downs between myself and the town. The weather broke with the hunter's moon. At night the temperature went down below freezing point. I got rather sick. And about the time I got sick, I discovered a city in the Downs; but this one wasn't white and black, or grey and black, it smouldered blood-red as though the sun went down in it, the buildings were very close together and seemed all gables and spires, nothing flat anywhere. When I got a little better I tried to find the city, but I never came to the right one, they were all white and black, or grey and black, whereas my city had been on fire, the streets and walls

208

flaming around you as you walked. I never found it. They found me first.'

'Did they expel you?' Hannah asked.

'Far from it! I was a hero. I had lived up there for several weeks. It was a remarkable feat of survival for a ten-year-old. A great test of character and physique. They approved of that.'

'How are you going to manage about coffee?' she asked.

'You are rather a Martha, aren't you, Hannah? Well, I think you are going to take that packing case over there and put it just below the window sill, and you are then going to put the cup of coffee on it. From time to time I shall relax sufficiently to sip the coffee. I don't think Neil is going to rush me, are you, Neil? FOR GOD'S SAKE, MAN! Are you?'

Hannah pulled up the packing case and put the cup of coffee on it, then she poured out black coffee and took it to Neil. 'This is black, good and strong,' she said. She wanted him to be strong, because she needed to let go and she could not do it while he was like this. All the time she continued to hang on, she was being carried inexorably further and further from reality and she was afraid a time might come when she could not get back. Instead of taking the cup, Neil took her free hand. He gripped it very tight, while his body shook and his face contorted grotesquely; he cried, silently, the gash of a mouth gaping.

'Neil,' she whispered. 'Come to the window. You may feel better then.' But he shrank back against the wall and hunched his shoulder in front of his face, trying to hide himself.

'So, you see, I can't ask Braithwaite for a walk on the Downs,' Cope said. 'I've, as you might say, "done the Downs".'

The carnation walls of *The North Star* were bathed in brilliant sunlight, and the glare was now fiercely reflected in the half-window of Moray's office. Cope could have asked for no more effective cover. Two policemen, reputedly crack shots, were installed, one in the upper room of the

Chinese restaurant, the other in a bedroom at *The North Star*. Neither man was confident that he could be sure of killing Cope with his first shot.

The chief constable, who was a believer in swift, decisive action, was angry with the two policemen, with the sunlight, and most of all, with Lomax and Brophy.

'A clear picture doesn't seem to be emerging, does it?' he said grimly. 'Is he a cool customer who's got everything well organised, working to some plan, or is he just a maniac with a rifle?'

'He's a very good organiser,' Brophy said cautiously. 'He did wonders during the campaign.'

'But he didn't commit himself to it in advance, did he?' Lomax said. 'In fact, he came into it as a result of a spur-of-the-moment decision at a party.'

This had been going on for some time. First Brophy said one thing, then Lomax contradicted it. To the surprise of the chief constable, Lomax was emerging as by far the more dominant personality of the two. He watched with distaste as Brophy once again retracted. 'Always thought that was odd. Must agree with you there. An odd fellow. Unpredictable.' He finally threw in the sponge. 'Think you probably know him better than I do.'

'It doesn't seem as though either of you can be much help,' the chief constable said.

'It isn't easy to find a solution once he has been allowed to get into the office carrying a rifle.' Lomax was deliberately offensive because this was something the chief constable understood and equated with strength. 'And particularly as no effort was made to stop Miss Mason going in a quarter of an hour later.'

'That kind of thing is of no help now.' The chief constable was angry, but he was reluctant to dismiss Lomax; Cope's attempt on the man's life gave him status of a kind. He said, 'Have you anything to suggest?'

Lomax was desperately anxious and uncertain. He knew, however, that certainty was the only thing the chief constable would settle for.

'I am absolutely certain,' he said with what resolution he could command, 'that the only chance of getting Moray and Miss Mason out of there alive is to give Cope time to play this out in his own way.'

'But he may kill them.'

'Yes, he may. But you won't stop him doing that by rushing him.'

'And what do you mean by "playing things out in his own way"?' It went against the chief constable's principles to indulge a criminal in this fashion.

'I think it is possible that in time Miss Mason and Moray may lose their importance for him.'

'They are hostages, damn it!'

'Yes, but he's not consistent; he loses sight of things, or they cease to be relevant to him. It could be he won't want to take anyone else over the edge with him.'

'If you imagine that that type would spare anyone else. . . .'

'I'm not talking of sparing people. I am suggesting there are experiences he will reserve for himself.'

'I've never heard such nonsense! And if he has a brainstorm?'

It was this possibility which chilled Lomax; indeed, it seemed to him to be rather more than a possibility. He said carefully, 'If he had a brainstorm, you wouldn't want to have done anything to precipitate it, would you?'

He could see that he had made his point. If things went badly wrong now, the blame would be his.

There was a ripple of laughter from the street. A plain-clothes man by the window explained, 'Says he'd like Ted to lend him *Morning Cloud*. Seems to be enjoying himself up to now.'

'You won't be needing me any more,' Lomax said. He left the saloon bar and telephoned Allinson at the *Gazette* office. Then he went into the street. He looked up at the room where they were. Cope had drawn the sliding window so that there was only a slit of darkness from which the rifle pointed. The reflected light was very bright now and it was impossible to see any of the occupants of the room.

211

How disaster simplifies one's feelings for a person! Only this week, as he watched Hannah coming down the road to meet him, he had realised it was already too late to question their relationship and he had been filled with misgivings. Now, he loved her without reservation, a state of loving he had never achieved before and would probably not sustain were she to be restored to him. The fear that she might not be restored to him was so terrifying that he felt he could not see this through, that he must go back to the office, get a few of his impressions down while they were still fresh in his mind. Those women who wait at pit-heads, hour after hour, how do they do it? It was something he had never asked before, they were so much an accepted part of the pattern of disaster. He remembered that when he was a reporter on a northern newspaper he had seen a girl trying to drag her mother away; the older woman had said, 'I can't leave him.' It hadn't made sense. But now, without it making any more sense, he could not leave Hannah.

'There's nothing you can do here, sir,' a constable advised. 'Better go in.'

'I'll stay if you don't mind,' he said.

People were coming up from the beach, the usual holiday entertainments abandoned in favour of the surprise attraction of a man holding two people to ransom. The police were having difficulty in keeping the street clear.

'If no one gets hurt they'll ask for their money back,' the constable said to Lomax.

Three acrobats from the pavilion show were staging a free demonstration in an attempt to get a better view. The knife thrower had already offered his services to the police.

By half-past four, nothing had happened and the ice-cream vendor was doing brisk business.

Cope said, 'I think I shall have to ask for an aeroplane soon.' It was such a small room: stalemate and a small room! 'But if I had an aeroplane there would be nowhere really interesting to go. There never has been, of course.' He had created a situation for other people to deal with, just like starting a fire. He began to walk up and down the room.

212

Hannah watched him. 'And even if there was somewhere still to go, I would have to take myself along. There are two people inside me, Hannah. One of them wants to be free of the other. You don't seem surprised. Is this true of all of us? Am I the last to be told about it?' The skin was drawn tight so that the skull showed, the eyes were very bright and becoming more protuberant; it was as though someone was indeed trying to escape, Hannah could almost feel the pressure behind the eyes.

She went to the window. He did not seem to mind, or even to notice. Her strength was nearly spent, the effort of keeping her head above panic-level would soon be too much. She must take in something of that sane world outside and try to store it away, releasing a little at a time to keep her going until the next opportunity. But the view was not reassuring. The people seemed pathetically unmotivated, policemen standing aimlessly, looking up but not seeming to focus on her, a man with a ladder and nowhere to put it, a fire engine without a fire; farther away, sightseers jostled one another, a man hoisted a child on his shoulders, a girl stood on the roof of a car and a boy scaled a lamp-post, Chinese faces smiled from the Chinese restaurant kitchen, television cameras were in position on the flat roof of the building behind the Lantern Shop. Yet nothing was happening. They were all playing make-believe. She remembered how, as a juror she had seen the policeman and the prisoner standing shoulder to shoulder, the one face impassive, the other sullen, boxed in together, the truth locked between them, condemned to watch a charade which bore no resemblance to what had really happened: and now, she and Neil and Rodney were boxed into this room while the people outside indulged in an absurd fantasy of their own devising.

'Telly,' Cope said, coming up beside her and pointing the rifle at the cameras. 'In every sitting-room in the land they will be living through this great experience with us. Can't you imagine them, the little voyeurs. . . .' He spat out the last phrase with something more than contempt. He was becoming desperate. Whatever else is handed out to us, there

213

is only one death apiece, so it is worth taking trouble over it. He should have thought of this before; it was hideously wrong to go into death blazing away with a rifle like any mad Jock. There must be something else, some other way. He said, ' "*A flower on a tall stem and three dark flames.* . . ." '

Hannah no longer listened or attempted to understand. At first she had thought that if she kept with him, it might be all right, that even if it involved a glimpse of his alternative world, it might be the only way to survive; but now she began to realise that it was a world that could only be entered by those who are prepared to risk their sanity. This did not mean that she doubted its reality. Indeed, at the moment, it seemed more real than anything else. It swirled around them. Neil was witness to this. For some time, he had been feeling the edge of the packing case as though it was a one-man ark in which he was now marooned. He appeared not to realise that it was not his body, but his mind that was at stake, and he constantly readjusted his limbs. Now he was taking off one shoe, muttering, 'Must keep circulation going. . . .'

Cope said, '*Is* fire the answer, as long as one doesn't run away from it?'

Hannah looked out of the window and saw that Will had come into the street. He had his arm in a sling and he, too, was looking up, but like the others he seemed unable to see her. Yet he remained there, gazing upwards. Through the invisible screen which separated them, she gazed back at him. After a moment or two, it no longer bothered her that he was unable to see her, they would only have wasted the precious time, like one did on long-distance telephone calls. It was better to have him like this, quite still, so that she could draw from him what she needed which certainly wasn't a smile, a wave of the hand, a frantic attempt to convey instant reassurance. What it was she needed, she could hardly have said. At times, Will had seemed to her to be an elusive and not entirely safe person whose mind darted ahead of hers, questioning more, accepting less. And now, he was, by his stillness, detached from all the busy little people down there; essentially solitary, not obviously a comforting person.

214

But more than comfort was needed now. She concentrated on Will, trying to shut everything else out of her mind, Rodney prowling round the room, Neil huddled on his packing case; and all the time she was conscious of a note, which although soundless, she could hear rising and rising so that if she opened her mouth it would even out into one incredibly high, sustained scream which would tear everything apart and put an end to all resistance. It seemed the pressure must burst her ear drums; she clenched her teeth and concentrated on Will until gradually everything around him blurred and dimmed and there was only one point of light which trembled on his face.

Cope said, 'We can rip up the packing cases. There may even be some paraffin in the store cupboard.'

The sun went down behind the tall chimneys in Scotney Square, throwing out gaudy streamers of orange, turquoise and crimson; in Pont Street, there was already a blueness as though arc lights had been switched on. From the open window of a car a young man was saying, 'This is Martin Penney speaking from the radio car in Pont Street; behind me is the network of alleys called The Warren, but this evening the prey is not in The Warren, he is still . . .'

'Is anything happening there, Martin? We've got an urgent news item waiting.'

He had to admit that nothing was happening.

But then a raggle-taggle group of youngsters came to the end of Pont Street. One of them, a long-haired lad with a gay impudent face, had a tambourine, and he was an artist: he saw the expectant faces, the unused props—fire engine, ladder, television cameras—and the street beneath the window, waiting like a stage for something to come to life on it; and he made his contribution. Raising his tambourine, he began to sing:

> ' "I danced in the morning
> When the world was begun
> And I danced in the moon
> And the stars and the sun. . . ." '

He moved through the crowd and people made way for him.

> ' "And I came down from Heaven
> And I danced on the earth,
> In Bethlehem
> I had my birth...." '

The constable said to Lomax, 'We only need Brighton to send the dolphins now!'

People in the crowd began to sing and clap their hands. The young man and his followers had reached the police barrier. Cope said, 'Marvellous! Marvellous! Just when something was needed.' He leant out of the window and shouted imperiously, 'Let them through! Let them through!' The police humoured him to the extent of letting the young man through the barrier. He pranced beneath the window, shaking his tambourine and singing:

> ' "Dance, then, wherever you may be
> I am the Lord of the Dance, said he...." '

'Come on, Hannah!' Cope implored. 'Come *on*! Sing!'

'No!' But she felt a terrible desire to become a part of his madness. She tried to think of Will, but this no longer helped. She clenched her teeth and repeated his name over and over in her mind, but it didn't work. He was sane but it didn't make her sane. Her legs were beginning to shake and soon the shaking spread up her thighs.

Cope said, 'Sing! Sing!'

The young man swayed, side to side, back and forth, arms now extended wide, now raised high above his head; in the cramped room, Cope gyrated, feet stamping, head nodding more and more vehemently to the beat of the music as though it was something with which he must contend, an issue to be settled once and for all. He cried, 'Sing! Louder, louder!'

Hannah had lost control over the lower half of her body; urine was running down the insides of her legs, but the worst thing of all was the shaking which was so violent it seemed that every bone was working loose. The singing of the crowd grew louder. The young man's head lolled back, rolled forward, the shoulders hunched, braced, every muscle in the writhing body jerked and quivered. Cope banged the butt of the rifle on the floor, louder and louder and louder, but still he cried wildly, with as much despair as exultation, 'Louder! Louder!' Neil was wiggling the toes of his left foot and repeating 'one little piggy went to market'. The young man with the tambourine sang, *'I'll lead you all/ Wherever you may be/I will lead you all/In the dance, said he. . . .'*

Hannah stretched her arms out in front of her. She was not aware of what she was doing and was surprised to see them there, the fingers straining as though trying to grasp something; although the strain was intense, the arms were not shaking. She stared at the hands, the fingers within an inch of deliverance. She gathered all the strength that was in her, drew a long deep breath and held it; then, as the fingers clawed, she felt in her stomach the pull of something small but strong as a core of steel. There was one moment of tremendous effort and then she seemed to float free of the force of gravity. She was high up, looking down on Cope, quite dispassionately, and seeing that he was driven by impulses beyond his control and would probably kill her. She was not afraid, because she was outside the action which was not relevant to her; the only source of danger was Hannah Mason and once she was reconciled with this creature there was no one else she need fear. All this seemed to be laid out beneath her like a picture and at the same time it was like music in perfect harmony, and as she looked and listened, marvelling, she thought that she had overcome the world and would not have to return to it; but no sooner had thought begun to form in her mind than she felt herself spinning down.

Outside, the volume of sound swelled in spite of a policeman shouting through a loud hailer, 'People's lives are in danger, will you please. . . .' His voice was drowned in the singing. *'I danced for the fishermen/For James and John/ They came with me/And the dance went on. . . .'*

Hannah took her place in the room again. She felt as

217

though she had missed a reel in a film but that it didn't matter very much; she did not think that the policeman or anyone out there could help her. She was on her own and it was as well to know it. She sat down at the table. There was a sheet of paper in the typewriter. She thought that perhaps she should demonstrate that she had no part in what was going on around her. Automatically, her fingers typed "Now is the time for all good men to come to the aid of the party." This was not very inspiring, but before she could type anything else Cope had come up and was looking over her shoulder at the typewritten words. He said, 'I don't think I can have this,' quite mildly, as if he had caught her playing about in class. Then he hit her a great blow across the face and said, 'Get out! And dispose of that disgusting creature over there while you're about it!' Something clattered on the floor. The policeman was shouting through the loud hailer again. Cope rushed to the window and leant out. 'Let them sing! Everyone must sing!'

Hannah looked down. The front door key was at her feet. She regarded it warily because hope could be dangerous to her; already her knees were beginning to shake. She closed her eyes and took a deep breath, testing that core of steel in her stomach. It held. She was no longer so disinterested as in that one supreme moment, but she felt calm. She picked up the key and went across to Neil. 'We're going now.' She was afraid he would not move and she knew she could not lift him. She came closer and whispered, 'Come on. This little piggy is going to market.' At this, he got to his feet where he remained, holding one shoe in his hand. She guided him to the door. Cope was singing:

> ' "I danced on a Friday
> When the sky turned black—
> It's hard to dance
> With the devil on your back...." '

They were through the door; in front of them the window-less stairs were dark. She did not dare to put on the light in case it distracted Cope. Moray shuffled, feeling for each tread like a blind man.

> ' *"They cut me down*
> *And I leap up high—*
> *I am the life*
> *That'll never, never die...."* '

They had sung it twice. Would they begin once again, or would they stop? She did not dare to hurry Neil in case this frightened him and he refused to go on; but if they delayed too long the music might stop. She was convinced that Cope would do something terrible when the music stopped.

'Shoe's tight.' Neil leant against the wall, whimpering. 'Foot's gone to sleep.' Hannah concentrated her mind on Neil's foot. It was important not to think in terms of escape; the next step on the stair was all that mattered. She bent down and unlaced his shoe, jerking it off while he swayed against the wall and giggled. When she had the shoe off, he went down another two steps and said, 'No. Still asleep.' There were three more steps; she ran down them and flung open the door. There was a great gasp and the singing stopped. Lomax and a constable started towards her and a shot rang out. Lomax and the constable ducked back. Hannah ran up the stairs and pulled Neil down; he stumbled and she half-dragged him across the threshold. Someone shouted to her, 'Stay there! You're out of his range there.'

A girl was screaming. The crowd had moved back when the shot was fired, but someone had remained behind, crumpled on the ground beneath the window; Hannah could see his arm flung out, fingers still holding the tambourine. Lomax and the constable began to edge their way towards him. There was silence now. And blood, more blood than Hannah would have believed possible. From the window, Cope watched motionless. Lomax and the constable reached the young man; the constable took off his jacket and laid it over his head and shoulders. Then Lomax and he crawled on towards Hannah and Moray. The constable said, 'Edge into the doorway of the bakery, just in case. . . .'

From the opposite building, the chief constable exhorted Cope to throw down his rifle. Whether he did or not, no longer mattered; they were going to get him now one way or another. The light was going. In the dark, men would edge along the wall and get in through the open door. He could wait for that, or come down now; he had that much choice. He came down. He ran into the road, zigzagging in the direction of The Warren. Two shots were fired and then he was too near the crowd for the police to risk another shot. The crowd scattered, as far as was possible in that confined space, and the way was clear for him. He was in The Warren. The police made no effort to stop him. There were only three ways out of The Warren, and the other two had been sealed for some time.

In the radio car, Martin Penny was saying, 'There are going to be a lot of questions which will have to be answered. Why was Cope ever allowed to reach the office, and having reached it, why. . . .'

'And, Martin, there's going to be a few questions for Neil Moray to answer, surely?'

'The way he looked when he came out, George, it will be some time before he answers any questions.'

The police were moving in on the Pont Street entrance to The Warren. They were armed and accompanied by dogs. There was no way out for Cope, but it would take time to comb the narrow alleyways and shops.

'He used to come in to buy prints,' a young woman was telling Basil Todd. 'I always had a strange feeling about him. . . .'

A doctor knelt beside Hannah murmuring persuasively. He wanted her to go to hospital; Moray had already been taken away.

'It's all over now,' the doctor soothed.

'But it isn't. I must stay to the end. Please !' She had to know how it ended, she couldn't have Cope left loose in her mind. 'I've tried so hard to be good,' she pleaded. 'Please let me stay.'

Will said, 'Let her stay.'

220

Someone put a rug round her shoulders. She sat in the doorway of the baker's shop and Will sat beside her. If she lay on her back, she would have a fine view of the sky, all those red giants and white dwarfs....

The crash of breaking glass.

'He won't come out alive.' A woman's voice. '*They'll* see to that.' A stirring in the shifting sands of pity.

Searchlights had been switched on. The Warren was like a glass labyrinth. Cope showed little awareness of his pursuers, although for a time he evaded them effectively. It was the antique shops which drew him and he broke into one after another, hurling himself through panes of glass, breaking with his bare hands every mirror, every showcase, until his hands were hewn so lumpishly out of shape as to be useless; and still he went on, thrashing about with his feet, as though he must destroy his own image wherever it appeared. The cramped passageways facilitated obstruction and his pursuers were hampered by pyramids of splintered wood and broken glass. He still had some advantage over them when, at the end of a blind alley, he broke into a clock shop. Here, the fine sweep of destruction which had carried him forward was fragmented by the meticulous precision of the smaller timekeepers. He blundered from one to the other of these exquisite things, hurling them to the ground and stamping on wheels and springs as though he feared the intricate mechanism might have power to reassemble itself. Around him, the larger clocks continued with unvarying busyness, second hands described their inexorable circles, pendulums swung unremittingly, pulses beat to well-regulated measures. His own rhythm was fractured, his movements uncoordinated. The staring dials seemed to grow in number and to close in on him, until at last a heavy grandfather clock bore down on him, and, burying its great benign face in his, held him prisoner with a delicate frill of glass around his neck. Although the police shouted at him not to move, he struggled violently to free himself from this strange embrace and one of the jugular veins in his neck was severed.

It was quiet. In Pont Street voices petered out. A discarded ice-cream wrapper skittered briskly along the gutter, a black cat strolled across the road. People watched the alley which led into The Warren, dim turnip faces upturned to the light of the street lamp. A child began to cry. Then, farther away, a long, low 'aaah!' swelling and dying away. Someone shouted, 'They're taking him out of the Villiers Street entrance!' People began to run, pushing and shoving. Hannah bowed her head on her knees.

Voices again.

'You're going to have something to tell your pals after this holiday, aren't you, lovey?'

'It's too late. They've gone now. You wouldn't have liked it anyway. Messy.'

'If only someone could have *talked* to him.'

Hannah said, 'I am going to lie on my back.'

There was a swathe of sky above, stretched between roofs and chimneys; a crescent moon snarled up in fairy lights and stars tangled in wire; television aerials sailing down the Milky Way, a whole fleet of them. . . .

Will said, 'You *must* come now.' The ultimate gentleness which cannot be denied. She sat up reluctantly while the street with pallid lamps and dark disfigured buildings pitched into view and the ground rocked beneath her. She held Will's hand as the world settled again, a poor tatterdemalion gathering its threadbare rags about it. She felt herself being drawn towards it, but not quite inside it yet.